CAST OF CHARACTERS

FAMILY
SECRETS

*Five extraordinary siblings. One dangerous past.
Unlimited potential.*

Matthew Tynan—The jaded playboy had steered clear of his gorgeous—and guarded—secretary, Carey Benton, but when he needed her help to look into a CIA cover-up for friend Jake Ingram, resisting her sweet, small-town charm could prove to be mission impossible.

Carey Benton—The Kansas-born beauty had Matt's trust and respect, but what she really wanted was her handsome boss's undying love. One makeover later, she's intent on tempting Matt to give up his bachelor days for good.

Jake Ingram—One of the Extraordinary Five (X5) genetically engineered supergeniuses, he's in a race to find his missing siblings before rogue government agents get to them first and and use them to destroy the world.

Agnes Payne and Oliver Grimble—The evil scientists missed nabbing X5 brain Gretchen Wagner thanks to the double-crossing private investigator they'd hired who fell in love with her. But they're hot on Jake's trail....

About the Author

EVELYN VAUGHN

Evelyn Vaughn (aka Yvonne Jocks) can trace much of her joy in writing back to childhood, when she loved not just to read but to play make-believe with her sister and friends. The opportunity to join the fine writers in the FAMILY SECRETS series, therefore, was a dream come true. Working with so many other authors—brainstorming continuations and mutual story lines, and sharing characters—has felt remarkably similar to the games of "Let's Pretend" she used to play as a child. She didn't want it to end.

Evelyn, an English teacher at Tarrant County College in Arlington, Texas, has written forever, first publishing in 1993. She lives with her cat and her imaginary friends near Dallas-Fort Worth airport, loves movies and videos, and is an unapologetic TV addict. She's still trying to figure out both how to time-travel and how to meet up with some of her favorite characters, and she loves to talk about stories and characters, especially her own. Please write her at Yvaughn@aol.com, or at P.O. Box 6, Euless, Tx 76039. Or check out her Web site at www.evelynvaughn.homestead.com.

EVELYN VAUGHN

THE
PLAYER

Silhouette Books

Published by Silhouette Books

America's Publisher of Contemporary Romance

Special thanks and acknowledgment are given
to Evelyn Vaughn for her contribution
to the FAMILY SECRETS series.

SILHOUETTE BOOKS

ISBN 0-373-61370-9

THE PLAYER

Copyright © 2003 by Harlequin Books S.A.

Visit us at www.silhouettefamilysecrets.com

Printed in U.S.A.

FAMILY SECRETS

Henry Bloomfield (d.) m. Violet Vaughn 2nd m. Dale Hobson (d.)

Susannah Hobson

Extraordinary Five

Connor Quinn (d.)

Jake Ingram

Gretchen Wagner m. Kurt Miller

Marcus Evans

Faith Martin

"Uncle" Oliver Grimble m. "Aunt" Agnes Payne

Gideon Faulkner

Ingram Family

Clayton Ingram m. Carolyn Cook

Zach Ingram
m.
Maisy Dalton

Evans Family

Charles Evans
m.
Sarah Alexander

Russell (Russ) Evans
m.
Lynn Van Allen

Drew Evans

Honey Evans

Seth Evans

Laura Evans

Holt Evans

———— Birth Family

------ Adoptive Family

m. Married

d. Deceased

This book is the group effort of so many wonderful women, I hardly know how to begin! With a full heart, I dedicate it to them. This includes:

* My incredible editors, especially Leslie Wainger, Margaret Marbury, Julie Barrett, Melissa Endlich, Tina Colombo, Stephanie Maurer and Selina McLemore at Silhouette Books who helped create the incredible FAMILY SECRETS saga.

* All the FAMILY SECRETS authors with whom I had a chance to closely share characters, especially: Cathy Mann (for Ethan and Kelly), Anne Marie Winston (for Gretchen and Kurt), Cindy Gerard (for working so closely with me on Violet Vaughn), Virginia Kantra (for Samantha), Jenna MIlls (for Eric and Leigh) and Beverly Bird (for Honey!).

* And my dedicated critique-mates and brainstormers, especially Toni, Matt-and-Kayli, Virginia Kantra, Deb Stover and Maureen McKade.

Thank you, all of you, for this.

Prologue

Carey Benton adored Mondays.

She gladly left the still-gray summer morning to descend deep into the Eastern Market Metro station with other business-clad "Hill Rats." Lawyers, staffers, lobbyists and interns looked vaguely grumpy at the new workweek. Carey felt energized.

Hearing the echoing rush of an approaching train, she ran for the platform. After two long, quiet days, she would ride back into the heart of the free world and help make a difference.

And after two days, Carey would see Matt Tynan again.

Not that her day-to-day happiness balanced on one man. She was twenty-five, not thirteen! And she sure wouldn't stake her happiness on someone like Matt, even if he was the closest thing to male perfection she'd ever known. He was ten years her senior. He was far more worldly. He was a player.

Worse, he was her boss.

But those, rationalized Carey as the Blue Line train screeched to an impatient stop, were reasons not to pursue a romance with the president's top troubleshooter. She had no such delusions...so why not enjoy the scenery?

Doors slid open and she merged into the crowd to board, excited, alive...happy. Large Plexiglas windows reflected the train's crowded interior back at her. She faced a workday of at least ten hours, probably longer, the first in a whole week of them, and she was *happy*. How many women could say that?

She noticed her reflection—tall and slim in a modest linen suit, long brown hair pulled back in a ponytail. Flushing, Carey quickly tugged the pink scrunchy loose and pocketed it.

Ponytails were for Kansas City, not the White House.

5:45 a.m.

"WDCN traffic and weather every fifteen minutes," blared Matt's shower radio over the massage-strength spray. Matt, ducking to rinse shampoo out of his hair, groaned. Then he spit, because he was brushing his teeth while showering.

To keep the schedule he had, a man had to multitask.

Not that he had anything against traffic *or* weather. But it got in the way of the real news, and it meant he was running late. For him, anyway. He liked to get into the West Wing as early as possible, especially on Mondays... especially lately.

He'd be more efficient if he brought dates back to his high-rise apartment instead of staying out all night, he mused, opening his mouth to catch the pulsing water, then spitting again. It would save a significant step in his morning commute.

He killed the water, dropped his toothbrush back into its cup, slid open the frosted-glass shower door and grabbed a towel. He had good reasons not to bring women home. Not that his bare apartment seemed particularly homey. He'd long ago determined to never mislead women that he was offering more than he ever had or ever would offer, which was honest fun.

Matt loved women. He loved sex. But he avoided commitment at all costs. As his father and grandfather proved, men in his family weren't any good at it. Why mess up someone else's life attempting to prove otherwise?

Without the shower, the radio screamed out its prediction for muggy weather. Matt toweled his hair, swiped on some antiperspirant, then grabbed his electric razor. As he strode into a bare bedroom, a second radio detailed the usual crises for the Beltway above the razor's whine.

God, Matt loved Mondays. They were like the whistle at the start of a game. *His* game.

The meteorologist finished. Matt perked up. Now came the real stuff.

Bond market—bad. Stock market—worse. April's World Bank heist hadn't ruined the economy but, despite White House cautions against fear, panic still might. Small banks had begun to fail and corporations were downsizing, all on President Stewart's watch. Matt listened intently while he shaved and, with his free hand, scooped socks and briefs out of the drawer of his bureau and tossed them onto the neatly made bed.

Janeen Sullivan, his current lady friend, had been great, but he should've come home last night.

National news—iffy. He finished shaving, yanked on his socks and underwear and stepped into the walk-in closet for the rest of his clothes. Nobody in his right mind could blame the president either for the floods in the southwest or the latest rumors about secret genetic research labs. But this was D.C. Matt's job as a troubleshooter, aka advisor, included worrying about people *outside* their right mind. He needed a plan to deal with them before he hit the office.

He dressed in a button-down shirt, charcoal slacks, jacket and tie.

International news—not great. The heist had hurt the European Coalition even worse than the States, making for cranky allies. The government of Rebelia still dominated the old Eastern bloc, its dictator too dangerous to be ignored. Combing his damp, dark hair as he walked, Matt stepped into his shoes en route to the bathroom and silenced the shower radio. His return trip took him past the bureau for his wallet and keys, but he hesitated inside the bedroom door until he heard the magical announcement, "A word from our sponsors." Then he switched that radio off, too.

He had four minutes to get down to his car before anything else important would be said. He caught his mobile phone out of its charger on his way into the kitchen, flipped it open and commanded, "Florist."

While the ringing started, he squinted woefully into the refrigerator's barren interior, then shrugged. Damn.

He shut the refrigerator as the florist's answering machine picked up. On his way out, he identified himself, asked that a dozen pink roses be sent to his date's hotel room with the usual note, then thumbed the end button as he locked the door behind him. Okay, so he didn't encourage commitment. That didn't mean he had to be an ass.

And asking his staff to do his romantic follow-ups for him would be way out of line. It wasn't as if Carey Benton couldn't; Matt had never had a more competent assistant. And it wasn't as if she *wouldn't*. In fact, Matt suspected that Carey would do more for him than any boss should rightly ask…though that might be wishful thinking. It was sure *dangerous* thinking.

Still, some things a man shouldn't delegate. Just the temptation to delegate was probably a bad sign. He'd liked Janeen just fine...but Matt still felt relieved to be heading back to the office and its staff.

On the elevator to the parking garage, he called ahead to the drive-thru bagel shop and placed his order. He even remembered Carey's favorite; pecan cream cheese. He reached his Mustang and turned on the radio just in time for the next announcement of "WDCN traffic and weather every fifteen minutes."

6:08 a.m.

Was it Monday?

Unable to sleep, Violet Vaughn Hobson sat up in bed for a long while, then stood and wandered to the window of her second-story, generic downtown motel room. She drew the curtains to look out at the unnaturally white, still-lit Washington Monument, half visible in the distance. Traffic seemed busy out there. She supposed it must be Monday.

She shook her head, frustrated with how time was beginning to blur for her. She was aging, true, but hardly old. Yet so much had happened....

After more than a twenty-year burial, Violet's bizarre past life had resurfaced. It began in April, when she'd recognized the preternatural brilliance behind the World Bank heist as that of her stolen son, Gideon—the youngest of her and Henry Bloomfield's five miracles, the son she'd thought had been killed. Then she'd learned that financial wizard Jake Ingram had been hired to head the task force investigating the robbery, and she recognized her oldest son, as well. Jake hadn't known it at the time, but his genius was just as preternatural as that of his brother the thief—and every bit as dangerous.

Since then, Violet had contacted Jake and convinced him

of his fantastic origins *and* his danger. Mere days ago, he'd located his twin sister, Grace—now called Gretchen. And she was newly married!

Married as their scientist parents—both sperm donor and surrogate mother—never were. In love....

A lifetime had passed since Henry's murder, since Violet had tried to buy their children's safety by sending them off to new identities and new lives. But the past was rising, full of mistakes and guilt...and love.

It had been love, hadn't it? Never sanctified in marriage. Never even spoken. But such a love....

How much precious time had Violet wasted, adoring Henry, her older employer, from afar. How much of their lives had been misdirected into their job. And why—

Violet's eyes abruptly focused on a man across the street, looking up at her window. She stepped quickly behind the draperies.

Was he watching her?

After a minute of steady breathing, to calm her racing heart, she peeked out—and was relieved to see the man wave at a clearly different window, then head into a café. He was no enemy spy trying to use her to get to the children.

But spies were out there, all the same.

Violet's twenty-plus years of peace were clearly over. She had too much to do before any of her and Henry's extraordinary children—whom the press in ignorance and fear had dubbed "gen-eng'ed, biotech babies," even mutants— would be safe. She had too much to make up for.

But sometimes Violet still woke early and, instead of making plans, simply dreamed she could go back in time. She wished she could change things so that her own love story could have ended more happily than it had. Happy endings were possible for some people, weren't they?

But some wishes never came true.

One

Carey was taking a message from *the* Jake Ingram—well-known financial wizard from Texas—when Matt breezed into the West Wing. She heard him coming, exchanging bits of news and approval numbers, greeting staff and assistants by first name. The perfect charmer. The closer he got, the happier she felt.

"He's walking in now, Mr. Ingram," she said, unable to keep the smile from her voice. "Would you like to hold?"

"Please." Not only was Mr. Ingram investigating the World Bank heist, he was an old college friend of Matt's. She knew her boss would want to take this call.

Then Matt spun into her outer office, his arms full of blue bags from Bagel Biz. At the sight of him, Carey could easily forget her own name, much less that she had one of the nation's movers and shakers waiting to the sound of patriotic Muzak.

"Morning, glory," greeted Matt with a winning grin, unloading the bags onto a sideboard she kept clear for just such luxuries. "How are things in Ogallala?"

It was a joke between them, pretending he couldn't remember where she was from. Matt Tynan could remember everything from the gross national product of Paraguay to the general population of Baton Rouge. Surely he could remember Kansas City, Kansas.

But it wasn't just Matt's sharp mind that had Carey's insides melting in slow appreciation. Nor was it his palpable sex appeal, his athletic build or his dark good looks. He was Hollywood handsome, enlivened by mercurial eyes, a quick grin and the fact that he was almost always in motion—ducking his head, rolling his shoulders, stuffing his hands into his pockets. His previous assistant, a kindly woman who'd trained Carey, had called him exhausting. She'd smiled as she said it.

Carey had yet to meet a woman who didn't smile when talking about Matt Tynan.

That was what truly fascinated her. Matt was a man who clearly adored women, all women. Young and old. Slim and fat. Shy and extroverted. He was so unlikely to commit to any of them that the White House staff was betting on whether he would marry before he reached the age of forty. Even President Stewart, Carey heard, had bet no. But neither would Matt deliberately hurt anyone; even his ex-lovers adored him. Women responded to his undiluted appreciation.

Carey was no exception.

"I didn't go home this weekend," she said, as if Matt had been serious about Ogallala. Her need to stay efficient got her to her feet and forming words at the same time. "Along with the usual meetings, you've got a nine o'clock with the Alaskan environmentalists, a ten o'clock with the Parents' Coalition and lunch with Josh O'Donnell about the O.S.E.P."

Matt unloaded bagels and spreads. "Aye aye, Skipper."

"I've left phone messages and the A.P. printout on your desk, and a birthday card for your stepmother that needs signing."

"Marie or Taffy?" asked Matt. "Or the new one…?"

Carey narrowed her eyes, fairly sure he knew his stepmothers' birthdays and names, even his current, common-law step. "Taffy. And Jake Ingram's holding on line one."

Matt crumpled the now empty bags together, arcing the blue wad across the office and into the wooden wastebasket. He'd started to slide his miniature tape recorder from his pocket but stilled when the name registered. "Jake? Really?"

His grin returned, complete with dimples, as he spilled a microtape out of the recorder and tossed it to Carey.

She caught it. "That, or someone pretending to be Jake Ingram, who does a remarkably good Jake Ingram imitation."

"You don't find many of those." Matt cocked his head, his gleaming eyes softened by laugh lines crinkling the outside corners. "Richard Nixon, John Wayne, Marlon Brando—those are easy. Jake Ingram imitations though...."

Carey played along. "Few and far between."

He winked. "If you can have the letters on that tape ready for signing by end of day, I'll love you forever."

"Promises, promises," she teased, to hide her pleasure.

"Oh, and see if you can get me ten minutes with Senator Bermann this morning, and call my housekeeper about restocking the fridge, okay?"

"Yes on the letters, the senator will insist you go to his office so you'll need at least a half hour, and Serina already said she'd bring groceries this..." Mmm. When he circled past her, Carey almost lost her train of thought just breathing in the scent of him. "This afternoon."

It wasn't so much his smooth aftershave as the soap he used. Sandalwood or something. And just plain Matt.

"You're too good to be true, Skipper. Stay that way. That's an order." But in the doorway of his office, he paused, frowned, then shook his head. "It's barely 6:00 a.m. in Dallas."

Dallas was Jake Ingram's home base. Now that he was

heading an international task force, he could be working anywhere.

Matt shrugged off whatever concerns that gave him. "One way to find out. Hold—"

"—your other calls," finished Carey, winning another heart-stopping, wink-and-grin combination.

Then Matt shut his door behind him, diluting whatever power he wielded over her, sexual or otherwise.

Wow.

Carey sank into her office chair, catching her breath. If she felt this unbalanced admiring Matt Tynan from afar, thank goodness she stood no possible chance with him from anear.

"Did I hear bagel rumors?" asked Rita Winfield, White House Press Secretary, peeking in. Her eyes lit on the sideboard, and she made a beeline for it. "Goody! I think this is how Matt became one of the Top Twenty Beltway Bachelors last year."

Carey laughed, determined not to let her crush on Matt handicap her professionalism with the rest of the White House staff. "Bagels?"

"He feeds his women very well. Want one?"

"I can get it."

Rita waved Carey off. "I'm already here. Pecan cream cheese, right?"

There were moments at this job that Carey just had to stop and marvel. Sometimes it was something as simple as crossing Lafayette Square, between the Metro station and the White House, or striding into the West Wing via the staff entrance with her blue identification badge. Sometimes it happened at a monument, or a museum—she had yet to grow jaded about D.C. and hoped she never would. And then there were times like this: a woman hired personally by the president of the United States was fixing her breakfast. Amazing. "Thank you."

"Private call, huh?" Rita nodded toward the closed door. She was several years older than Matt, a walking testimony to how well one's late thirties could treat a woman. Apparently she and Matt went back a long way.

Whether they'd ever been lovers was anybody's guess.

Knowing Matt Tynan's reputation—probably.

Carey still knew better than to offer more information than was needed. "Uh-huh. Would you like me to get you five minutes?"

"I want to show this to him." Rita handed over the society page of the *Washington Post*. Carey automatically swept her long hair back from her face as she looked at it.

Stepping Out, read the caption of a picture above the fold. To judge by the mirrors and chandeliers, it had been taken inside the Kennedy Center. Looking closer, Carey felt a stab of unbidden yearning. Matt had been born to wear a tux. And the sleek redhead draped across his arm looked more sexually satisfied than was probably legal without warning labels.

Not that Carey could do more than guess about that—at least, not until she went over his credit card bill for him. She knew what a dozen pink roses from the florist meant.

"A peanut heiress." Rita licked cream cheese off her fingers. "Sister, I can milk this one for a week."

"Where do you even *buy* a dress like that?" Carey mused, taking a bite of bagel. Something about the cut and drape of the gown—or of the heiress—made her feel like a complete yokel. Or maybe a nun. The peanut heiress had probably never in her life worn her hair in a scrunchy.

It was yet one more reason Matt would never see Carey as more than his competent, efficient assistant. He dated sophisticated women. Older women. Experienced women.

Despite her best efforts, Carey sighed.

"I could find you a dress like that," offered Rita. "With a little polish, maybe our guy in there—"

"No." Carey had never admitted her feelings to the press secretary; Rita was just remarkably perceptive. "Don't even joke about that. He's my boss. If anything ever happened—" fat chance, she thought "—I'd have to change jobs. And I love this job."

Matt made a difference. By assisting him, Carey felt as if she made a difference, too. She wasn't the good woman *behind* him; she had the desk in *front*. And she loved seeing him every day. Not one of his many dates could make a similar claim.

"Well, you know where to find me." Rita helped herself to a pen from Carey's desk and reclaimed the society page. "When he's free, give this to him, will you?"

When she handed the newspaper back to Carey, Rita had drawn a little monocle and top hat onto the picture of Matt's date, resembling a popular, brand-name spokes-peanut.

The phone rang again and Rita, with a self-satisfied laugh, left when Carey answered it. "Matt Tynan's office."

"When are you gonna leave that ugly bum and come work for me, huh?" asked Josh O'Donnell, Assistant Secretary for the Office of Special Education Programs. He always asked that.

Carey politely turned him down, just as she did every other time, and took his latest message for Matt. Maybe her life *was* a form of slow torture. She was in love with a man who exuded sexuality...at everyone except her. And that was probably just as well.

But it was miles better than Kansas City.

Matt turned on and muted the three televisions crowded into his office, glanced at the small video screen on his desk and dropped into his chair. He wasn't sure when he'd started noticing. Three months ago? Six? But some mornings, Carey Benton was so pretty she was dangerous. Shiny brown hair. Smiling blue eyes. A wholesome, fresh face that belonged on the cover of *Seventeen* magazine more than it did inside the Beltway. She was too good to be true, yet there she sat, a sweet, dependable constant in his crazy life, and damned if she didn't brighten his mornings. And noontimes. And afternoons.

But no nights. If Matt wasn't so careful about workplace romances and younger women, he could easily screw up one of the best relationships he'd ever had.

His determination reinforced, he picked up the phone. "Talk to me, Jake. Are you postponing your wedding again?"

"Hey, Tynan." At the tension in his friend's voice, Matt forgot Carey—which was saying something. "I need a favor."

"Anything," Matt said. "You know that."

Jake Ingram never asked for favors. Hell, Jake had so much more money than Matt, he'd never needed them. All Matt had was a way with women—and his job as White House Advisor.

The screen on his desk beeped to indicate that POTUS— the President Of The United States—was on the move.

"Anything that I can," he qualified.

"I need information—nothing that would compromise you," Jake hurried to add. "I'm hoping you can get details faster than I can. It has to do with an old CIA project—"

This didn't sound good. "CIA?"

"*Old* CIA," insisted Jake. "The project started almost forty years ago, and my information indicates it was discontinued in 1980. With Freedom of Information, at least some of it should be declassified by now. But response time is a bear, especially with the red tape.''

''And you're hoping I can pull files from Pennsylvania Avenue faster than you can from Dallas.'' Matt drummed the end of a pencil on his desk. ''I hate to disillusion you, pal, but I'm not sure even my boss has the power to speed up bureaucracy. Especially with those covert-op types.''

''I know it's a long shot.'' Jake sounded like he used to during finals: short on sleep and pumped on challenge. ''But there may be a connection between this project and the World Bank heist.''

''Whoa, there.'' Matt's pencil bounced off his desk. It had been two months since some techno-whiz called Achilles had hacked into the World Bank and transferred three hundred and fifty billion dollars into a series of dummy accounts and corporations. Matt knew that Jake had been hired to help the FBI investigate the crime. But the CIA? ''Connected with the World Bank heist how?''

''I can't tell you yet.'' At least Jake sounded truly regretful. ''Hopefully once I've got more information, I can, but for now…it's just too dangerous.''

''Yeah, you daredevil math guys like to ride the ragged edge.'' Matt scrubbed a hand through his hair, concerned despite his joking. ''I'll look into the matter, no problem. Would you mind if I put my assistant on it?''

''Carey? How much do you trust her?''

Matt considered the young woman on the other side of his closed door, ducked his head and smiled. His admiration of her went far beyond appreciation of her shiny hair, welcoming eyes and willowy curves. He'd come to trust her more than his three-and-a-half mothers put together. ''Implicitly.''

''Then go for it. Um, Matt…'' There Jake went, sounding furtive again. ''I'll check back with you next week. But if you don't hear from me by that Friday, send the data to a woman named Gretchen Miller. Here's her number.''

It was a foreign exchange. Matt didn't recognize the international calling code. "Someone you trust, huh?" he only half teased. "What's Tara think about that?"

Tara was Jake's fiancée—his lady of perpetual waiting.

"I trust Gretchen implicitly, too," said Jake. "So does her new husband. Read me back the number."

Matt did, increasingly suspicious. "So why wouldn't you be able to call back next week, Jake?"

"You've got enough to worry about with Code Proteus."

"Proteus?" The name sounded vaguely familiar.

"That's the project's handle. It was run under the Medusa branch of the CIA, working out of a North Carolina town called Belle Terre. I have some names to attach to it—Agnes Payne, Oliver Grimble, Violet Vaughn and Henry Bloomfield. Try not to let Payne or Grimble know you're digging into their pasts."

"Vaughn and Bloomfield?"

"Vaughn's in our column." Jake's voice softened with a touch of what could be loss. "Bloomfield died just before the project shut down."

"Got it." But Matt wasn't close to satisfied. "Is everything okay, Jake? Your brother's been all right since the kidnapping? Your parents?"

"My brother's in love," Jake said, as if that were any guarantee. "He's doing great. My family's fine."

Matt must have just imagined that his friend added, under his breath, "That one, anyway."

Carey was typing the third of the letters Matt had dictated in his car when he leaned out his office door. "Hey, Skipper, can I see you a minute?"

She stood, snagging the newspaper Rita had left for him.

Then she considered how serious he'd sounded and put the society page back down. The peanut heiress could wait.

She was glad she did when Matt closed the old wooden door behind them with a thud. His TVs were on, but silent.

"Is something wrong?" She turned as he started to pass her and they bumped shoulders, her light linen jacket grazing his darker suit coat. Matt easily steadied her with a warm, solid hand on her arm. It helped her physical balance, but threw her emotional balance into a whole new dizziness.

"Not wrong, no. Just…private. Have a seat."

She did. He leaned a hip against his desk, cocked his head and asked, "You're some kind of Liberal Arts guru, right?"

She nodded. "Double major in literature and history."

"Huh. Does the name Proteus ring any bells?"

"Sure." When he widened his eyes, encouraging, she continued. "Proteus was a sea god in Greek mythology, a son of Poseidon. He could see the future, but apparently he didn't like looking. Whenever someone approached him for a prophecy, he shape-shifted to frighten them away."

"Changeable," mused Matt, nodding. "Protean."

"The only way to win his help was to hold on to him, no matter what kind of monster he became, to remember his shapes were an illusion. If a person held on long enough, Proteus would revert to his true self and offer the future. Matt, is there some other reason you called me in—"

He held up a hand in silent reassurance that all would become clear. "I'm going to ask you for a favor, but please don't feel obligated to say yes."

Yes, yes, yes, she thought—but tried to look efficient. She might never manage sophistication, but at least she could avoid slapstick. "Tell me what you need," she said, as she often did, "and I'll tell you if we can do it."

"It's personal." He dipped his head in warning, dragging out his words. "And it's confidential."

She nodded, increasingly intrigued.

"Jake Ingram has asked me to gather information about an old CIA project called Code Proteus." Matt pushed himself up from his desk and circled it. "It's a closed project, hopefully declassified, but he needs a rush. I wouldn't ask except that on top of my usual crises there's that vote on the education budget coming up at the end of the month."

Carey nodded. President Stewart had won the election—barely—based on his education initiative. If he lost this vote in either the House or Senate, he lost most of his credibility.

And if anybody knew how full Matt's calendar was, it was the woman who kept it. "I'd be honored to help."

"It'll mean overtime. You already work ten-hour days."

Usually longer. But there was a reason for that, and at least he noticed. "I'm glad to do it, Matt. Really." Carey smiled. "It sounds kind of cloak-and-dagger."

Even Matt's snort seemed sexy. "At the first sign of cloaks or daggers, you call me, got it?"

Carey felt her smile widen at the fantasy of Matt riding to her rescue. "Yes, sir, Mr. Tynan, sir."

He rolled his eyes at the formality and stuffed his hands briefly into his pockets. "I mean it, Carey. If this thing's still active, or people notice us asking questions, I don't want you involved."

But he wouldn't have asked her if it wasn't important. "I'll be careful. I always am."

"Good." He came around the desk again and handed her a half sheet of notepaper on which he'd jotted prompts: CIA, Code Proteus, Medusa Branch, started 60s, ended 80s. His fingers brushed hers during the exchange and Matt fell still beside her, eyes particularly bright, particularly intense.

Carey had to work not to shiver. He stood so close, smelled so good....

"I'll get right on it." Her promise barely wavered.

Matt's head ducked toward hers, hesitated, dipped closer. As though they were conspirators, sharing danger, sharing trust. "Thank you," he said, low. He held her gaze a moment too long, long enough that his grin began to relax into something softer, slower, more intimate.

Almost as though he not only liked her, not only needed her, but found her attractive.

Almost as though he, Matt Tynan, was interested in her, Carey Benton, for reasons far more primal than her banter, typing speed and organizational abilities.

Carey always felt unusually conscious of her own body around him; the way he radiated sex appeal she'd have to be dead not to. But for maybe the first time she suspected he was aware of it, too. This new awareness felt both delicious…and dangerous.

Someone knocked on the door and they both jumped.

"Okeydoke, then." Matt backed away from her faster than a recovering alcoholic from a tall bourbon. "Let me know when you learn something important."

But Carey had the unsettling suspicion she just had.

Two

"And then his hand brushed mine," said Carey at lunch in the downstairs mess. She'd carefully avoided mentioning what she and Matt had discussed, referring to Code Proteus as "an extra project." Even if Carey hadn't promised discretion, her friend Honey Evans—who worked for the Telephone Office in the basement under the West Wing—probably wasn't a high security risk. But other than the interns, who rarely stayed more than a few months at a time, Honey and Carey were the youngest employees in the West Wing and thus gravitated to each other.

Also, opposites attracted.

"So you jumped him," finished Honey with a happy bounce, popping a Tater Tot into her mouth. "You ripped the buttons right off his starched shirt—no, you *bit* them off!—and you pushed Matt Tynan back onto his desk and crawled on top of him like you've been longing to do since forever—"

"Stop!" Carey could hardly force the word past her horror-tightened throat. Worse, the crazy image kind of turned her on. "What if someone hears you?"

"Ya think?" Honey brightened and looked around them. But to her clear disappointment, and Carey's immense relief, no one was listening to them discuss their love lives...or their lack thereof. Carey had no love life because the only important man in her life, outside of family, was her boss. Honey had none because....

Well, to hear Honey tell it, she enjoyed a different man every night. The more Carey got to know her friend, though, the more she wondered if that were true. Sometimes she got the oddest feeling that Honey was talking a big talk, trying hard to seem more like a wild child than she really was.

But why?

"I'm just teasing." Honey tossed blond curls back from her face. "Of course, *I* would have jumped him long before now. *You* probably just sighed and thanked him for favoring you with his barest touch, then decided you'd never *ever* wash that hand again."

"Mock me if you will," said Carey. "But the way he went still for a moment, right after our fingers touched…it felt significant, is all."

Honey's eyes sparkled with mischief. "Not as significant as biting off his shirt buttons would be."

Carey sighed and stabbed some Greek salad, biting it instead of Matt Tynan's shirt buttons. Even if he *were* interested, she wasn't. Not outside her fantasies. So why did it matter?

Honey said, "I don't see why you accepted this new project. You already get here ungodly early, leave ungodly late and shun all signs of a social life. When does Tynan think you can fit in more work—carry a laptop into the bathroom with you? Are you going to start spending the night here?"

Carey took another quick bite of salad, and Honey sat up, intrigued. Shorter than Carey by four inches, she wasn't opposed to climbing onto her knees in the chair to get the extra height she needed. "O-oh! So that's your plan—late nights in the office, huh?"

"It's not like that," protested Carey. But was it?

"You'll wait until everyone else has left, turn down the lights, put on a sultry R & B CD. He'll have his tie off and his sleeves rolled up, maybe his shirt collar unbuttoned…."

Carey felt herself blush again. "Stop it, Honey. For one thing, there's *never* a time when everyone else has left. For another, there's nothing romantic between Matt and me."

"Which is why you talk about him every day at lunch." Honey took a decisive bite of another Tater Tot.

"That's not—" Carey groaned, unsure she could defend herself. But Honey had settled back into her seat, downright intrigued, so she tried. "I *do* like him, sure. What's not to like? But even if I was fool enough to consider dating him, he likes sophisticated women." The kind she would never be.

"Like Ms. Peanut," said Honey. Apparently the operators downstairs had been passing the society page around, too.

Carey was beginning to feel bad for the heiress, who'd done nothing worse than accompany Matt to a fund-raiser and get her picture taken on his arm. "She's probably not a bad woman. Just because her family made its fortune in peanuts isn't any reason for us to make fun of her."

Honey stared. "You've got to be kidding."

"Peanuts are very useful plants," added Carey, playing with an olive. Okay, so she was reaching.

"This isn't George Washington Carver we're talking about here. It's some rich bimbo with a boob job." Honey narrowed her eyes. "Not to mention, while you were home in your flannel nightgown, crocheting socks for war orphans or something, she was probably screwing Matt Tynan like a lightbulb. That makes her your enemy. Live with it."

"I wasn't wearing flannel," protested Carey, more than a little uncomfortable with the images Honey had just painted. Matt naked. Matt in bed. Matt naked in bed. "It's June."

"Please," said Honey again. "In fact, if Tynan's got such a phobia about virgins, just find some stud to relieve you of that little problem. Then you can join the ranks of the grown-ups, right?''

''I'm older than you! Besides, he doesn't have a phobia about virgins.'' As far as Carey knew, anyway; it wasn't exactly something they discussed between the budget, national security or the new Supreme Court justice. ''Which doesn't matter because we're not dating! And I've told you before, being a virgin isn't some problem to be solved.''

''That,'' said Honey darkly, ''depends on who you're talking to.''

''It's not like I'm saving myself for marriage. And it's not like I'm particularly uptight—flannel nightgowns aside.''

Honey's eyes and mouth widened. ''You *do* have one!''

''For the winter, yes, but that's beside the point. My body is my business, and when I find a man I can trust, a man I can love and commit to, then we'll see. Even if…''

Even if Matt Tynan tempted her toward rethinking that policy. Not that he was offering.

She shook off those fantasies. ''Until then I've got an exciting life and an important job. I'm happy.''

''And you don't want to do it with anyone but Tynan.'' Honey rolled her eyes, but relented. ''I suppose there's something marginally sweet about that. Hopeless and melancholy, but sweet. So spill. After he touched your hand and went all still, what happened?''

''Rita Winfield came by.'' Carey shrugged. ''And I went back to my desk.''

Honey shook her head. ''Your stories suck.''

Thursday, June 5

''Senator,'' protested Matt again. He rarely got to finish the title. Normally he only managed ''Sen—''. But he was losing patience.

Wendell Bermann was old and powerful. He looked powerful, with his long jaw adding a touch of class to an otherwise solid, Midwestern frame, leathery skin and iron-gray hair. He'd represented Missouri since before Matt was born. Maybe that was why he had little new to say. "—fine servicemen live in the city of Harper, and I would be remiss if I did not defend the job they are doing for this great nation during these troubled times!"

"With all due respect, Senator," said Matt as the man took a breath. He forced a smile. "We don't fire servicemen. If the base closes—and it's been running on minimal personnel for almost a decade now—they'll still have a job elsewhere."

"And what about their wives?" demanded Bermann.

Or husbands, thought Matt, shoving his hands into his pockets. You sexist son of a—

He made himself smile harder.

"And what about those hardworking, loyal Americans whose businesses will dry up without that base there?" As if nobody had thought of them, despite the last hundred times Bermann had mentioned it.

"Well, sir." Matt freed a hand to spread it. "A Harper Chamber of Commerce study shows two private colleges in town carry more business than the base. The chancellor of their county's community college district said that with the tax breaks offered in the president's education budget, they hope to build a new campus in Harper. That would attract a larger student body to support local business than the base has personnel."

"You fellas are trying to confuse the issue with numbers," said Bermann, and he launched a diatribe against the president's popular Fight Fear With Knowledge campaign.

Confuse the issue with numbers. Matt imagined how math whiz Jake Ingram would react to that statement.

But thinking of Jake reminded Matt of Code Proteus and of Carey, who'd stayed late the past few nights hunting for the secret project. It was after seven and she was probably still back at the office, her face illuminated by the light of her computer screen, her chin propped on her fist....

Bermann. Remember Bermann.

"...the average American. The working-class American. The American who wants good solid values, not liberal college brainwashing. Information age, my aunt Fanny. There's too much damned information out there, if you ask me!"

Matt rubbed a hand down his face. "Being on the Appropriations Committee, I'm sure you're aware that eighty percent of the benefits from the president's education initiative is aimed not at colleges but public schools, with an emphasis on identifying both gifted and special needs children—"

"And I don't give a good doggy damn," interrupted Bermann, ending today's dance. "Unless Stewart reverses his decision to close that base in Harper, I'm gonna put that education initiative of his out of its misery when the Senate votes. You know I've got the markers to do it. So you stop wasting my time and go do something useful, like tell your boss to give it up."

Not likely. Besides, the president was running for reelection in a year, and education was his rallying cry.

It always came down to elections, one way or the other.

Matt said, "If you'd just look at my ideas to preserve the spirit of the base—"

"Wasting," said Berman. "My. Time."

Matt took a deep breath. This man wasn't just Wendell Bermann. He was the Honorable Wendell Bermann of the United States Senate. And damn it, Matt would respect the office even if he despised the man. That was the only way democracy survived.

"Thank you for your time, sir," he said. Then he escaped the Dirksen Senate Office Building.

It wasn't dark yet but a stillness hung over D.C. as Matt drove back to the White House. Though the city stayed open twenty-four hours a day, a lot of people had gone home to their families or friends for the night.

Matt once overheard Carey defending his grueling hours in her unique, Kansan way. She'd said that Old West cowboys on a summertime cattle drive were told they'd have plenty of time to sleep "come winter."

Much of the White House staff followed a similar philosophy. They'd get outside lives when the president's term was up. But when that happened, Matt would just find someone else to help get elected. He loved politics. He loved how the system worked, how it took voices as diverse as President Stewart and Senator Bermann and so many more, and mixed them and tugged them and tempered them until one mutual voice was reached. It sometimes sounded too strident, sometimes too lax, but it was the voice of America, for better or worse.

If there were a greater ideal for flawed humans in a flawed world than democracy, Matt hadn't heard it. He couldn't foresee ever giving it up—reason number God-knew-what for him never disguising himself as family material. Spouses and parents shouldn't vanish during elections or other assorted crises.

He should know. His mom had walked out on them when Matt was twelve, and his first stepmom had dumped them his junior year in high school. His dad tended toward sudden "business trips," at the expense of his marriages. The Cleavers, they were not.

Parking in his White House space, Matt jogged up the stairs, past the indoor security check, into the stately lobby and past the Marine guard into the West Wing proper. The stillness outside hadn't made it here yet. Rita, a phone to her ear, was talking while she read sheets sliding out of the fax machine. The Chief of Staff chatted with the Director of Communications, nodding as Matt passed.

And there sat Carey at her computer.

Her chin propped on her fist.

Her pretty face illuminated by the light of the screen.

Looking at her, Matt felt a comforting stillness wrap itself around him like his paternal grandmother's quilt. His original grandmother's, not one of his many steps. He wasn't completely sure which bit of Carey's magic, in the office, had made it so homey. She'd mounted plants in high, unused corners—ivies, flowers, ferns. She'd set up a sideboard across from her desk, often setting out cookies or brownies for him and other staff members. Much of what she'd brought into the office was wood; desk, cabinets, pencil cups, inboxes and outboxes. She'd mounted and framed different prints of the White House, a uniquely Carey kind of choice. And a soft green throw draped over the back of her chair. Sometimes when Matt worked through the night, grabbing a quick nap on the sofa in his office, he used it as a blanket...and smelled Carey in it. And dreamed hot, inappropriate dreams.

Too young, he told himself. Too important. He dated women without strings, and Carey came with more strings than macramé.

As if hearing his thoughts, she looked up. Immediately she brightened at his presence. But she said, ''Uh-oh. Someone's talk with the senator didn't go well, huh?''

Understatement of the week, Matt thought. He took those last few steps into the office and half sat on the edge of her desk, drawn by her sympathy. He picked up her stapler and began to turn it over in his hands. "Depends on your definition of 'well.' Distract me from my diplomatic failure, Carey. Tell me what you've found on our other project."

"Not a lot." She took the stapler away from him. "The first thing I did was request files using Freedom of Information. Nothing's come of that yet, even with me throwing your name around like a Superball. But when I started looking for some kind of money trail, I found an invoice—"

The phone rang, and Matt nodded his assent for her to answer it. While she did, he picked up her paper-clip holder, shook a few neon-colored clips into his palm, and grinned to himself. *Like a Superball.* Carey made him think of old toys like that, of ice-cream cones and backyard campouts and vacant-lot summertime baseball games. Innocent times. Idealism.

"Matt Tynan's office. This is Carcy." She took the paper-clip holder firmly away from him, put it out of his reach, then opened her free hand in a silent demand for the extra clips. "I'll see if I can catch him. Please hold."

Then she looked up at him. "It's your mother."

She clearly meant the original. Reluctantly he handed Carey her paper clips and stood. "You found an invoice?"

"If it's really related to Proteus, which seems kind of iffy. It's for a toy store. Does that make any sense?"

He shook his head, backing toward his office. His mother hated being on hold. It brought out her abandonment issues. "Nothing else?"

"Don't lose faith yet." She sounded so confident that, even as he closed his door, he believed her.

He sank into his chair, surrounded by photocopies that needed reading, forms that needed signing, the ever-changing POTUS monitor on his desk. None of it could unbalance him like a phone call from his mother. "Hi, Mom."

"I think Harry's cheating on me," she announced.

Matt closed his eyes, wishing his sympathy weren't tempered with frustration. "What makes you think that, Mom?"

His mother had terrible luck with husbands, starting with the father who'd raised him and continuing with Matt's bastard of a stepdad. Those innocent days of home-baked cookies and simple parent-teacher nights had ended long ago.

While his mother began her list of suspicions, Matt glanced at the closed door and thought of the family picture on Carey's desk—one mother, one father and a handful of siblings, all happy, all younger than him in so many ways.

Some days there were far more than ten years stretching between him and his assistant.

Carey listened to the door snick shut, then sighed.

Staying late wasn't anything like Honey had predicted. Having just met with the senator, Matt still wore his tie, and Carey wasn't about to strip off her panty hose and bra with the office so busy. But she enjoyed the opportunity to help out, especially for something as big as the World Bank investigation, and she liked the extra time with Matt. She couldn't remember him ever sitting on her desk during regular working hours; surely she would've remembered the proximity of his slim hip to her hands, the way his knee, pressing out the crease of his trousers, had jutted toward her suddenly heavy breasts....

She realized she was still clutching the paper clips he'd handed back to her—as if his casual touch had imbued them with meaning. She forced herself to sprinkle them into the holder and turned back to her computerized goose chase. That one invoice, among a simple list of paperwork saved on an old five-and-a-quarter-inch floppy disk, was all she'd found. Other than the notation of "Proteus" that had supposedly been scribbled on it, she couldn't even be sure it was a real clue.

Invoice, read the database file. *FAO Schwarz. R & D Dept. $48.72. "Assorted beta toys." Dated November 17, 1973. Handwritten across the top: "Medusa—Proteus."*

But why in the world would a CIA project purchase toys?

Carey felt her interest in this research project deepen to something more. Toys implied children, right? People.

"People." She rolled the word across her tongue as she cut-and-pasted the data into a word-processing document to print. Why hadn't she considered that before? People could rarely be neatly filed. They had parents, friends, spouses, children, pasts. People touched each other in any number of ways, and they could leave indelible marks—even when, like Matt, they tried not to.

Maybe that was where she'd gone wrong in her hunt so far. She'd forgotten to factor in simple humanity.

Carey took the page that slid out of her printer and tucked it into a file marked P & C: personal and confidential. She noticed the light for Matt's line, on her phone, go out, and she felt oddly sad. Matt rarely enjoyed conversations with his mother.

When his door opened, he had his gym bag.

"I'm hitting the O.E.O.B. before the gym closes. If I don't catch you before you leave, have security walk you out to your— You don't drive, do you?"

"Not here, I don't." At his telling expression, she sighed. "This is the White House, Matt, and tourist season. There are more police between here and the Metro than you have ex-girlfriends. And the sun sets late. And I have pepper spray."

"I'd rather you had a car."

"If wishes were horses..." teased Carey. Not that she

was a beggar, though the White House pay scale was a lot leaner than most citizens realized.

Matt lifted his free hand in defeat and headed out for the Old Executive Office Building. She wondered what his mother had said to make him so desperate for a workout that he'd forgotten their project. He seemed…lonely.

Then she regained her senses. Matt Tynan lonely?

If wishes were horses, then beggars would ride.

He'd always been changeable, she reminded herself, and smiled softly at the parallel. Protean.

Instead of further pursuing her week's worth of near dead ends, Carey logged onto the Internet and rested her chin on her fist as she started a whole new search. Both the money trail and the paper trail might remain top secret, out of reach.

But Carey would bet dollars to doughnuts that she could find a *people* trail.

Three

"Gone to library," read the note taped to Matt's POTUS screen in Carey's familiar, curvy writing. She knew how often he glanced at that. "Remember your 9:00."

Back from the gym, his hair damp and his skin tingling from the shower, Matt folded and tucked the note into his pocket. He told himself he was relieved by Carey's absence. The office was quieting down—as much as the West Wing ever did—and it seemed wiser not to enjoy too much privacy with his sweet assistant.

Some men weren't meant for commitment, but some women weren't intended for anything else. Mixing the two generally resulted in disasters like his parents' marriages. Matt had no intention of turning his fresh-faced secretary into the kind of lost soul his father had made of his mother.

Instead he headed out for his nine o'clock appointment with Congresswoman Judy Riley. They were meeting not at her office but at the Hawk and Dove, a noisy pub well down Pennsylvania Avenue from work. She sat to the left of the bar with the rest of the pols, and Matt ordered himself a beer as he angled in beside her. He didn't bother requesting a receipt. The way Judy's eyes flirted at him as she said hello, she seemed intent on discussing more than funding for the National Endowment of the Arts.

"Hello, yourself," he said with his usual grin—but without his usual interest. Judy was attractive in her tough, mature way. And Matt did favor women who could take care of themselves.

But she didn't have shiny brown hair or blue eyes.

Matt didn't brush her off. But he flirted back without ever crossing that line from fun into seduction. The congress-woman, being one sharp lady, figured it out and quickly adapted. They had an enjoyable half hour.

Then Matt found himself on his own in D.C.'s busiest bar. At least the TVs here on Capitol Hill showed cable news over sports, and the beer was good. Since his empty apartment held no attraction—he couldn't remember the last place he'd considered *home*—he talked some aides into joining him for a pool game. Pool and politics. God, he loved this town.

It was maybe nine-forty and their debate about diplomatic relations with Rebelia had just gotten fun when his mobile phone rang. The number—a D.C. exchange—didn't look familiar as he answered, but few people had this line. "Talk to me."

Nothing. All he could hear were the noises of the pub— clacking pool balls, clinking glass and the laughter of one of the female aides when her date tickled her.

He pulled the phone back from his ear and frowned at it. The line had disconnected.

Flushing, Carey hung up the payphone at the Library of Congress, the minute she heard the woman's laughter. Then she stared at the receiver. What was wrong with her?

She'd gotten an image of what Matt might be doing with his smiling mouth and practiced hands to encourage such a happy, social sound—and suddenly the information she'd found about Dr. Henry Bloomfield of Belle Terre, N.C., seemed far less important. Was it the congresswoman, she wondered, or someone else?

She disliked the suspicion that he might have another charge for pink roses, dated tomorrow morning, on next month's credit-card bill. As if it was any of her business.

How naive could she get? He obviously had other more important, more urgent…more *available* fish to fry.

"Miss?" prompted one of the librarians, detouring to the bank of phones near the elevator bay to urge her out. "The library is officially closed."

It had closed at nine-thirty, making Carey one of the worst stragglers. But she'd just *had* to print out that last article from the *Belle Terre Bugle*. And then she'd had to tell Matt. Or so she'd thought.

"Yes, sir," she said, clutching the precious sheaf of printouts to her traitorously aching chest. "Thank you."

She felt small and unimportant as she crossed the main foyer, its floor so shiny that it reflected like a mirror the tall, white statue of James Madison. The six-story Madison Library was huge, the third largest building in D.C., and built in a clean, modern style of architecture that made it seem boxy and plain against the other landmarks on Capitol Hill. Normally Carey preferred the library's Jefferson Building, just across Independence Avenue as she descended the main steps. But newspapers and periodicals were in the Madison.

Just as well. The last thing she needed to make her feel even more provincial was the Jefferson Building's marble stairways, galleries, fountains and gilded copper dome. Even if that kind of elegance *was* part of what had won her heart to this city on her first high-school visit.

The elegance, and the fast pace, and the power.

Carey hesitated on the well-lit sidewalk, still holding tight to her printouts. She didn't want to go home yet. She didn't want to revert from a West Wing employee investigating a top-secret CIA project to simple girl from Kansas in her neat, too homespun apartment. Especially not while some congresswoman might be... How had Honey put it?

Screwing Matt Tynan like a lightbulb.

"The fountain," she remembered out loud, to distract herself from what Matt might be doing right now, why he wasn't doing it with her, and why she even cared.

Instead of doubling back toward the Metro station, she crossed Independence Avenue at 1st Street to the Court of Neptune. She sank onto the fountain's marble edge, close enough that bits of the spray misted her hair, and forced herself to face her cowardice in hanging up on Matt. It wasn't as though she didn't know he had a sex life. He was the president's top advisor; the whole U.S. of A. knew he had a sex life! Politically incorrect or not, his experience might even be part of his appeal. Just because Carey wasn't willing to have sex until she met the right man didn't mean she wasn't curious. And if practice made perfect, then Matt Tynan must be....

Really perfect.

Flushing, she turned her face more directly toward the cool spray of the fountain, green-lit from beneath the water's surface with watery lights. The Court of Neptune showed just that—the god Neptune, sea people, their steeds and water-spitting turtles. All were aged green, spread out against neatly arched grottos of white marble. Carey had heard that at least one of the figures was Neptune's son, Triton.

Now she studied those bare-chested sea studs, looking for another of Neptune's sons—the mysterious Proteus. She fixed on one whose athletic form vaguely reminded her of a certain political advisor.

"C'mon," she whispered, under the patter of water. "What's going on with this project, anyway? Why'd they use your name?"

But of course, none of the statues said a thing. They remained frozen in their timeless choreography, so enduring that she had to reconsider whether any of them portrayed the ever-changing Proteus. Common sense told her she would find more information in the printouts. She could tell just by skimming that she'd found more than she ever expected—if not on the CIA project, then at least on its head scientist.

Her people trail had paid off. She'd attacked genealogical records and then microfiche with her usual enthusiasm—until the library closed and she'd called Matt and embarrassed herself. What did it matter what he was doing? She could sit around feeling jealous and petty like all the other dispensable Tynan worshipers in this city. Or she could do the job he'd asked of her; the one person who *could* do it.

She took a last deep breath of the fountain's delicious mist. Then, before the sheaf of papers she held got any more damp, she headed back toward the Capitol South Metro station.

But not to go home.

She had some heavy reading ahead of her, and she should see Matt about it as soon as he…as soon as possible. Better to do that at the office than hang out with an imaginary sea god so jealous of the future that he never shared it without a fight.

Matt strode into the office at six-fifteen the next morning, mentally preparing to meet with the rest of the senior staff, then stopped still. Carey's desk sat empty, although she usually made it in by six. How late had she stayed last night, anyway? How safe was her walk home from her own Metro stop?

He frowned as he turned into his office, more concerned than usual, and stopped at the sight of someone on the sofa.

His pretty assistant lay sound asleep, wrapped in that soft green throw of hers…and what looked like photocopies.

Unaccountably relieved, Matt stepped quietly closer.

God, she was beautiful. Young, for one thing; she was normally so self-possessed, he too often forgot that. Asleep, with her fists curled under her jaw, there was no missing it. But it sure didn't dissuade him from looking.

She had the soft, clear skin of youth. Full lips. An innocent expression on her resting face. Her shiny brown hair, pulled into a ponytail, swept across the arm of the sofa, and her curves, under that soft throw…

He looked slowly down Carey's body, where the green throw outlined its rises and dips, until her bare legs and feet poked out from beneath it. She wore pink polish on her toenails. Somehow, eyeing her bare feet seemed truly intimate. Lecherous, even.

Matt sank reluctantly onto the low table beside the sofa, sitting on more papers, ending his voyeurism by brushing a lock of hair off her face. "Carey?"

His voice stuck on her name the first try and he had to clear his throat to do it right. "Carey."

"Mmm." She smiled at the sound of his voice, turned her soft cheek into his palm. His breath hitched in his chest.

Maybe he shouldn't wake her, after all.

No. This was his office and he had work to do. In under an hour, he'd be in the Roosevelt Room with the most powerful leaders of the nation. He had a press summary to review, bond market numbers to check and a dedication speech to approve before then. He couldn't do it all with Carey lying here, where she shouldn't have spent the night in the first place, making him wish he'd spent the night, too. Beside her.

"Hey, Skipper," he murmured more firmly, deliberately curling his fingers back from the warmth of her cheek, drawing his knuckles across it instead. The change didn't dilute the effect of her softness. "I thought you went home."

Her eyes fluttered open. They focused on his face, and her full lips curved into a welcoming smile. "Matt."

"Morning, glory." He longed to seal her welcome with a kiss. He stood instead, blaming it on bad habits.

Belatedly, her eyes widened. *"Matt!"* She sat up, the throw sliding to her hips. She still wore her short-sleeved white blouse and pale blue skirt from yesterday. Their wrinkles, and her sleep-fluffy ponytail, made her look younger, less efficient...and more approachable than ever. "How long— What time is it?"

"Almost six-thirty. Time for you to go home."

"But work's starting!" She passed a nervous hand over her hair, finding and yanking out the elastic holding her ponytail. Matt decided she must be the prettiest woman he'd ever seen first thing in the morning. Most women transformed without their makeup, or hairstyles, or clothes. Or, most importantly, without the confidence those extra little details seemed to give them.

Carey Benton looked reassuringly like *Carey*.

Just with messier clothes and fluffier hair than usual.

Matt braced his hands firmly on his knees in an increasingly desperate attempt to keep them out of trouble. "I'll call someone in from the temp pool until you get back. Go home, eat breakfast, take a shower."

Not that she smelled bad. She smelled good. First-thing-in-the-morning good. Real. Nor did picturing her in the shower much help in keeping his distance, or his libido, in check.

He said, "I know how cruel that sofa can be."

"It was fine." Carey's stretch pulled her blouse tight across her bosom. Her pert, firm bosom. She clearly hadn't removed only her panty hose to sleep.

Matt swallowed hard.

"Really, I didn't mind," Carey continued, recovering with the easy resilience of youth. "I wanted to be here in case you came back last night, and I got busy reading, and then it was after midnight." The D.C. Metro didn't run past midnight, one of several reasons Matt always drove. "I've learned more about Henry Bloomfield, Matt. The scientist who runs Code Proteus? A *lot* more. The Library of Congress carries issues of the *Belle Terre Bugle* on microfilm, all the way back to 1914, and the *Charlotte Observer* and the *Atlanta Tribune*. I wasn't able to print anywhere near enough. What I got is right here."

She reached to tug a sheaf of papers out from under him.

He felt very aware of the nearness of her hand to his thigh. Matt pulled the papers free himself, even if that meant his hand briefly collided with hers. It was either that or stand, and since she was still sitting—

He didn't want her face at crotch level; he might embarrass them both. Matt liked seeing women first thing in the morning, liked learning how they really looked, how they really smelled without the disguise of fresh perfume or mouthwash. But if they all smelled like Carey, he might never get out of bed again.

"Apparently he was a real hermit," his assistant continued, thankfully innocent of his thoughts. Presumably she meant Bloomfield. "One of those eccentric intellectual types. But his obituary still had some interesting—"

The video screen on Matt's desk beeped to indicate that POTUS was changing location, probably leaving the residence for his jog. Matt held up a hand, flat, to silence Carey.

"Wait. You need to get breakfast and a change of clothes. Whatever you found can wait."

"I'm not sure it can," she insisted with a flash of blue-eyed determination. "Listen for a minute. Dr. Bloomfield was a biologist." She said that as though it meant something important. "He was a professor in Atlanta for a while, and in the early sixties he wrote this ground-breaking paper on genetic engineering."

Matt's first meeting was in under half an hour. He still hadn't reviewed the summary, checked the market or read the speech, much less scanned his calendar. And here he sat, fisting his hand to keep from reaching out for Carey Benton's unusually fluffy hair. "It's probably fascinating stuff," he admitted, rubbing the back of his neck instead. "Especially considering all those stupid 'mutant' rumors lately. But unless you found—"

Then he stopped. Instead of her lips, or her hair, or even her unrestrained breasts, he finally focused on Carey's eyes. They were no longer sleepy. They were clear, excited and begging him to catch up. He forced himself back to his earlier train of thought...*All those stupid rumors*...

"Genetics?" he asked.

Carey nodded quickly. "Some coincidence, huh?"

A person couldn't catch the news without overdosing on reactionary misinformation about genetic engineering: *Government Hides Super Children...I Married A Clone...They Are Here—And What They Want.* Despite good repetition of the president's now famous "Fight Fear" message from April, at least three new bills had been introduced to the House in response to the public's rising concerns about genetics, from cloning to super-soldiers to medical privacy issues. Genetics was shaping itself into the issue of the new century and possibly next year's election. But still.... "The sixties?"

"Forty years ago." The same time government labs had supposedly created those rumored Super Children.

Matt shook his head, resisting the idea that was trying to

push past all logic. "This project is about the World Bank heist. You don't honestly think it's connected to—"

But he shut up, because with every word he spoke, she looked less excited. She even started to look embarrassed.

He suddenly felt like the spoilsport, the party pooper, the—God forbid—mature one. It was a role he'd never wanted. Carey wasn't trying to convince him of the existence of Santa Claus here. She was making a leap, but it wasn't completely off center.

Just, as she would put it, a half bubble off plumb.

And more than anything, more than even running late, he hated being the cause of her lost enthusiasm.

"So what do you need to find out more?" he asked—and was rewarded with Carey's smile, brighter than any sunrise.

"I'd like to use a long lunch to go back to the library," she said. "There was a discrepancy in one of the obituaries, but if Bloomfield was that big in the scientific community, some of the journals may have covered his death. I'd like to see which version gets repeated most, maybe learn more about his research. I also want to go through more microfilm from Atlanta, for the time he was teaching at Emory University. It may have nothing to do with Code Proteus, of course, but…"

But the guy was a geneticist long before DNA became a common term—and rumors about top-secret genetic experiments from the sixties were now rivaling stories about Area 51 and Roswell. Whatever illogical mess this was, Jake was the one who'd gotten him into it. And Jake was always logical.

Matt glanced at his watch and made a decision.

"Go. Take a long breakfast instead of a long lunch. Just get me an in-house temp first, okay?"

Carey hopped to her bare feet and started to tuck her

wrinkled blouse into her wrinkled blue skirt. Matt caught a glimpse of her bare waist and swallowed hard. "I'll see if Suzie's available," she said.

"And get yourself some breakfast."

"Pushy." But she smiled as she slid her bare feet into pumps. Between her boldness and hiding those toenails, she didn't seem quite so young or approachable. A mixed blessing.

Matt disliked the idea of anyone who looked and smelled this good in the morning, much less someone as smart as her, being too young for him. Not that she really was.

"Hey." He caught hold of her wrist as she started toward the door, then quickly let go. Her skin felt so soft, it took all his meager self-control not to hang on. "This is big stuff, Care. Why didn't you call me when you found it?"

Carey glanced back at him, then shrugged and smiled— too brightly. "I thought it would be more efficient if I waited until I had further information." Which was why he'd put her on this project, right? Her efficiency. So why…?

Matt watched her go and frowned. He hadn't gotten this far in politics without being able to read people. But this was too-good-to-be-true Carey. *His* Carey.

What possible reason could she have for lying to him?

By the time Carey got back to the West Wing, lunchtime had come and gone and she suspected she'd sacrificed more than one tree for the sheaf of printouts she carried. But even if she was embarrassed to have woken with Matt Tynan this morning, she couldn't stay away forever. And really, it was just work. Right?

As soon as she'd dismissed the temp, she settled down at her desk and called Matt's mobile phone to pass on his latest messages and to share her discoveries as best she could on an unsecured line. "Wait until you hear about you know who!"

"Sorry, Skipper," interrupted Matt, "But *wait* is the key word. I'll check back."

As his phone was audibly being shut, Carey heard voices in the background saying, "Good afternoon, Mr. President."

Damn. But it was so full of...possibilities!

She wanted to bury herself in Bloomfield's tale of tragedy, to reread the printouts and highlight pertinent parts and arrange them into more significant order. Jake Ingram would need a binder, tabs, table of contents....

But she'd been gone all morning. She had mail to sort, answer or delegate. She had photocopies to run and computer backups to make. She had phone messages to return or redirect and Matt's calendar to shuffle, yet again. And a blanket to fold.

Honey Evans, who'd called to see why Carey had missed lunch, used her afternoon break to deliver a sandwich and cola. She wanted payment in gossip, of course. Grateful though Carey was, she didn't have time to either confess about chastely spending the night on Matt Tynan's sofa or to hear about Honey's plans for the Matchbox 20 concert that night. And Bloomfield was *her* secret—hers and Matt's. Her friend had to return to the Telephone Office disappointed.

Even when Matt spun back by, they had time for no more than a few prioritized sentences. The Chief of Staff, the latest FDA court battle, and the five minutes the assistant secretary of the O.S.E.P.—Office of Special Education Programs—needed were more immediately priorities than a project that had been closed more than twenty years earlier.

Unfortunately, it became one of those days that didn't seem to end. The next morning's edition of the *Post* called ahead to inform Rita of a damning quote about the president, which, by hitting on a Friday, could easily become a three-day story. Rebelia's Hitler-like dictator was causing more trouble in Eastern Europe. The First Son got a D in Civics on his report card—who knew how that leaked—and Senator Bermann and his supporters were still blocking the president's education initiative.

By eight o'clock that night the Marine guards had changed and most of the press corps, who normally lurked in waiting in their own room in the West Wing, had gone home. Carey got her chance to reread, highlight and organize what she'd found on Henry Bloomfield. The more time she spent on this, the more the scientist fascinated her. She took extra care preparing a professional report and slipping it into a large P & C envelope, lest Matt needed it for Mr. Ingram before she got back from the weekend.

The long, quiet, relatively boring weekend.

Maybe she should have gone to the Matchbox 20 concert with Honey, after all.

Matt swung back in the doorway. "Good," he said, his gaze darting from her jacket to the purse in her hands to the light she'd turned off over her desk. "You're still here."

"Just barely." She was done, after all, even if she didn't want to be. "I put the Bloomfield report on your chair, along with your letters, a requisition form and some statistics I found about great men who had bad grades as kids. Do you need anything else?"

"We-ell…" Matt stretched out the word, stuffing a hand into his pocket. "I don't have a lot of reading time. Would you mind staying long enough to give me an overview?"

"Long or short version?" she asked, always glad for a chance to prove herself. The phone rang, yet again. She reached for it but Matt caught her hand to stop her.

"Anyone really important can page me," he said, his eyes gleaming.

The shiver that washed through her at his touch didn't feel at all efficient. It felt wonderful. No wonder women so rarely told him no.

Foolish or not, Carey suddenly wanted to know what it felt like to be one of those women.

"I can stay," she told him hoarsely.

"I know where we can get some privacy," he promised—and abruptly headed for the door.

Still holding her hand.

Four

Violet Vaughn Hobson never used the telephone in her hotel room. Any of her hotel rooms. Instead she found public places such as bus terminals or convenience stores. Alternating payphones made her harder to trace. Long-distance calling cards could be purchased with cash.

Tonight she chose the Smithsonian Metro station, glad for the commuters and tourists who crowded it even on a Friday night. The risk of being overheard was nowhere near as great as the risk of being caught alone.

As a child, Violet had fought her loneliness with knowledge. Data rarely let a person down. Facts and scientific evidence just *were*. Then she'd gotten a biology scholarship to Emory University and met a man who was just as fascinating. Henry Bloomfield.

She often thought of Henry since the World Bank heist and this foolishness about clones had hit the press. If she could believe that he'd truly loved her, perhaps she could justify having done what no self-respecting woman would. But she doubted it.

All she knew for sure, forty years later, was that *she* had loved *him*. And what she'd done for that love...

Before she lost her nerve, Violet found the bank of payphones, inserted coins, then began the lengthy trial-by-numbers that such calling cards required.

"Ingram," answered a man's voice after the first ring.

She tried to hear Henry in it, but Henry's gentle drawl had been East Coast, not Texas. "Who is this?"

Violet's eyes stung with unshed tears. "Jake?"

She'd only seen him once as an adult, once since she'd sent them all away with false identities and the hope of a normal life. It was a false hope—she and Henry had guaranteed that from the children's conception. But her very cells knew him. "Jake, it's Violet."

His breath rushed out. "Violet?" Of course he wouldn't call her Mother. "Hello."

"You sound tired."

"I'm fine. I just have a lot…" His voice trailed off. They both knew why the man publicly charged with solving the World Bank heist while privately tracking down the rest of Henry and Violet's special offspring might be tired. "I've asked a friend to look into Code Proteus. He works at the White House."

The government? Violet's hand tightened on the phone receiver. "Are you sure that's wise?"

"I trust Matt Tynan like my own brother." After a long pause, Jake carefully added, "Zach."

His adopted brother. Long ago, Violet had watched as a hypnotist stole young Jake's memories of his true brothers, Mark and Gideon, and of Faith and his twin sister Grace. She'd watched them sent to new lives. Last month he'd found Grace again—but even now he only knew her as Gretchen Wagner Miller, the person she'd become.

The person that Violet and Henry's secrets would not allow her to remain, any more than they allowed Jake the illusion of normalcy.

Guilt weighed on Violet even more heavily than the safe-deposit key that hung, along with two gold rings, on a chain around her neck. "We need to meet again, Jake. I have something important to give you, and I'm afraid to wait too long. If Croft knows who you are—were—he may not just be hunting Mark and Faith. He might want me for what I know about the files.''

"And as leverage." Jake's suggestion terrified her—not for her safety, but theirs.

"You mustn't let them use me against you."

"You should go to Brunhia, Violet. It's safe there. Gretchen and Kurt would be glad to have you."

Her heart ached to do just that, to see her daughter again, to meet the new husband. Perhaps Violet was greedy. God had given her not only Henry Bloomfield and their five deliberately perfect children, but Dale Hobson and his daughter Susannah. She'd even found Jake again. But she wanted them all.

Still, what she wanted and what she deserved were two different things. "Gretchen and Kurt don't know me."

Jake said, "We're starting to remember. Beyond the dreams, I mean. We're working with Maisy Dalton—Zach's fiancée—to recover more memories through hypnotic deprogramming."

No thanks to her. "Well…perhaps I can telephone them."

Jake gave her a number, which Violet wrote down.

"Call her," insisted Jake. "And call me within the week, so I know you're still all right. I'll be back in D.C. soon. We can arrange a meeting."

"Good." Violet felt someone's gaze on her. She turned quickly, but saw only a cluster of young adults running for the escalator down to the train platform. "Jake, is everything else all right with you? You're keeping in touch with your fiancée despite all the complications, aren't you?"

"Work has me pretty busy," hedged her oldest son.

"Don't take after Henry in that, Jake. Please. Allow—" Her throat caught. "Allow yourself to be loved."

"Tara will have to know the truth first," he reminded her. He meant the truth of him being one of the so-called mutants being sought by tabloids and conspiracy theorists alike. "It's not something I can tell her on the phone."

"No," Violet managed over the guilt that squeezed her chest. "Of course not. I'll call you next week."

"Good night, Violet."

Then she was alone again, among the city crowd. She'd been alone most of her life; secrets had isolated her even in her late marriage to Dale Hobson. And her time with Henry...

She'd been so lonely, and loved him so desperately, that she'd let him use her without him even knowing he had. He'd thought her only goal was the experiment, their hopes for a better world. But she hadn't given birth to five experiments—six, if you counted the child who was stillborn, the one she'd never seen or held. She'd given birth to *babies,* real and whole, and more perfect than should have been possible. That was her and Henry's foolish triumph.

But it was their children's curse.

"Henry Bloomfield," said Carey, over the clink of china and gentle piano music, "lived a tragic life."

Matt felt a smile pull at his mouth—more because of Carey's earnest work ethic than Bloomfield's alleged tragedies. The restaurant they were in, Where or When, had a great Art Nouveau atmosphere with gilded arches and wall sconces, blue-and-gold upholstery and carpeting, black marble tables and inset lighting in the ceiling to imitate a starry sky. Its tall booths provided near-perfect privacy, too. The ambience made you feel as though you'd tumbled into an old 1930's musical complete with happy, make-believe times and long, romantic, night-on-the-town sequences. Carey, in her yellow sweater set, made the perfect ingenue, which, he guessed, left him as the sophisticated city fella out to show her the wide world.

He could think of worse fates. Except that in the movies, the ingenue would make an honest man out of the city fella in holy matrimony. Matt knew those happy endings didn't really exist. Maybe for Bentons. Not for Tynans.

He fidgeted with his dark blue napkin, practicing knots, watching her. "So how was Bloomfield's life tragic?"

Carey folded her slender arms on the table edge. "For one thing, he was an only child."

"This is tragic?" Matt was an only child, which was probably a blessing, although Carey made a good enough advertisement for larger families.

"For another," she continued with her usual efficiency, "Henry's parents died together in a plane crash while he was in grad school. He inherited a huge fortune, but he was all alone."

When the waiter arrived to take their orders, Matt saw through Carey's request for a simple salad. He managed to bully her into steak by teasing that it was as good as anything back home in Texas—where, of course, Carey *wasn't* from.

"So poor Henry was all alone with his money and education," he then prompted.

"After his Ph.D., he took a job at Emory University in Atlanta. He met and married an assistant professor there, and they started a family." Her eyes grew sad. "They had twin boys, but the babies died within hours of being born. They were identical—including identically defective hearts. Faulty genes."

Matt winced. "That's rough."

Carey nodded, solemn, and said, soft-voiced, "Three months later, Henry's wife killed herself."

The pianist's old piece about unrequited love seemed

downright underhanded. "You've convinced me. Tragic's the word."

"Henry was getting press for a paper on genetic engineering, which is probably why his own suicide attempt made the papers." Carey fell silent when the waiter brought their appetizer, then said, "I found very little about him in Atlanta, after that. But I think he must have started doing more research for the university. Even though schedules show him carrying less class hours, his income didn't drop."

She looked so intrigued that Matt, fiddling with a slip knot, felt torn between his usual admiration and something strangely similar to…jealousy? She'd sure gotten wrapped up with this mad scientist of Jake's, hadn't she? "Have you considered a career in espionage? I may just know somebody."

At least it earned him a wan smile. "I'm too good an administrative assistant, and you know it."

He did know it. That was the only thing keeping him from slipping off his shoe and finding her leg with his foot under the table. For the first time, seeing how involved she'd gotten in this case, it occurred to him that she might be *too* good. "So how does this connect Bloomfield to either Code Proteus or the *uber* children the *World Inquisitor* says are infiltrating society? Try some of this." He held out a piece of warm French bread.

Hopefully the food would distract her while he decided how to play this.

Carey took the piece of bread he'd torn off for her and dipped it into the cheese-and-artichoke dish. Matt watched her take a bite, watched her chew, watched her close her eyes to savor the sensual delight of the dish…and flat-out forgot to breathe.

He felt the impact in his gut and places lower. Sheer, raw

attraction. Carey's pleasure made him feel both male and hungry—hungry for far more than the steaks they'd ordered.

Carey swallowed, slowly opened her eyes and smiled at him, beautifully sated. "That's incredible!"

"Yeah." He stared at her, slowly losing the battle he'd been fighting for months. "It's a favorite of mine."

Even *she* wasn't that good an administrative assistant.

Not if it meant going another night without kissing her.

Carey was in heaven—heaven with blue velvet, an imitation starry sky, good food and Matt. She knew this was just business; bosses often fed employees who worked late. But she'd rarely been in restaurants this fancy. The few times she'd dated, even since moving to D.C., she'd been with men younger than Matt who had neither the money nor the taste to take her someplace like this.

Nor the status, she thought, eyeing how the restaurant's maître d' guarded both the entryway and his book of names. Matt had gotten them in, underdressed and without a reservation, because he was Matt Tynan, the president's top advisor. That sort of thing shouldn't impress her, but it did, on instinctive levels she didn't wholly understand. She wondered what it would feel like to be here on a date instead of business, and felt a not unpleasant tremor deep in her midsection. From what she'd heard, if this were a date, the whole dinner would be an appetizer.

All the more reason to be efficient and businesslike. "Here's where I see the connection," she explained, scooping more bread into the dip under her boss's intense scrutiny. "In 1966, the university started heavily supporting a research project."

Matt leaned forward, his attention caught. "Genetics?"

"No, organ transplants. But get this. They called it the

Prometheus Project, because of how the mythic Prometheus regenerates his liver each time the eagle eats it.''

"Code Proteus. Project Prometheus. What a coincidence.'' Matt's sarcasm seconded her suspicion of no coincidence at all.

"Also, I didn't see any big push to raise funds, which makes me think the school already had funding in place. Since that's the same year Henry Bloomfield moved back to Belle Terre—''

"—they may have taken the money from whatever research project he'd been working on before that. Damn, you're good.''

She flushed, pleased. "Either he quit his research, or his funding was canceled. Either way, that was in 1966.''

"The same year Medusa adopted Code Proteus. The CIA moved in with the money and took over the research.'' Matt's gaze lingered on Carey's mouth before he went back to fidgeting with his napkin. "God knows what they wanted with genetics research.''

"I doubt Henry Bloomfield would be party to anything immoral.'' Carey wanted to wipe her lip, then noticed Matt's stilled hands and incredulous expression. "He was probably trying to keep more babies from dying the way his own did.''

Matt's dark brows climbed his forehead, both amused and amazed. "And you think that because…?''

She hadn't gotten into the West Wing by being easily cowed. "Because I have no reason to think otherwise. All the obituaries say he was a good man.''

Matt went back to the napkin, his gleaming eyes playing between that and her the whole time. "It's the rare obituary that calls someone an asshole, Skipper. So what did you find out about him, after he moved to North Carolina?''

"Not a lot,'' she admitted. She'd skimmed more issues

of the *Belle Terre Bugle* than she could count. Only the 1980 obituary mentioned him—with a reference that, if it wasn't a printing error, opened up whole new mysteries. "Which I guess supports the idea that he was working on something secret. But still…"

"The CIA wouldn't have funded him out of sheer altruism. And if this guy was a genius, he would've been smart enough to know that." Matt leaned back in his seat, pensive. "How'd he die?"

"Accidental drowning near his family home." Her eyes had stung when she'd read that. What an ignoble death, for a man with such high ideals. "He wasn't even fifty years old."

"And were there witnesses to this alleged accident?"

Why did Carey get the feeling Matt didn't like Henry Bloomfield? He didn't like *something,* anyway. "No. But if he wasn't alone, he might not have drowned."

"Or maybe he didn't drown at all." Matt looked up quickly. "Here comes the food. Let's order some wine, relax, and celebrate a job well done, okay?"

What? Carey stared at him as the waiter left their steaks. Then she challenged, *"Done?"*

"I can courier the report to wherever Jake needs it. You've done more than enough for one week."

Carey's appetite wavered. She liked the extra responsibility of working on Code Proteus—and yes, maybe she liked the extra connection to Matt. Being the only other person involved in this project had made her feel special to him in the only way their professional relationship seemed to allow.

"We haven't gotten any of the records I requested," she reminded him. "And I still don't know why Code Proteus had an invoice for toys. If children were involved…"

"Right." He sounded reluctant. "The clone rumors."

Actually, she'd been thinking more that if children were involved, she felt honor bound to find out how. Especially after reading that obituary in the *Bugle*. "I also have questions about Henry Bloomfield's next of kin."

Matt cut a piece of steak, but paused, his brows pulling together. "The guy who lost everyone?"

"The national obituaries implied as much. But the *Bugle* had a line like, 'Bloomfield's wife and children have absented themselves from public during their grief.'"

She'd actually gasped when she read that, right there in the Library of Congress.

Matt blinked, suspicious. "Wife and children?"

"Exactly! No record of a second marriage, nor of any births. And only the local paper mentioned them. I can't stop looking now! What if they're still alive?"

"Or what if they're really anxious to protect their privacy?" Matt leaned closer, wearing his serious face. His long eyelashes tended to undermine his expression, but interfered with her breathing, all the same. "I don't want you getting too involved in this, Care."

"I'm already involved, so it's too late. You might as well use me." She almost winced at her own words. *Use me?*

He opened his mouth to reply, then closed it, his lips flirting between a smile and a scowl. After a long moment he chose the scowl. "It could be dangerous."

"Over twenty years later? I know you're a troubleshooter, but do you always have to assume the worst possible outcome?"

"Some people shouldn't be trusted."

But from Matt's troubled gaze, Carey got the impression that he wasn't just talking about spies or Henry Bloomfield anymore. He was talking about himself and… What? *Her?*

Surely not her. Possibly someone elegant and sophisticated. Probably a lot of someones.

"Maybe if we expected more from some people," she said gently, "they might surprise us. Or even themselves."

He let his head fall forward as if in defeat, then lifted his gaze to hers, and she forgot to breathe. His dark eyes, always intense, held hers. "And what if it's a bad surprise?"

She was imagining things. He was talking about Code Proteus, nothing else. There could be nothing else.

"I'm willing to take my chances," she whispered.

She means with Bloomfield, Matt's common sense insisted. His gut, where her words had impacted most solidly, was already turning Carey's statement into a sultry challenge. *She means the* research *project Romeo.*

Common sense didn't stand a chance, sitting this close to someone as pretty as Carey. Someone he'd come to trust, to admire, even to care for more than was wise. He wasn't sure when it had happened, but subtly and surely, it had. It was happening still.

"So what made you become a secretary, anyway?" he asked, a desperate reminder to himself of why he shouldn't flirt. Only then did he consider the personal, tell-me-about-yourself overtones to his question.

Too late.

She blinked at him. "What about Henry Bloomfield?"

Shut up about Henry Bloomfield. "You're just going to keep looking no matter what I say, aren't you?"

Her smile sparkled through him. "Yes. Pretty much."

He groaned. "At least tell me you'll be careful."

"Of the CIA, the scientists or the genetic mutants?" She laughed at his expression. "Yes. Of course I'll be careful."

"Then Bloomfield can wait until we know more. Tell me why a woman as capable and intelligent as you settles for support work." *The only reason I'm not kissing you right*

*now, much less peeling that soft yellow sweater down your
bare arms...*

To his immense relief, she accepted his change of topic.
"First of all, I'm an administrative assistant, not a secretary.
Second, you think I'm *settling?*"

Wasn't she? "I know how much you get paid."

She snorted. "As if the size of a paycheck reflects the
importance of someone's work! Tell that to the firefighters
and nurses and teachers. I know how much you get paid,
too, buster."

That was humbling. Most of Matt's dates thought the
prestige of working in the West Wing translated into big
bucks. But if his finance-savvy college friends, including
Jake Ingram, hadn't advised him into a great stock portfolio,
now tucked into a blind trust, he'd probably be feeding
Carey a Big Mac at this moment.

He realized with a rush of affection that she'd probably
be eating it as happily as she was eating her steak.
"'Buster'?"

She nodded. "I'll have you know that my father's plumb-
ing business almost went under before my mom took over
the administrative side of things."

"I thought she was a stay-at-home mom."

"She was. A stay-at-home, working mom." As they ate,
Carey admitted that she'd considered pursuing something
with more prestige. But after getting her degree, she'd been
drawn back to clerical work. "I'm good at it," she said after
he ordered a slice of pecan cheesecake, with two forks, for
dessert. "I'm involved. I make a difference. You work behind the scenes, too, and for nowhere near the money you
could be earning."

"'Behind the scenes' might be pushing it." Matt had
done his share of national interviews. He even got mentioned in the tabloids now and then, when genetic mutants

weren't hogging the headlines. "But I see your point. There are people out there who could make a real difference, with the right support, and I can do that. Or at least try. They're worth the gamble, you know?"

"I know."

Carey should know better than to gaze at any man with that kind of adoration, her eyes shining, her sleek brown hair catching liquid gold shimmers in the candlelight. This not only felt like a date, it felt like a damned good one.

The sensation was more delicious than the cheesecake the waiter set between them...and just as bad for him.

She asked, "Have you ever considered running yourself?"

"What, you like my stand on women's issues?" He knew Carey was at least peripherally involved in such groups as Emily's List and the League of Women Voters, something else he admired.

"I didn't know you had a stand," she teased. "But you'd get the women's vote, all the same."

Oh. She meant his looks and bachelor status—and his disappointment was as palpable as it was unreasonable. He was a political professional; he *avoided* taking a stand on issues. But he was, like she said, good with women.

Matt slid his fork through a creamy wedge of cheesecake, speared it, then held it across the table for her. Hell, she probably expected it.

When Carey obediently opened her mouth, it was all he could do to keep breathing. He carefully inserted the treat and she closed her teeth almost to the fork tines. He pulled the fork slowly free, watching her lips.

"Bachelors are less likely to get elected," he admitted. Then he quickly added, "Anyway, of all the lousy reasons to marry, an election is one of the worst."

I'm not a marrying guy, Carey. You do know that.

She said, "So you'll buck the odds. At least nobody can accuse you of adultery, right?"

After the fallout he'd seen from his father's cheating? His grandfather's? His stepfather's? "No," he said tightly.

Maybe Carey saw something. She reached across the table, put her hand on his arm, and he felt his body temperature shift at her light touch. Her eyes were solemn. "I was just teasing."

He forced a grin. "Also, I've got this thing about people counting too much on me," he half joked, half warned. "Dependability isn't my strength. Irresponsibility runs in my—"

The beep of his pager kept him from digging himself any deeper. The page didn't surprise him, not in this job. Nor did the office phone number. His disappointment was another matter; that, and the time. Had they really been here for two hours?

"Better finish that last bite, Skipper." He snapped his beeper back onto his belt. "I'm needed back at the salt mines."

Carey didn't ask what was wrong—something he couldn't tell most dates anyway. He liked that. He liked that he *could* tell her. He liked too damn much about her tonight.

The code the Chief of Staff had keyed in after his number indicated something international and urgent. Matt didn't bother to call in for more details; they had his mobile number if they wanted to talk, and he could be in the Oval Office getting the scoop in person within ten minutes.

"So what do you think *is* your strength?" Carey asked, taking a final bite of cheesecake before retrieving her purse.

"Winning people over." He savored the pleasure on her face as she chewed, the way she closed her eyes and slowly inhaled. What would Carey look like truly satisfied? Only as she opened her eyes did he think to stand, and his grin felt rueful. "I just don't always know what to do with them when I have them."

"That," she teased, accepting his offered hand, "is not what I've heard."

He did an exaggerated double take. "Oh, really? And just what kind of rumor-mongering have you heard?"

Staring up at him, she parted her lips but managed no words. Her cheeks pinked, visible even in the light of candles, sconces and artificial stars. He knew damned well what she'd heard. He was a playboy. A ladies' man. Recreationally popular.

She'd heard right. Truth was truth, and despite good reasons for keeping his distance these months, he was tired of playing against type. He had honest urges. Basic urges.

And for once, at least briefly, he wanted to live up to someone's expectations. Or in this case, down to them.

Matt leaned nearer, to taste Carey's innocence, to breathe in her idealism, to reassure himself that women like her existed—women from two-parent homes and happy families, women who still believed the best of even mad scientists and politicians. He twined his fingers with hers, pulled her willowy, yellow-suited body up against his with aching slowness, lowered his head toward hers. His face neared hers...his lips touched hers.

With a sigh of total completion, Matt kissed the wholesome promise of her. Carey...

Her lips opened under his, willing, accepting. When he stepped back—barely back, still breathing her nearness—her gaze seemed even more open, willing and accepting against his own.

The kiss, at least, seemed to have met her expectations. It had blasted away all of his. Except...

Somehow Matt made himself pull farther back, instead of leaning in for another kiss. The reflection of himself in

Carey's eyes was heady, dizzying. But it was an illusion, an image he could never maintain. He was her boss. There were good reasons bosses shouldn't romance their employees, even outside the White House. Inside the scandal-ridden West Wing...

Damn it. Having even the president count on him *definitely* didn't play to his strengths.

He turned away from her and frowned his frustration across the restaurant, hoping nobody from the press was here to blow his screwup out of proportion. "I shouldn't have done that."

Instead of protesting, Carey stepped closer, watching his face. She still held his hand, and he didn't have the heart to release hers. When he turned his head, she was gazing up at him with honest confusion, silent questions.

"I'm sorry," he insisted, awkward with the unwieldy burden of doing the right thing. "It won't happen again."

Then he saw the man staring at them from outside the restaurant's front window.

Five

"Wait here," Matt murmured, and strode out of the restaurant, leaving Carey to blink dazedly after him.

What just happened?

Reeling from both the power of his kiss and the speed of his desertion, Carey clutched her purse in one hand, then both hands. She felt as out of place in this fine restaurant as she should feel with someone as worldly as Matt—although a moment ago, with him had seemed like the perfect place. Her cheeks burned, and she wondered if other patrons were staring at her, if they'd recognized Matt, if they thought she was just another of his women.

One he hadn't even stayed to escort home?

The maître d' guided her to the entryway. "Did you enjoy your dinner, miss?" he asked while Carey faced the truth that, at this moment, she *was* just another of Matt's women. How many others had the nice man with the brass name tag reading Jacques assisted?

"Thank you," she responded. "It was wonderful, really."

Matt's reappearance through the doorway only marginally relieved her. He was scowling. The no-nonsense way he claimed her hand helped. "Come on."

No explanation. No "please." Even disoriented, Carey found the strength to balk, digging her heels into the carpet.

When Matt realized she wasn't meekly following, his expression softened. "I saw someone watching us."

"No!" Jacques shook his head, tsking. "Not here!"

Carey realized that not only were the booths in Where or When high-backed for privacy, but she hadn't yet seen a flash go off. Privacy. No wonder Matt brought his dates here.

Matt shifted his weight, clearly tempted to stalk back out, maybe run down whomever he suspected of spying. To Carey's relief, he put a hand on her waist and drew her back to his side. "It's not your fault, Jacques. Don't worry about it."

"But if someone disturbs you here, it reflects on us."

"I, uh, I could have been mistaken." But from the way Matt's dark eyes slid back to the window, the coiled stillness of his stance, he clearly doubted that. He was just being nice.

Carey touched his arm, to perhaps soothe some of his annoyance or just to touch. Matt turned to guide her, barely brushing the small of her back, through the door Jacques opened for them. The kiss still lingered on her lips, a tingle, an awakening, but Matt could probably kiss three women a day like that and hardly notice. Maybe his kiss was just kindness.

Kindness, and world-changing. The traffic on the street was the same. The corner lamps and neon signs and illuminated nearby monuments all reminded her that they'd left the private world of their dinner behind. But the world had changed, all the same.

He'd kissed her. But he'd said it wouldn't happen again.

"Damn it," muttered Matt as a valet parked his Mustang at the curb for them.

"Damn it?" Carey tried her best to make her question sound lighthearted, as if she fielded heart-stopping kisses from powerful men on a regular basis. *Why* wouldn't he kiss her again?

"I…" His words faded as he stared down at her, as if searching her face just for the pleasure of the search. Then he pressed his lips together and straightened, more determined. "I'd meant to drive you home," he explained, circling the car to open the passenger door for her. "Not back to the office."

"I can take the Metro," she assured him, both flattered and disappointed as he helped her in.

"I don't like you taking the Metro." He shut her door.

Carey frowned to herself. Either the kiss had truly disoriented her, or Matt was acting strangely. When he climbed into the driver's seat, she said, "*I* like me taking the Metro."

He stared at her, then shrugged and turned his attention to the traffic. "McPherson Square station it is."

When he started the engine, his radio came on—set to a news station—and he said nothing else, not even about the kiss. Carey couldn't think of anything *but* the kiss. She'd fantasized something more melodramatic, such as him yanking her tightly to him, covering her mouth with his. She hadn't known that he would go so very slowly, as if he wanted to savor every breath, as if they had all the time in the world.

But they hadn't. They didn't. Not according to him.

Too soon, they drove toward Lafayette Square. The north portico of the White House lay beyond it, a flood-lit jewel atop its wide, fenced lawn.

Matt was double-parked outside the Metro entrance.

"I'm sorry," he said stiffly, not looking at her.

"You're a busy man," she reassured him, unfastening her seat belt. "And I really do love the Metro— Oh." He wasn't talking about not driving her home, was he? "You already apologized for that."

A car behind them honked. Matt switched on his hazard lights. "I was out of line, and you deserve better."

Did better than that exist?

"I won't file a complaint if you don't." She was trying to sound worldly, sophisticated. It came out sounding stupid.

He turned the radio off, then planted both hands on the steering wheel. "You're the best assistant I've ever had."

She blinked at him across the car's interior. The best assistant? An hour ago his words would have thrilled her. "Oh."

"It didn't mean—" But he stopped himself. He didn't say, "It didn't mean anything." Maybe he couldn't say it.

She knew she couldn't. But that wasn't the efficient reaction, the professional reaction. That wasn't the best assistant's reaction. "They need you at the office," she said softly, and got out of the car. She didn't look back.

She had work to do. At least she was important for that.

The emergency that demanded Matt's presence concerned more trouble in Eastern Europe from the Rebelian dictator. Matt had a special interest in Rebelia's neighboring country of Delmonico, since an old friend of his had become the pro-tem ambassador after her husband's recent death. Predicting public reaction to varying strategies kept Matt blessedly busy through Saturday. Then he lucked into a last-minute date with Janeen Sullivan, the heiress his friend Rita had dubbed Ms. Peanut.

"Meet at Where or When?" she suggested over the phone.

"No," he said. His favorite restaurant made him think of Carey now. He didn't want to think about Carey when he was with Janeen…or to be with Janeen while thinking about Carey. "You're at the Ritz-Carlton, right?"

"I like the way you think," she purred.

But they hadn't made it through salad before Matt was certain—he had no desire to take his girlfriend upstairs for dessert. Well…maybe he had some desire. He wasn't dead and buried. But even if he couldn't control his body's interest, he could damn well control what he did with it.

For some reason, Janeen wasn't enough. Not tonight.

"I've missed you." She flirted with her necklace. "I loved the roses you sent."

A family, two tables over, seemed to be looking at Matt. One girl had that, isn't-he-someone-important look on her face.

He felt somehow embarrassed. He wasn't used to feeling embarrassed.

Janeen pouted at his disinterest. "It's a week and a half until the state dinner," she said.

"The teachers' tribute," he remembered. "Yeah. I'll have Carey process the paperwork for your security clearance."

"Carey?" She arched a carefully trimmed eyebrow.

Carey. He still wasn't sure how much he honestly regretted that kiss, though he knew he should. "My assistant."

"Is she pretty?"

She has a beauty you couldn't buy for all the peanuts in Georgia. But Matt didn't say that, not just because it was uncharacteristically cruel, but because his internal alarms were sounding. "You're jealous of my assistant?"

"Not jealous, just territorial."

Even worse. "Janeen, we've only been dating a couple of months."

"I know, I know," she assured him. "We're not exclusive."

Actually, Matt tended to be monogamous, even with casual sex. He prided himself on never going to bed with one woman until his previous lover knew they were through. "No, we're not."

Janeen ran a manicured nail slowly along the low neckline of her dress. "That doesn't mean I can't do my best to ruin you for all the others, though, does it?"

This was a bad idea.

"Come upstairs," she cajoled. "Just for one drink."

Oh, hell. "Room service?" he suggested, digging a bill out of his wallet to toss on the table.

"My treat," she agreed eagerly, nevertheless waiting for him to stand and pull out her chair.

They made it as far as the elevator bay before he began to have second thoughts. "Actually, Janeen, maybe—"

He couldn't finish, what with her tongue down his throat. But her searching hands didn't have their usual effect.

Then the elevator dinged its arrival. Janeen retracted her tongue—and she was blond. And he didn't want her. He probably *should* want her. It wasn't as if he should be thinking of sweet, wholesome Carey at this moment, and Janeen, whom he *was* dating, might be just the cure for his temporary insanity.

But he just didn't—

Flash! Even as Matt squinted angrily away from a familiar burst of light, several more followed. *Great.*

"What's your name, sweetheart?" called the photographer as they ducked into the open elevator.

Janeen rolled her eyes and kept her mouth shut; Matt really *didn't* date just anybody. Tabloids paid too much for tell-alls.

Matt joked, "Tynan. T-y-n—"

Janeen laughed as the elevator doors slid shut. Then she backed Matt against one of the mirrored walls and tried to unbutton his shirt.

Damn.

"Ah, sweetheart. Just a minute." Somehow he managed to sidestep her and check his pager. "I've, uh, got to make a call."

"Your beeper didn't go off," she protested.

"It's set on vibrate," he lied, flipping open his phone. "Rita," he commanded, assuming she'd recognize the name of the U.S. Press Secretary.

But Janeen pouted. "Who's Rita?"

They'd reached her floor and stepped out of the elevator by the time Rita answered. "Winfield here."

"You paged me," said Matt, trying to look apologetic for Janeen.

"No, I didn't," said Rita. He could hear conversation in the background, as though she was at some kind of meet-and-greet.

"That sounds serious," said Matt, while Janeen tapped her foot impatiently on the hallway carpeting.

"Oh-hh." One thing about Rita; she caught on fast. "This is one of *those* phone calls, is it? Are you with Ms. Peanut?"

When Janeen leaned in, he took a quick step backward. "Now?"

"This very minute," agreed Rita. "It cannot wait. The fate of democracy—nay, the free world—depends on your escape."

"Yeah," said Matt. "Okay. See you there."

It was one of his clumsier saves, but it worked. He extricated himself from Janeen and by time he got back to his empty apartment, his body barely minded. He considered calling Carey—just to hear her voice, maybe to see her. Then he remembered the photographer at the Ritz-Carlton and considered that he was a freaking idiot. One kiss was an incident—bad enough. But if it happened again, it would be a pattern. And Carey working for him equaled a scandal.

She didn't have to work for him. The thought horrified him. This was Carey's *job!* Not only that, but he needed her—as an assistant. The best he'd ever had. The best *assistant.*

That was when he knew he had to get serious about corralling whatever he felt for Carey before it got out of hand.

Rita Winfield's phone call the following day gave him the ammunition he needed.

"Talk to me," he said, answering his phone.

"At length, pal," his old friend assured him. "But in the meantime, I got a call from the *World Inquisitor,* wanting official comment on a story I think you'll find amusing."

She'd called him on a Sunday about the freaking *World Inquisitor?* "Yes, they got a picture, but so what? It was human, heterosexual kissing, no nudity, no mutants, no cowheaded aliens involved, so I don't see why they'd care."

"Goody, another one for my scrapbook," said Rita. "But this isn't about any of that—except maybe the mutants."

Monday, June 9

Carey loved Mondays. A long, lonely weekend remembering Matt's kiss—and researching rumors of secret government labs, to keep things focused on business—hadn't changed that.

Matt's expression, when she reached their office, did.

"You're here early," she said, then felt stupid, and not just for stating the obvious. Seeing Matt again, after that kiss, put her off balance. Something about the way he was looking doubled the effect. The way he'd folded his arms. The way he'd raised his eyebrows.

"'White House Investigates Mutants,'" he said, clipped.

Now she felt even more off balance. "What?"

He lifted a sheet of paper off her desk and offered it to

her like a subpoena. "It's the headline from this Wednesday's issue of the *World Inquisitor*. Apparently 'President Stewart's top aide, Matthew Tynan, is actively seeking the truth about governmental cover-ups in genetic experimentation.'"

"Why would they think that?" Was he angry with *her?*

"Let's think about it," he said. "Do *you* know of any reason they'd have to connect me to their super-babies story?"

And it hit her, like a punch in the stomach. "Oh, no."

He slapped the paper back onto her desk. "You called the *Inquisitor?*"

"As me, Carey Benton! I didn't mention your name, much less the president or the White House. I would never— How did they even—?" She felt sick, and his obvious anger wasn't helping. "I just wanted to ask Mr. Cantrell where he got his information, such that it is, that's all. How did they connect me to you?"

"Gee," said Matt. "I don't know. A computer, maybe?"

Of course a computer. A database. Federal employees….

"Oh, Matt, I'm so sorry, I don't— What are we going to do?" She wanted to reach for him, if only for the balance. Something about his stiff posture and frown kept her back.

"What are *we* going to do?" He turned and walked into his office, then faced her from the doorway. "The White House is going to do what it always does with the *World Inquisitor*'s bull, which is, ignore it. I'm going to call Jake Ingram, apologize, and hope this doesn't impact his investigation. And you, Carey—*you* are going to leave Code Proteus alone. Got it?"

"*What?*" He couldn't mean that. "But, Matt—"

He shut the door in her face.

Carey sank into her chair, physically shaking. How could she have been so stupid as to give her real name? And how could Matt, the charmer, the same Matt who had kissed her—

She saw that he hadn't brought the Monday bagels, and pressed a fist to her mouth to keep from crying.

By the time Matt came out of his office for the senior staff meeting, she'd collected herself enough to make a better case.

"Matt," she said. He looked wary as he stopped for her. "I made a mistake, and I'm sorry for the trouble I've caused. I'll do whatever I can to help fix things. But I can't be of much use if you're so angry that we can't even talk about it."

He considered that, dead still and expressionless. But at least when he spoke, his voice didn't have that awful stiffness to it. "Yeah. Look, Skipper, maybe we've been talking a bit too much, anyway."

She shook her head. "What does that mean?"

But he was already leaving. "I'll be late for my meeting."

By Wednesday, things had only gotten worse. Even Honey Evans noticed, at lunch. She interrupted her own story of some retired CIA agent so lonely he was calling the White House just to chat and asked, "What's wrong with you?"

"I may have to quit working for Matt." Carey spoke the words with a stunned wonder, but she recognized their truth. She'd prided herself on her efficiency, and now she couldn't even do her job. Not if Matt didn't trust her. Not if he felt he had to constantly be on his guard.

Whether it was because of the kiss or the goof-up with the *Inquisitor,* she didn't know. She wasn't sure it mattered.

"No way!" Honey almost poured cola on herself before she noticed and put down the can. "Why?"

Carey hesitated. Despite Honey's wild ways, the bouncy

blonde hid a core of honor; Carey felt sure of it. It was no coincidence that Honey came from a family of overachievers. "Do you promise not to tell? I mean *anybody?*"

"Hey, I'm no sheep who just bleats for the hell of it."

So Carey told her—not about Code Proteus, of course, but about dinner and the kiss and the brush-off. She hadn't realized until her words started tripping over each other how badly she'd needed to share this. Her only other real confidante in the office, Rita Winfield, had more important matters to deal with—matters of national security. And Rita was Matt's friend.

Honey was Carey's. Clearly. Only a true friend would slam down her cola can so hard that some of it fizzed out the top, as she exclaimed, "The bastard!"

"You promised not to tell," insisted Carey.

"I know I did, and I won't. But first he sexually harasses you—"

"Honey, he did no such thing!"

"And then he decides to punish you for whatever it was he says you did, which I'm sure was completely innocent, you being you. What gives him the right?"

Carey felt some of the tightness in her throat ease with the support of her friend's outrage. "He's not punishing me, Honey. But he won't let me work late, which is ridiculous. I still haven't caught up this morning. He doesn't return my pages as quickly as he used to, as if he's afraid to even talk to me. Sooner or later, this is going to cause bigger problems than just for us. I think—" God, but it hurt to even consider! "I think maybe I should leave before that happens."

Honey took a long draft of cola, wrinkled her nose at the can, then offered, "I hear if you make him fire you instead, you can get unemployment benefits. The getting fired part can be cathartic, too, depending on how you play it."

Carey's laugh sounded uneven, but at least it was a laugh. "I can get another job. It would probably pay better."

"Leave the White House? Who am I supposed to eat with?"

The idea of seeing Matt every day, just from a distance, hurt too deeply to consider. "I can't do this halfway."

Honey considered the idea gloomily, then brightened. "Carey, that's brilliant!"

For some reason, Honey's enthusiasm always made Carey nervous. "Brilliant, how?"

"Once you're not working for Tynan, you can seduce him with a clear conscience. True, he's a jerk now. But he's a sexy jerk."

Carey knew better than to buy into that. It wasn't likely that Matt would want to date her, even if she did quit. The way he'd been acting, she wasn't sure she wanted to date him, either. Despite that kiss.

She'd sleep on it. She owed them both that much.

But how could she keep working for him like this?

"I'm sorry, Jake," said Matt on Thursday, pacing. He hated being tethered by the curly phone cord, but it was the only way to assure a secure line. "Your name didn't get mentioned, though, and the *Inquisitor* has the credibility of gruel. Rita didn't even give them a 'no comment,' she just blew them off."

"It's not a problem," said Jake Ingram. "Really."

"It's just that things are moving a little more slowly this week. I took Carey off the project."

"Did something happen?" Somehow, Jake put a dozen emotions into that question. Exhaustion, resignation, uncertainty, suspicion.... What the hell had he gotten himself into, anyway?

Matt closed his eyes and shook his head, afraid he might simply be projecting. "No. Not with her work, anyway."

Jake's side of the line was silent for a moment. Then he said, "You've got to be joking. Not Carey, too."

They'd been friends too long for Matt not to recognize either the assumption or the pending lecture. Of their old gang in college, Jake was second only to Eric Jones in toeing the line. "Too? There is no *too,* Jake. Nothing happened."

Well, almost nothing. He'd stopped matters before anything significant had happened between him and Carey. Despite his dreams and memories of their one not-quite-innocent kiss.

"Tell me you didn't put the old Tynan moves on Carey."

When in doubt, counterattack. "Postpone any weddings lately, Ingram?"

Jake said, "Ouch. You're a real pal. She's still trustworthy on this, right? She won't start talking?"

Matt was just as glad for the chance to turn the conversation back to where it needed to be—the World Bank heist, Code Proteus and genetic engineering. None of which Jake Ingram was yet willing to explain. "Point being that, without Carey on this, and with some other crises, it may be a few weeks before I can get another package to you."

"That last report gave me plenty to consider," Jake assured him. "Just get back to me when you can. Okay?" The words sounded more calm than the voice.

"Yeah." Matt jiggled the phone cord to watch it bounce.

"Don't screw up with Carey," added Jake.

And yet, almost as soon as they'd hung up, a knock sounded at Matt's door. Carey peeked in. "Can I talk to you a moment?"

Matt stared at her and thought that, in a kinder world, she could talk to him for eternities. Her hair looked so shiny and natural, and her white blouse did nothing to dispel that innocent image of hers or to hide her willowy curves.

He'd missed her. But he'd be damned if he let that tempt him into doing worse by her than he already had. Her job could be at risk, if it got out, and she deserved this job.

One of the hardest things he'd done all day was to start gathering reports together. "Sorry, Skipper, I'm heading back over to Bermann's office, and I've got to review some numbers."

"It will just take a minute." And his door snicked shut behind her. That snick unsettled him. They were alone.

Over the past few days Carey had looked increasingly confused, even hurt—an expression that twisted his gut, no matter how necessary his behavior. But this afternoon she was no victim. She looked strong, focused, in control.

"Just a minute, then," he agreed, shifting the reports to his other arm. They made a lousy shield between him and her.

She handed him a sheet of paper, and for a moment Matt felt a surge of relief. He put it on his reports and started to reach for his pen, assuming it was something he had to sign. Then he saw the subject line, and he went completely still.

"I'm sorry things have turned out this way, Matt," said Carey with gentle firmness. "But I'm giving my two-week notice."

Six

"**Y**ou can't give notice." It wasn't the smartest thing he'd ever said, what with the page of stationery staring him in the face. Carey's resignation was as impeccably typed as everything else she did for him.

But she wasn't doing this for him. She was doing it *to* him.

She squared her slim shoulders. There was a reason she made such an efficient front line of defense for his office. "Of course I can. No matter whose fault it is, I'm no longer an asset to you or this office. The sooner we face that, the sooner I can start training someone better qualified to take my place."

"No." Matt dropped the letter and his files onto his desk, and spread his hands. "Nobody is better qualified than you. I've been an ass lately, I know it, but that's no reason to quit."

She did not contradict him about being an ass. "You haven't trusted me since I messed up with that *Inquisitor* reporter."

"It wasn't the reporter!" He saw her eyes widen. So much for that ruse. "Bad press happens even when you *don't* make mistakes, and I had worse things printed about me in high school. I only came down on you that hard because—"

"This is about Friday," she said.

"It is. Was. Partly." He tried to smile, but maybe Carey

had built a resistance over the months. She just stared at him. He said, "We can pretend Friday didn't happen."

"The way you've been pretending all week?"

She had a point, damn it. But Matt was willing to ignore logic, even pride, if it meant not losing Carey. "Look, I screwed up. I screwed up on Friday, and I made things worse in damage control. But I can fix this. I've got a strategy."

She shook her head. "Your 'strategy' is to keep me at arm's length, Matt, as if you're afraid at any moment I'm going to..." She blushed. For some reason she'd focused on his shirt buttons.

"I'm not afraid of that, Carey," he reassured her, shifting his weight. "Of all the many problems I'm facing this week, fear of your baser urges is not one of them."

"Well, you fear *something* about me, and I can't work that way. Neither can you, if you'd just stop deluding yourself long enough to notice how these last few days have gone for us."

Us. That was why everything was going to hell. Somehow, in one kiss, he'd given her the hint of an *us.* Actually, he must have done it before the kiss; she wouldn't have been so receptive otherwise. A woman like Janeen, sure. Not Carey.

How could she know him on so many levels and still think he had any *us* potential? Even Jake, from hundreds of miles away, knew Matt better than that. *Don't screw up with Carey,* he'd warned.

Too late.

He scowled down at that damned letter on his desk, then pushed it aside just to stall. He had to stop this. "I don't want things between us to end this way."

"Well..." Carey hesitated. "They don't have to end."

His gaze cut up to hers, searching for any hint that she

meant...that she wanted...well, something that she'd be an idiot to want, but that quickened his pulse all the same. He thought of that kiss, of how she'd tasted, smelled, felt.

Even if she didn't work for him, she came with strings.

To his guarded relief, she looked away and said, "I mean, I'd like to continue working on Code Proteus."

"You shouldn't be doing unpaid work for me."

"I'm not just doing it for you," she insisted. Although he'd kind of wondered about that, at first, he now believed her. Of the two of them, she was clearly the more mature, despite their age differences. "I'm doing it for Henry Bloomfield, and the wife and children he may have had when he died, and whatever children the CIA was buying toys for. I'm doing it because Jake Ingram's working on something very important to the country right now—I heard the president's speech on fighting fear, too. Finding the criminal who pulled off the World Bank robbery is bigger than all of us. And it's not like *you* have time for anything else."

He didn't. Of the president's multipronged approach to fighting fear, capturing the elusive Achilles was only one part. The president's central solution, his ultimate weapon against the nation's fears about everything from retirement funds to DNA experiments, was knowledge—education. And Senator Bermann was blocking the education initiative as stubbornly as ever. It would come to vote by the end of the month, and if Stewart lost...

"That's true," he started. "But—"

"And," Carey reminded him, "I've already got clearance. You don't want to have to bring in another set of eyes, do you?"

He wouldn't trust anyone's eyes over her baby blues, which was one more reason why the idea of losing her was so devastating. But not the only reason. Not even close.

And yet lose her, he had—Proteus or not. In one kiss. The reality of it hurt on deeper levels than he wanted to consider. He knew he couldn't go through their parting slowly. "You're sure?" he asked, both admiring and resenting her for being adult enough to admit something he was still fighting, something so damned obvious, so damned tragic.

She lifted her chin and he saw a kindred pain in her eyes, along with determination. "Yes."

"Then don't take your two weeks."

Carey actually took a surprised step back. "What?"

"Of course you'll get your last two weeks' pay—"

"That's not what I meant!"

"Bring in someone new tomorrow, this afternoon if you can, and catch her up as quickly as possible. And at least consider leaving Proteus. It may not be safe, and it won't help either of us to draw this out."

Carey shook her head again, and Matt felt bad. Bad? He was in hell. "I'm not doing this to hurt you, Carey," he insisted, fisting his free hand to keep from reaching for her. He'd said that before, to other women. He'd never meant it this much. "But as long as you're here, you leaving is going to loom over us. It'll distract me." More than she knew. "And I can't risk distraction right now."

"But it's a big job, Matt! My replacement can't—"

"I mean it." It was the only way he could stand to lose her—fast. Like pulling off a Band-Aid. "You've always said that if someone else can't sit down at your desk and take over on a day's notice, you aren't doing your job right. We got by just fine the week your mom had her emergency gallbladder surgery."

Actually he'd missed her like a limb. Like an organ. The office felt incomplete without her—and so had he. But business had limped along, even so.

"All right." Damned if Carey didn't look confused again—and hurt. Well, *she* was the one who'd resigned. Recognizing his own childishness didn't drown that thought. "You're the boss."

"For a little while, anyway," he muttered, turning away to his filing cabinet.

If he didn't turn away, he might say or do something they'd both regret.

Regret even more than this.

Carey made herself go though the motions of arranging a replacement from the White House temporary pool—a man who'd filled in for her when she went on vacation, one Matt seemed to get along with well enough. Then she packed up some of her personal belongings, including a picture of her parents, a calendar from Denver that Matt had given her last Christmas, her green chenille throw. She didn't want to have to carry everything home at once. Even if she got Honey to drive her, Honey's convertible only had so much room in the trunk.

She hugged the blanket. What had she done?

She had the best, most exciting administrative job in the country. Maybe Matt was right. Maybe they could pretend the kiss hadn't happened. Maybe they could move past it.

Then the door from Matt's office opened. He looked so dark and tired and handsome as he came to stand beside her desk, she longed to touch him. To rub his shoulders, or his temples, and ease away the tension of his day. To just touch him.

"I, uh, hate to ask this," he said, putting an armload of files on her desk. "But I've flagged the pages with the statistics I need and I was hoping—"

"I'm still your assistant through the end of the week."

Carey felt proud that her voice barely wavered. "I'm completely capable of making copies and returning files."

Still he lingered, shifting his weight, tall and hesitant. He smelled of warmth and sandalwood and man—the most consistent man in her life. And once she left here…

He took a deep breath. "Look, Skipper, I'm sorry for how I've behaved. On Friday, this week, this afternoon. I've been selfish, which I guess should be no surprise, since I've been a selfish boss all along."

She tried to protest, but he shook his head.

"You've barely had a social life since you got this job—don't think I haven't noticed. With our schedule, how could you? Maybe now you can, uh, act and date and live like any beautiful, intelligent woman your age."

He thought she was beautiful? Intelligent, yes, but beautiful? It shouldn't send a shiver through her the way it did. Even if she wasn't his employee, he wanted her to date someone else. Not him.

He said, "Anyway, if you need more time, that's fine. I'll deal with it. Let's do what's best for you, for once."

There he went, being helpful again—helpful and sweet and far too accepting of her departure. "No, you were right," she said. "Fast is the only way to do this. I'll work through tomorrow, and leave my number in case anything comes up during the interim assistant's transition. It's Kip Davis, by the way."

"Good," said Matt. "He's…he'll be fine." But his gaze paused on her folded green throw, and he frowned.

"Is there anything else?" asked Carey, wishing for things she couldn't even fully conceive much less ask for. But she could feel them, and they felt like Matt Tynan, like his kiss.

"No," he said, and headed for the doorway. "See you tomorrow, Skipper," he called over his shoulder.

It was the last time he would say that to her, and Carey could barely hold back her tears. She'd done the right thing.

She just hated it when the right thing hurt so badly, she could barely breathe through it.

Friday, June 13

Matt's new assistant, Kip, was a slim blond man maybe three years older than Carey. He was starting as a temporary, but after a day's training, Carey had high hopes for him—even if she recognized on his face some of the same primal reactions to Matt Tynan's good looks and easy manner as she felt herself.

"Damn shame he's straight," murmured Kip to her the next morning after Matt's first hit-and-run entrance and exit of the day. "Though I guess that'll keep things less complicated."

Carey considered how much easier her life would be at this moment if Matt didn't date women at all—as opposed to just not dating *her*—and she sighed. "You don't know the half of it."

"Ah, well." In the spare desk chair they'd brought in, Kip turned back to her computer. "Real life can rarely outdo those impossible dreams anyway, can it? Never knock the fantasy."

He *really* didn't know the half of it. But he spoke four languages, had been doing administrative and clerical work in trusted positions for almost ten years, and knew the White House staff's computer systems inside and out. He had great people skills, a flexible schedule and a bachelor's degree in political science, unlike Carey's double major in Liberal Arts. He probably deserved her job more than she ever had, but his lifestyle choices still turned off too many potential bosses.

Of all Matt's weaknesses, insecurity about his masculinity was not one of them. He'd always gotten along with Kip just fine. At least some good was coming out of this.

It was midmorning when, after taking yet another phone call, Kip looked surprised and put the caller on hold. "It's for you."

Nothing in his expression indicated that it might be Matt, and Carey rarely got personal calls at work, so she was at a loss as she answered. "This is Carey."

"Who the hell was that?" demanded Josh O'Donnell's Bronx accent. "What good does it do me to bring O.S.E.P. business to Tynan's attention if I'm not allowed to talk to you first?"

"Actually, Mr. O'Donnell, I'm not working for Matt after this week," admitted Carey. "So you may have to get used—"

"You got a new job?" he asked. "Otherwise, work for me."

Carey stared at the phone. "You're serious?"

She hadn't even revised her résumé!

"I've been asking you for forever, girl! Come across the street and work for me. It's still government wages, but the O.E.O.B.'s got prettier offices than the West Wing any day."

"I'd have to interview with you first, Mr. O'Donnell. Make sure it's a good match for both of us." But by the time she'd arranged an appointment for the following week and written down directions to his office in the Old Executive Office Building, she couldn't deny her relief. She had scant savings, and this would minimize her loss of wages. Just as important, she truly supported the work the O.S.E.P. was doing. Their work was one reason Matt was trying so hard to pass the education initiative.

Determined, competent, confusing Matt…

He came and went particularly quickly that day, taking more meetings than most mortal businessmen would ever dare. Carey should know. She'd helped him schedule them long before she'd known this day was coming. He had no winks or grins for her.

He was out when, in midafternoon, Rita Winfield carried in a red, white and blue sheet-cake singing, "For she's a jolly good fella." Other staff—assistants, speechwriters, clerks and interns from departments as diverse as the Travel Office, the Gifts Office, and the Telephone Office—crowded in as Kip stood and heartily joined the singing. Now Carey *did* cry, but it was through smiles. The next half hour or so blurred into a daze of kisses and hugs, a few last-minute presents and cards bearing more important names than seemed possible.

"Be careful with those signatures," warned Rita with a laugh. "A forger could do a lot of damage to this nation if he got hold of some of those!"

"Are you plotting to overthrow the government again, Rita?" chided a familiar voice behind her—familiar, but not Matt's. Simply from the way people began jostling backward into each other to make respectful way, Carey knew it wasn't Matt. She'd stood before she even noticed the Secret Service agent at the door.

"You'd think," said the President of the United States as he turned into the office, "that I'd be more careful whom I hire as press secretary. Hello, Carey Benton. My friend Matt tells me this is your last day in the trenches with us."

"Yes, Mr. President." This time, Carey's voice *did* waver.

"Well, I couldn't let that happen without wishing you well." And President Stewart offered his hand to her—which she of course took. A fit man in his early fifties, balding but handsome, the president had a powerful grip and an earnest smile. Several flashbulbs went off—his official photographer capturing the moment for posterity. "Any woman who can keep up with Matt Tynan for a year has my complete respect. And some sympathy."

"Thank you, sir," said Carey. "But you've put up with him a lot longer than I have. You appointed him."

The president's smile deepened. "Touché." Turning back toward the door, he caught Rita Winfield's gaze. "Why do you suppose I make these kinds of personnel choices anyway, Rita? Dare I hope we've sufficiently hidden my streak of insanity from the American people?"

"We haven't hidden it at all, sir," said Rita with a grin. "I think it's part of why the American people love you."

"God bless 'em." But the leader of the country was already on his way out, back to a schedule that even Carey—after a year working with Matt—had a hard time imagining. "Good luck in the future, Carey Benton," he called. "Thank you for your service."

How could the rest of her professional life be anything but a letdown after this?

Honey Evans broke the spell of the moment. "Now you're never going to wash *that* hand again, either."

After that, Carey's attempts to get Kip up to speed were regularly interrupted for the rest of the afternoon. The Chief of Staff ducked in long enough to wish her well, as did the Vice President. The First Lady stopped by. None of these were people Carey immediately worked with, of course, but despite its bustle and its importance, the White House had an old-world formality about it. That included thank-you notes, matching china and cordial farewells when an employee tendered notice.

The people who worked more closely with her, and so were less formal, of course had questions about her departure. Carey fended them off with the simple excuse of "Personal reasons." When possible she added, "Luckily, Matt's okay with it."

After all, they'd still be working with Matt after she left. And the tension wasn't his fault, certainly no more than hers.

"I'll get to the truth sooner or later," teased Rita when Carey gave that answer. "Either out of you or out of Tynan."

But Carey wouldn't be around anymore to be questioned.

The one person she really wanted to see, of course, had meetings all afternoon. She lingered late in the office with the last of her boxes, and with Honey and Kip—who were getting along well, flirting futilely and outrageously. Her throat felt tighter and tighter the later the clock turned. Rita offered to walk her out, to spare her the embarrassment of a military escort now that she'd turned in her blue pass, but Carey insisted on waiting.

Maybe she should get out of town, for once. Maybe she should celebrate instead of mourn her freedom. Finally, in deference to her friends, she had to say, "I guess I'd better get—"

Then she heard Rita call, "You almost missed her!" And her breath caught.

Matt jogged into the office, his coat unbuttoned, his tie loose. "Hey, Skipper," he panted, catching himself on the door frame. "I was afraid you'd leave without me."

You could call me at home, if I had, she wanted to say. *I'm not leaving D.C. I'm not even leaving you, if only....*

But she wouldn't dare say that, any more than she would risk the likelihood that he *wouldn't* call her at home. Matt had always been incredible, but his love life wasn't part of Carey's world. She'd preferred being unique. "I'm glad you made it."

"I'm sorry I wasn't here for the party." Matt picked up

her last box, Carey shouldered her satchel, and they started for the lobby. His tie still hung crooked, and his dark hair was mussed. His eyes shone at her, dark and earnest, and he'd never looked so good. "You deserve better."

She wished he wouldn't say that, when *better* meant *not him.*

"You know I've loved working here, don't you?" she asked as they reached the lobby. "This has been the best job, and you…"

But her throat closed off anything else she could've said.

With a slight groan, as if giving up on his better instincts, Matt handed his box to Kip, stepped forward and pulled Carey into a quick hug. For one long, blissful moment, his warmth and strength and smell surrounded her. She was wrapped in him, held by him, like something precious and desirable. He even kissed her cheek, his own scratching softly with afternoon roughness. Her eyes stung.

And then he let go.

"Take care of yourself." He backed toward the West Wing proper, clearly escaping. "Say hi to the folks in Kansas City when you see them."

Not Ogallala. Not Dallas or Phoenix or Albuquerque. Not Tombstone or Deadwood. Kansas City.

They weren't playing with each other anymore, and Carey hated that. But all she said was, "I'll do that."

"C'mon, Tynan," challenged Honey, hands on her hips. "Was that the best kiss you've got?"

Where was a nice hole in the floor when you needed one?

"Yeah," said Matt, not looking away from Carey. "It's the best kiss I've got for women who are too good for me, anyway."

Honey rolled her eyes. "Then I guess you better start cleaning up your image, huh?" Thank God, Carey's friend had stayed quiet around President Stewart!

Kip said, "I'll just help Carey out with this, then I'll be back for your notes, 'kay?"

Matt, with a final nod, turned and strode back into the inner sanctum, where Carey would no longer be allowed as anything but a visitor. Then he was gone.

And that was that.

So she readjusted her fat, soft-sided satchel over her shoulder and followed her friends out toward the parking lot. She would do it, she decided. She would rent a car at Union Station, get out of town and clear her head.

But she was taking this satchel with her.

It was, after all, her final connection to Matt Tynan. Her best hope of seeing him again. Her best chance of repairing past mistakes—to make up in efficiency what she clearly lacked as a possible date.

It held her copies of the Bloomfield research, newspaper clippings on the secret government genetics lab and photo-copies of her Freedom of Information files on Code Proteus.

Seven

Matt didn't last a day before he called her apartment, just to make sure she was okay.

Carey's phone rang once, twice, again.

Click. "Hello. You've reached Carey at 202-555-3712. Please leave a message at the beep. Thanks!"

Yes, she *thanked* people for leaving calls on her machine.

Matt hung up and went back to drafting strategy on his laptop while watching a late-morning CNN broadcast. So he'd buckled under the fleeting urge to hit speed dial. That didn't mean he'd go on tape with it.

If he wasn't careful, he'd say he missed her. He shouldn't start missing her until at least Monday. Failing that, he sure shouldn't admit it.

Worse would be if he suggested another dinner. He knew his own limits. If he went out with her again, without the implied Keep Off sign of them working together, only Carey herself could stop things from going a lot further than kissing.

Carey was a smart woman, but Matt could be damned persuasive when he wanted something. Better to just stay away.

He distracted himself with an early afternoon racquetball game with a personable congressman. Later, he had coffee with an attractive Wall Street broker. Then he called Carey, got her machine and hung up again.

When his phone rang, he answered it eagerly. "Hello?"

"Hi, handsome," purred Janeen Sullivan, the frustrated peanut heiress. "Wanna share some room service?"

Mere habit almost pulled a "Sure" from him. What a good way to forget about Carey for a few hours! Then he heard himself saying, "Tonight's no good. How about a rain check?"

"It's been a week!" He recognized the edge to her voice, not from her but from many women before her. Here it came: "And you gave me a rain check then, too. I'm beginning to think you don't take this relationship seriously."

Matt was tempted to laugh, but that would hurt her feelings. Harder to resist was the urge to remind her of a few things, such as how he'd said "You know I'm not looking for a relationship" when they'd first met.

He hated this part. *He* didn't change, did he? Wasn't he busy, unreliable and inconstant when the women met him? Yet the minute they said *relationship,* things went sour. He hadn't cheated. He rarely avoided the women. But his fun-loving partners eventually turned needy and shrill, and he knew that somehow, just by being himself, he'd done that to them.

That vague sense of guilt kept him from arguing the point.

"Look, beautiful," he hedged, scrubbing a hand through his hair. "We're still on for that state dinner Wednesday night, right? We'll eat fancy food, meet important people, and you can tell me at length what an ass I've been. How's that?"

She said nothing.

That was usually a bad sign. He knew he could salvage this, stay friends, but they had to be talking first. "Janeen? See you then?"

She sulkily agreed, and when they disconnected, he sat there and felt bad for a few minutes. Then he called Carey. Just to check.

Click. "Hello. You've reached…"

He hung up. It wasn't as though his phone number wasn't plastering itself all over her Caller I.D. Maybe she'd gone out on a date. If he were a better man, he'd hope she was enjoying herself.

He wasn't that good a man.

The cause of death wasn't listed as drowning but "blunt head trauma." And under "spouse," instead of a typed notation, someone had scribbled "Violet Vaughn?"

A wife? And the name struck her as vaguely familiar.

Standing in the county courthouse nearest Belle Terre, North Carolina, Carey quickly checked the name at the top of the death certificate. It was the same as on the voter registration material, tax records and birth certificate she'd found. Henry Bloomfield. Already, her two-hundred-fifty-mile drive down the coast in a rental car was worth it.

She had a name for Bloomfield's wife!

Carey looked for and found no marriage license. But another check of the voter registration listed a Violet Vaughn at the same address as Henry Bloomfield. Whereas his occupation was "Scientist/U.S. Gov't." Vaughn's was "Assistant/Dr. Henry Bloomfield."

An assistant. Just like Carey. But *un*like Carey, this Vaughn woman had *lived* with her boss.

Was North Carolina a common-law state?

"And to think," Carey said, after thanking the clerk, "some people minimize the importance of good filing skills."

After that, she drove to Belle Terre itself, a sleepy seaside village that seemed to be off the beaten track of summer visitors. She used the address she'd gotten from the assessor's office to find Bloomfield's isolated, antebellum home. It wore only a tattered dignity. Most of its windows were boarded and so much sand had blown onto the verandah that weeds grew there.

Carey parked and looked around, trying to imagine the gruff-looking man from the obituary pictures living here with his assistant. But the desertion of the empty estate—the graffiti, broken glass, beer cans and cigarette butts—just made her sad. Her throat ached from loneliness and lost chances.

Or maybe that was having ended her job with Matt Tynan.

After a few aborted attempts at a diner and the Belle Terre police station, she finally drove to the larger, neighboring town of Kent and played a hunch. She found Kent's one retirement home—Belle Terre had none at all—and introduced herself at the front desk. This time, she used her mother's maiden name.

"Do you suppose there's anyone here from Belle Terre who'd be willing to talk to me about the nineteen-sixties and -seventies there?"

The dark-skinned nurse looked Carey up and down, then shrugged. "You can go to the common room and ask. Just don't try to sell anybody anything or I'll yank your skinny butt out of there so fast you'll leave your empty shoes behind."

"Good," Carey said, and found her way to the common room. There, following her people trail struck pay dirt. Of seven residents who'd lived in Belle Terre, five remembered the Bloomfields—whom they spoke of in the plural.

"Stuck up," pronounced one leathery-faced old woman with carefully done finger curls as they settled onto a pair of sofas and two extra chairs. "They was kinda hoity-toity, keeping to themselves like that. Comes from getting so educated and living in Atlanta."

"Comes from livin' in that mansion of theirs!" A wizened little man with hunched shoulders, bright eyes and a walker nodded firmly. He shouted when he talked. But the woman beside him, perhaps in her seventies, patted his hand, and he lowered his voice. "Fine house."

These two wore matching rings, Carey noticed with delight. Now *that* was love, far more than Hollywood grins, hot kisses and fancy restaurants. Though for all she knew, they could have had both—the hot kisses and the longevity. Weren't both possible?

If both people wanted it, anyway. And Matt Tynan—

She flushed. This was about Henry Bloomfield, not Matt.

"We're the Johnsons, and they weren't so bad," insisted his wife. Other than a portable oxygen tank, she looked healthy—perhaps just not healthy enough to care for her husband alone. "They simply liked to keep to themselves, is all."

"You say 'they'?" Carey tried to hide her growing excitement as she scribbled notes. She felt marginally guilty for having told them she was researching a book but told herself that, from the thickness of her Code Proteus file, she might as well be.

"The whole family of them," agreed Mr. Johnson.

Family? So it was true? "I didn't find any marriage records for him."

"I always figured they was living in sin," said the woman with the finger curls. "Violet usin' her own name and all."

"I didn't find a license for his first marriage, either," Carey hurried to add. "And I'm sure that one was official, so—"

"Sure they were married," insisted a palsied black man in the corner. "I was a janitor in the emergency room, back in seventy or so, when that Mr. Bloomfield carried in a woman, pregnant and bleedin'. Said she was his wife, Violet. Scared enough for it to be true, too. He said it, and he owned it. To my way of thinkin' that makes them married in front of the only folks who count. He was right glad when she and the babies pulled through fine.''

Babies! Carey admitted that she'd found no records of births, either, but apparently the Bloomfield children had been born at home. Mrs. Johnson, who'd been a grammar-school teacher, had known all five of them before they left school to be home tutored. The three youngest, triplets, were Faith, Mark and Gideon. And the older Bloomfield children—the twins—had been named Grace and Jake.

Which was funny, since it had been a Jake who'd drawn her and Matt into this mystery in the first place. But of course Jake Ingram was from Texas, and... She did the math in her head.

How very odd. Ingram was the same age as Jake Bloomfield would be, if the children had survived.

Carey tried to ignore that tickle of coincidence.

''I think they died, not long after Henry,'' said Mrs. Johnson, turning to her husband. ''Wasn't that in the papers, Roy? Boating accident in Florida. So tragic.''

''Georgia,'' corrected her hunch-shouldered husband, loudly. ''Some kind of explosion. Four children and their mother.''

The woman with the finger curls nodded. ''That's right!''

Four? Perhaps they hadn't heard correctly at all. As Carey listened and took notes, her mind climbed from one possibility to another, each more incredible than the last.

Bloomfield was a geneticist, and his assistant gave birth to undocumented twins, then triplets. Carey was no expert, but didn't in vitro fertilization often result in multiple births?

And wasn't in vitro the way genetically altered eggs were replanted into a woman's uterus?

Was it even possible that Henry and Violet's children were genetically enhanced, maybe the secret "mutants" from the supermarket tabloids? Had they simply been babies from a loving relationship? Carey wondered, nodding at something Mrs. Johnson was telling her about how very bright the Bloomfield children were. Or were they part of a research experiment?

"They were smart?" she asked, the former teacher's announcement penetrating her wild thoughts.

"Oh, yes, the smartest children I've ever taught. Well, except for little Mark. He was better at sports, the poor dear."

"Smart how?" Carey's fingers cramped on her pen. "Spelling-bee smart?" *Read-your-mind smart? Melt-your-brain smart?*

"Grace won first grade spelling bees." Mrs. Johnson nodded, smiling at her memories. "Jake always came in second. Really, there was very little we could teach them—Belle Terre was an even smaller town then than it is now. But their parents wanted their family to have as normal a life as possible. Small towns are good for that. We accept folks for what they are, whether they're bringing frogs back to life, like little Faith, or always eating dirt and grunting, like Billy Anderson."

Several of her companions nodded and made sympathetic sounds; they also remembered Billy Anderson.

Carey asked, "Faith brought a frog back to life?"

"As her research project in the science fair, she froze a frog, then revived it. She excelled in science for so small a child. I'm sure she would have been a doctor or a veterinarian, had she lived."

"The others had special strengths, as well?"

"Oh, yes. Mark was their athlete, and Faith loved science. Gideon was their little inventor—transistor radios, cassette recorders, calculators. He could take any of them apart and then rebuild them, sometimes better. Pong games, too, and those arcade games at the corner store. What were those?"

"Asteroids," supplied the woman with the finger curls. "My Freddy spent so many quarters on that one! And Centipede and Space Invaders. Now folks have full-color computer games."

"And Jake and Grace," continued Carey, nudging them back on topic. "They were good at spelling? Maybe English classes?"

"Well, yes, but mainly Grace," said Mrs. Johnson. "She spoke more languages than any of the teachers, even in kindergarten. At first the principal thought she was making some of them up!"

"And what about Jake?" Carey underlined the word *languages* on her notepad. She was jumping to conclusions. Jake wasn't that unusual a name, and just because Matt's friend from the world of high finance had started them on this project...

"Math, dear," said the retired teacher. "Jake Bloomfield was particularly good with numbers. Numbers and money."

At 9:00 p.m., it made sense that Carey wasn't home. It was Saturday night. She had a life.

By midnight Matt threw out caution and tried her cell phone. A man could pretend to be casual when he called someone's home, but not so much her mobile.

Her line rang three times, then rolled over to her voice mailbox. "Hello. You've reached Carey's voice mail at—"

He hung up. Now he was worried.

By Sunday morning, despite a long jog and a quick skim of the *Washington Post,* the *New York Times* and the *Wall*

Street Journal, Matt was nearing frantic. Where the hell was she? Had she gone home to her folks? Or had her habit of hopping public transit at all hours finally gotten her into trouble?

Or what if whoever wanted Code Proteus to stay hidden was behind her disappearance?

He decided to drive to her place before too many streets got blocked off; it was the third Sunday in June which, in his Dupont Circle neighborhood, meant the annual Gay Pride Parade. That, and the following rally, would snarl up traffic for hours. So Matt headed down Massachusetts Avenue, taking D.C.'s traffic circles with practiced ease, all the way past the Capitol dome before turning south toward Carey's small apartment.

She wasn't there.

So he kept driving, aiming for Alexandria, what the locals called "Occupied Virginia" because of all the Yankees who lived there. Rita Winfield, the press secretary, was one of them; she lived in a half-restored Victorian row house.

He pounded on the door until she opened it.

Rita, wearing overalls, leather work gloves and a bandana tied around her red hair like on an old Rosie the Riveter poster, was completely covered with plaster dust. She stared at him unblinking for a moment, as composed as if she were facing down a hundred screaming reporters. Then she said, "Just in time to help me knock out a dividing wall."

"You've got to find Carey for me," he said.

"Do I?" Rita headed back inside her home, apparently trusting Matt to close the door and follow, which he did. "I don't recall you being my boss or my master, Matt. Not even during our relay."

That meant the two-and-a-quarter weeks they'd been lovers, almost ten years ago. It wasn't long enough, she often said, to be called a whole relationship, just a relay.

Rita stopped in the main hallway and handed him a huge sledgehammer. "Get to work and tell me about Carey."

Before he could protest, she also tugged off her gloves and pulled a slim cell phone from the bib pocket of her overalls. She was still a press secretary, even on Sunday.

"C'mon, Rita." At least he'd worn jeans today.

"C'mon, Tynan," she prompted, nodding toward the wall as she dialed a number from memory. "You're supposed to be knocking down a wall with that. Use the heavy metal end. Don't hit the parts I taped—those are the struts."

Matt had never felt more white-collar. "I've got more important things to worry about than your renovations."

"Not if you want my help you don't. Do you know how long I've been waiting for a free day to tackle this?" Her tone of bored competence brightened. "Hey, sweetie, it's Rita. How's freedom treating you? Call me when you get in, okay? Kiss, kiss."

She shut the phone, bored competence returning. "You didn't trust me?"

Actually, Rita ranked high on Matt's women-to-trust list—which, incidentally, was even longer than his men-to-trust list. The smooth way she'd managed to avoid dropping his name raised her several more notches. So he obediently swung the head of the sledgehammer into the wall where Rita pointed.

It made a truly satisfying hole in the plaster.

"She's not answering her cell, either," he warned her as she dialed a second number.

"Or maybe she's just not answering for *you,* sweet cheeks. Hi, Carey! Rita. I tried you at home and there was no answer, so I thought I'd take a chance here. Call me when you can. Ta-ta."

She hung up and her smile vanished. Carey merited

smiles. Matt didn't. "What the hell did you do to her, anyway?"

Matt checked himself in midswing. *"Me?"*

Rita's eyes widened. "O-oh! Did you? Did you finally put the old Tynan moves on Carey?" Then she wrinkled her nose. "You must have really screwed it up if she's avoiding your phone calls. They're usually stellar moves. I should know."

First Jake, now Rita? "I don't *have* 'old Tynan moves'!"

Rita laughed. "You just don't like being referred to as old Tynan. Come on, spill. Carey's not someone who'd leave a job on one day's notice without a really good reason."

"She gave two week's notice, but we decided it would be easier to make a clean break."

"Easier on whom?" Even as Matt considered how to answer that, Rita waved her cell phone at him. "And, hello, does this look like a clean break to you?"

"If you find out that she is, in a very un-Carey-like manner, just avoiding phone calls—"

"Or only the ones from you," Rita reminded him.

"—I'll be glad to leave it at that. But that's not like her, and she's not at her apartment." He swung the sledgehammer again, breaking through another section of wall. Plaster dust billowed through the air.

"Clean break, huh? You went by her apartment?"

"She's helping me with an outside project," admitted Matt. "It shouldn't be dangerous, but…"

"Really!" Rita scrolled through what was apparently her phone's search mode, then depressed a key, looking suspicious. "And here I thought you'd put the moves on her."

Matt tried not to choke on either plaster dust or guilt. "Who are you calling?"

Rita ignored his question. "Cute tape," she murmured

before adopting her leaving-a-message voice. "Hi, Honey. This is Rita Winfield from the Press Office— Oh, hi! I'm sorry, did I wake you?"

Matt looked at his watch. It was almost noon.

"Good. I'd hate to have woken you." Rita covered the phone and half whispered, half mouthed, "I woke her."

"I'm sorry to disturb you at home, but I'm trying to get hold of Carey, and she's not answering her phone. Uh-huh. You know, it didn't occur to me to call Kip. I suppose she *would* leave her number with him."

She nailed Matt with a dark look as she said that, and he groaned inwardly. Of course Carey would make sure her replacement could call her with any questions or problems.

"It wasn't actually a work question, but— You do? Oh, good. Just a minute while I write it down."

Rita shook her open hand impatiently toward Matt.

He was wearing jeans, not his usual suit, but luckily he found a pencil stub in a pocket and handed it to her.

She wrote a phone number on a section of the wall they hadn't destroyed yet, then read it back. "Thanks for your help, Honey. No, no emergency, I just wanted— Well, it *could* be about Matt, but that's up to Carey."

And she hung up, drawing dramatic, curly underlines on the wall. "Three phone calls and I have her. Read it and weep."

"Whose number is that?" He frowned at it.

"Maybe she's spending a long, romantic weekend with her new boyfriend," suggested Rita evilly.

Matt knew she was ragging him. He'd known Rita for years; they'd been lovers for a short time.

"Sure," grumbled Rita. "Clean break. If you must know, it's a temporary cell phone, which she apparently got at the car rental agency after forgetting hers at home. Our little

Carey decided to celebrate her newfound freedom with a road trip."

"Alone?"

"She's driving down the coast, Matt, not exploring deepest, darkest Africa. It's all right for men to drive alone down the coast, isn't it?"

He knew better than to argue the point with Rita, but he still didn't have to like it. "Out of town where?"

"What's it matter to you? You're not her boss or master, either, and last time I checked you weren't ready for anything serious. Despite that Carey could be the best thing that ever happened to you, if you'd just open your damned eyes."

"So where'd she go?" He used his pencil stub to write the cell phone number onto the back of a credit card receipt he had in his other pocket.

"Call her and ask."

"I don't want her to think I was worried," Matt admitted. "It'll just make things worse."

"You *were* worried, and how could it make anything worse?"

"She could think it's a sign of…" Of commitment. "Of something else. You call her and see how she's doing."

"I would," said Rita, folding her arms and narrowing her eyes, "but I'm cutting Algebra to meet Joey behind the gym after Home Ec. What the hell's going on between you and Carey?"

"C'mon, Red, please?" He gave her that look, the one that could get a surprising number of women to do anything for him. "At least say where she is. I can tell you know."

Rita withstood the look longer than most, but finally even she shrugged in defeat. "For some reason, our little Carey ended up in North Carolina."

Eight

Matt felt himself go cold. She *what?*

"What's going on between you two, anyway?" demanded Rita.

"None of your business." Carey had driven to North Carolina. Three guesses why. Alone. Without telling anybody—well, without telling him, anyway. He felt too stunned to be angry. Yet.

What if something had happened to her?

Rita unfolded her arms long enough to neatly drop her cell phone back into her bib pocket. He read the meaning behind her action. Favors were over, unless he cooperated.

"Fine. If you must know, I kissed her. Once."

"The old Tynan moves." She grinned triumphantly and punched him in the arm. "Good for you!"

Just what he needed, encouragement. "No, not good for me."

"Then bad, naughty Matt. What's my role here supposed to be, anyway, 'cause I'm surprisingly confused?"

"Yes, I'm attracted to her. Yes, Carey's an incredible woman. But we're working together."

"Not anymore," challenged Rita.

"She's still helping me on a project, and working relationships are deathtraps. Look at what happened to us."

"Oh, no, don't blame us on work. We don't make a good couple because we regularly try to bite each other's heads off."

"And she's too young."

"For what, the A.A.R.P.? To appreciate Rolling Stones concerts? To remember Princess Di's wedding? *She's* an adult. *You're* an adult. Considering how mature Carey is, and how immature you are, you two are practically the same age."

"And she deserves commitment. From someone… committed."

"Well, you've got me there." Rita took the sledgehammer and arced it into and through the side of her wall. She coughed on the plaster cloud. "And that's a damned shame, too. If only you hadn't been cursed by Gypsies to never be able to commit— But wait. No. I just made that up. There's no good reason in the world you can't commit to her, if she's the right woman. She's sure better than your usual choices."

"Easy for you to say," rumbled Matt. "It's not your life I'd be screwing up."

"Well, that's why I'm press secretary—my ease with the spoken language." Rita lowered the sledgehammer to the floor again with a solid thud; propped herself on the handle end as if it was a fat, heavy cane, and narrowed her eyes. "As for screwing up lives, is this about Carey, or your mom?"

He didn't want to go there. "'Bye, Rita."

She dogged him down the hallway as he sidestepped chunks of plaster toward the front foyer. "C'mon, Tynan! You're not your dad."

Matt laughed harshly as he stopped by the front door. "Will you look at the time? I'd better be going."

He did not check his watch. He was being sarcastic.

"Just because your father's the most charming 'Marriage Don't' in existence does *not* mean you'll follow in his footsteps. You know what I think?"

Matt didn't turn around. "Not a clue, you being so shy and retiring."

"I don't think you know Carey at all. Otherwise you'd see that she could chew you up and spit you out."

Matt opened the door. "Carey?"

"Don't let the mild manners fool you. She deserves a hundred percent, and she knows it. So either you stop driving by her house and calling her phone—which is stalking, by the way—and worrying, as if you have any right, or you give this commitment thing a shot. You may never find a better reason."

Matt kissed his friend's white-dusted cheek before ducking out. "Then as soon as I can get her off this project, I need to let her go a hundred percent."

She threw a glove at his head as he left. "You're an idiot! That's why you really need Carey. For damage control!"

And that was exactly why Carey needed someone else.

Carey sank to one bare knee, carefully laid her cellophane-wrapped supermarket bouquet into the mown grass, then sat back on her heels. Out of habit, from visiting her grandparents' and great-grandparents' graves, she wiped the marble free of dust and clippings. Her care still felt inadequate.

So did the headstone. All it had on it was:

Henry Bloomfield
1935-1980

No "Rest in Peace." No "Beloved Husband and Father." The lack of anything personal, even a middle name, stirred dissatisfaction in her, a tightness in her jaw, a pressure in her forehead. Especially today, Father's Day.

She'd mailed a funny card to her younger sister last week, to get their other sister's and brothers' signatures in time. It was a family tradition, to go in together on one card. And this morning Carey had telephoned her dad before checking out of the lonely motel room where she'd spent a sleepless night.

All night she'd dreamed impractical dreams about Matt Tynan. Not the real Matt Tynan, sadly. No, Carey had hugged her extra pillow close and fantasized about a Matt Tynan who not only wanted to kiss her, and make love to her but who loved her so much that he would never want anybody else.

Just her. Carey Benton. An unemployed woman from Kansas, kneeling in a cemetery in shorts and a T-shirt and a ponytail, mourning a man she'd never even met. Or two of them, if she counted the Matt Tynan who didn't really exist.

Plucking futilely at the flower arrangement, as if the angle of a blue carnation would matter to Bloomfield now, Carey sighed, stood and went back to her rental car. Maybe she should face the truth. She would be better off seeing less of Matt.

As she made the two-hundred-and-fifty-mile drive back to D.C., the idea grew increasingly sound. It would be one thing if he wanted her. Sure, she'd have to decide whether her pride could bear becoming one of the faceless many, but what a dilemma! As long as he didn't want her, then it was wrong to go on using Henry Bloomfield, Violet Vaughn and the extraordinary five children of Code Proteus simply as an excuse to keep seeing him.

It was sad, and it was beneath her. She risked becoming one of those groupies who sent him fan letters. Matt used to pretend to be impressed by them. He would laugh when he occasionally had to return a bra or boudoir photo that had slipped past the Gifts Office, to be registered, donated or destroyed. But by his own policy, Carey never sent back more than a simple thank-you-for-your-letter card, stamped with his signature. Matt did not respond himself. She'd seen him shred the letters with the barest of glances, and he'd looked…embarrassed. Not for himself. Not even for Carey, whom he'd tease about educational perks in her job. Embarrassed for those sad, needy women.

He really was a great guy. Carey didn't want to lose him from her life. But in that, she had to give him veto power. If her choices were to stalk him or to survive without him, she would survive. It was practical.

Then she got home, saw her answering machine blinking and checked the Caller I.D. Suddenly, practicality seemed overrated. Matt had called five times!

Carey bounced on her toes, pressed the play button and held her breath. "Hey, sweetie, it's Rita…"

Carey's heels came down onto the floor in solid disappointment. *This* was why she and Matt should cut their ties. If she checked her mobile and saw messages there, too, would she get her hopes up again?

She checked. She saw. Her hopes skyrocketed, better judgment be damned, as she dialed into her voice mailbox.

"Hi, Carey! Rita. I tried you at home…"

Throwing the cell phone into her purse, where it belonged, Carey felt a familiar tightness in her jaw, a pressure in her forehead. But this time her dissatisfaction was with herself.

She kicked off her shoes and flopped into the pillow-strewn seat of her bay window. She'd sewn the pillows out of old T-shirts she couldn't bear to give up, and she usually liked her view of the street, her glimpse of the Capitol dome in the distance. Now she barely noticed as she dialed Matt's unlisted home number first, on the excuse that he'd called the most.

When she got his machine, she tried to keep her message breezy and business-like. As if hearing his taped "Talk to me" wasn't the high point of her afternoon. Then, determined not to dwell on impossibilities, she called Rita Winfield.

Without preamble Rita said, "He kissed you and you didn't tell me?"

"What?" So much for not dwelling. And how'd Rita know? "Why do you think anyone kissed me?"

"Matt saying, 'I kissed her' was my first clue. Spill, woman. Where, when, how and was it worth it?"

Great restaurant. A week ago. Wonderfully. Yes, it was a dangerous memory, now that she had determined to survive without Matt. Her throat tightened in displeasure, despite that Matt and Rita went way back, despite that Carey had told Honey. "I don't think it's appropriate for me to talk about this, Rita. I'm surprised Matt did."

"I had to torture him first. But I knew *something* had to be going on for you to quit so suddenly. So have you called him, let him know you're home safe?"

Safe? She shifted, surprised. "Why wouldn't I be safe?"

"Because you weren't there when he called you, which took you out of his realm of control, which panicked him." Rita's explanation helped ease Carey's momentary concern. "It's a guy thing. You'll learn to find the balance between amusement and annoyance as you get older. So did you call?"

"I left a message on his home machine."

"He may not get it for a while yet. It's the third Sunday—"

"The parade," remembered Carey. Although Matt didn't

mind Dupont Circle's reputation, she knew he hated parade traffic. "Well, if he wants to call back, I'll be sure to—"

Her phone beeped. Rita said, "Speak of the devil."

Carey said, "Did you just want to badger me with personal questions, or is there something we haven't covered?"

The line beeped again. It wasn't necessarily Matt.

"We'll do lunch this week, barring crises, and I'll badger you some more then, how's that?" Rita hurried her words before Carey's other caller hung up. "Don't let go too easily. 'Bye!"

Let *him* go? Last time Carey checked, that was Matt's doing.

She clicked over to the other line, wishing her Caller I.D. box wasn't across the living room. "Hello?"

Silence. Then, as uncertainty began to creep back—just as Carey was about to demand "Who is this?" in classic horror-heroine style—she made out the noise of ambient traffic. Car phone.

Matt's dusty voice, tighter than usual, asked, "Carey?"

She sank back into her pillows with palpable relief—mainly just at hearing his voice. Merely surviving paled in contrast. "You were expecting my machine again, weren't you?"

"Well, I wasn't expecting you to spend the weekend in Belle Terre without telling me, that's for certain."

He didn't sound happy. "Did you need me for something? Kip didn't call me."

"This isn't about me needing you for something. It's about me trusting you not to go around endangering yourself."

"Endangering?"

"We don't know enough to assume otherwise."

"Well, I know a lot more now," she assured him. "And

you're going to want to hear it as soon as possible—on a secure line.''

There was a long silence on Matt's side, silence and traffic. Then he said, ''Courier it over to the office for me, rush. Charge it to my account. You remember the numbers, right?''

She sat up. ''Why don't I just tell you?''

''Because I'm not going home anytime soon, and I'm on my cell.'' He didn't offer to come by, not that she wanted him to.

''I know you're on your cell, that's why—'' She stopped, her new practicality warring with suspicion. Why was he acting so curt with her? It was more than simple anger. ''I'll bring them by the office myself first thing in the morning.''

''Don't do that,'' he said. ''Just courier them.''

And despite a two-hundred-fifty-mile pep talk, Carey demanded, ''Why?''

''Because—'' His words stumbled, then he tried again. ''Because I don't want to see you.''

She drew a shaky breath of surprise. Well! At the very least, she wasn't one of the many.

She'd never heard Matt be so blunt with a woman. Not the drunk who'd tripped him at the Christmas party. Not the female reporter who pestered him about a rumored vasectomy. Not the teen who'd flashed him on a school tour. Only she, Carey, got that.

And it wasn't worthy of protest. ''Oh.''

''Don't sound like that. I didn't mean— It's just—'' He swore softly. ''We agreed to a clean break, didn't we? Fast, like a Band-Aid? Well this hasn't been it. I spent the whole damned weekend worrying about where the hell you'd gone, and I've got more important—I mean, *other* things that need— Damn.''

A horn blared on his end of the line.

Clean break? He'd called eight times! Worried? He didn't exactly travel with a bodyguard! Matt was sending more mixed messages than the shape-shifting Proteus himself. If Carey had wanted to fight, she had ammunition.

She didn't want that. "Matt, just talk to me. What's wrong?"

"Don't do this, Carey," he pleaded, as if she were the one begging. "Would you just please courier over to me whatever you found in Belle Terre? Include copies of the paperwork for your expenses, so I can have someone cut a check."

And she gave up—only a few dozen words too late to salvage her pride or his. If he wanted to pull loose this badly, why was she hanging on? "I'll make sure you get everything by midday."

"Thanks, Carey. I'm sorry I— Thanks."

"Don't mention it." And she hung up, her eyes and throat burning. She'd told herself she could survive without Matt, and she believed it. She could survive without eyesight, too. Or hearing. Or her hands.

If she felt depressed, it was because tomorrow was Monday—and for the first time in a year she had no reason to look forward to it.

Violet Vaughn Hobson readjusted her sunglasses and tried not to look suspicious as she glanced around the busy shopping area of the Pavilion at the Old Post Office. She thought she recognized a man standing near the video arcade, and her heart sped. She tensed to run. She might be fifty-nine years old, but recent years of ranch work had kept her fit.

He'd vanished into the crowd before she could be certain if she'd seen him before or not.

The risk was growing, she decided, making her way to a

large bank of pay phones by the main entrance. After Henry's murder, she'd done all she could to lessen that risk for their children—including giving them up. But the Coalition that she believed had continued the Code Proteus experiments, albeit with corrupted data, knew the boat accident was a ruse, that Jake was alive. They must suspect she was, too.

It was only a matter of time before they found her.

If for no other reason than that, she had to make this call. Using her latest prepaid card, she punched the extended series of numbers into the pay phone, starting with the country code.

She almost hung up as the other end began to ring. But she no longer had time for cowardice, and her heart wanted this far too much to be denied.

"Hello?" It was a man's voice. He sounded wary.

"Hello, is Gra—" Despite her care, Violet almost blew her daughter's name on the first try. "That is, is Gretchen there? This is Violet Hobson."

"Violet?" His voice warmed immediately. "Gretchen is going to be so thrilled to speak with you. By the way, I'm Kurt Miller, Gretchen's husband."

Violet heard him put the phone down, then heard him exclaim, "Hey, Professor. It's Violet Hobson. It's your *mother!*"

Violet had to press a hand to her mouth, to hold back the sweet pain that almost escaped her. *Your mother.*

Unlike Jake, Gretchen had lost her adoptive parents.

"H-hello?" asked her daughter's voice, the first time Violet had heard it in more than twenty years. Not since she first saw Jake's picture had she felt such recognition in her soul.

"Hello, darling." Violet couldn't have withheld the endearment if she tried. "I hope I'm not interrupting anything."

And Gretchen burst into tears.

"Gretchen?" Violet looked wildly around her, as if she could summon help from here, in Washington, for a distraught daughter somewhere off the coast of Portugal. "I'm so sorry. I shouldn't have called."

"No," protested her daughter, through sobs. "Please don't go, *I'm* sorry, I'm just... It's my hormones. Please don't go."

Violet heard the real despair in her daughter's plea. "Of course I won't. I'm not going anywhere until you tell me to."

"I'm so sorry." A nervous laugh mixed with Gretchen's tears. "I didn't mean to upset you. I can't seem to go three hours without crying these last few weeks."

For a biology major, Violet had been particularly slow on the uptake. "Darling, are you expecting?"

Gretchen sniffed and laughed. In the background, Violet heard Kurt tease, "She can't hear you nod, Professor."

"Yes," whispered Gretchen. "Kurt and I are so happy."

Violet sank back against the wall beside the phone. "That's wonderful, darling! I can't tell you how pleased Henry would be if he were still alive."

They had never had that, she and Henry Bloomfield. Yes, they'd created these incredible children, but it had been through artificial insemination. Only in later years, as they realized what they meant to each other, had they become lovers. The children's big, solemn bear of a father had ended up wanting for them the very normalcy that he and Violet, with the purest of intentions, had nonetheless stolen from them at their conception. His efforts to give them that, or a reasonable imitation, had been in part what had gotten him killed.

"He would be *so* pleased," she said again.

"Tell me about him?" asked Gretchen. "Please? Maisy Dalton has been helping us to remember—Jake and me—but it's such a slow process, and I'm unsure what to trust. What was he like? When did you know you truly loved him? You did, didn't you?"

Hot tears ran down Violet's cheeks and she struggled to keep them from thickening her voice too badly. After so many guilt-ridden years, Gretchen's guileless faith touched her more deeply than she'd thought she was capable of feeling again.

"I loved Henry Bloomfield from the moment I met him." It felt wonderful to finally admit that. "I loved him for years before he ever knew it. I loved him almost as much as I loved the five of you." And she set about proving it, as best words could.

Thank goodness she had an expensive phone card because, unlike with Jake, once Violet and Gretchen started talking, they found no end of fascinating topics. Not surprisingly, Gretchen wanted to know about Violet's pregnancy and delivery, about her own infancy—how early she'd slept through the night, how soon she'd started talking. She wondered if her altered genes would affect her own baby, and Violet reassured her that, at most, the child might be as good with languages as her mother.

Violet, in return, loved Kurt Miller's pet name for Gretchen—Professor—since Henry had been a professor, too.

"He called me that the first time we danced together," admitted her oldest daughter, emboldened. "In Cairo."

"You love him," said Violet. "I'm so grateful."

Gretchen told her about the state-of-the-art intelligence system that she and Kurt were setting up for their safe house. So Violet gave her details about the fail safes that

Henry had arranged for his family, without which they never would have escaped the Coalition the first time. Those who *had* escaped.

"Come to us," urged Gretchen. "Stay here in Brunhia, where you'll be safe from those people. I know Jake wants you to."

"I want to," said Violet. "I *will*. But I must do a few more things here in the States. I have something important to give to Jake, and I want to try one more time to find Susannah, my stepdaughter. She ran away after her father died...."

So many lost children.

"I'd like to meet her," said Gretchen earnestly.

"I'd like that, too."

"Violet..." Gretchen hesitated, then rushed ahead. "What name did I call you when I was little?"

Violet could hardly hear over her heartbeat. "When you were very little, you called me 'Mama.' But as you got older, you and the others called me 'Mom.' Just like any children."

"Mom," she repeated. "Mom. I'd like to call you that, if it's all right with you."

Violet didn't bother disguising the tears in her voice. "It's more than all right."

Even the continued sense that she was being watched could not rob her of that moment, nor of her renewed determination.

Violet would take her knowledge of Gretchen, and the safe house and of Henry's future grandchild, to her grave before she would allow the Coalition to touch them.

Nine

Matt hadn't botched a breakup this badly since high school. That especially sucked since he and Carey hadn't really dated. And of all the women, she was the one he'd never wanted to hurt.

He told himself that it would be easier for her this way. Closure, and all that nonsense. But it made for a dismal start of his first week without her.

Receiving Carey's package on Monday—both the sparse CIA paperwork she'd requested through the Freedom of Information Act and the far more thorough report of her trip to Belle Terre—didn't help. Matt spent a disturbing night in the West Wing, without a green blanket, increasingly suspicious as he read.

One of his best friends might be a genetic mutant?

Bloomfield, the top scientist on Code Proteus, had fathered five exceptional children. That was the same number of children the more credible articles on the secret genetics labs of the 1960s reported. The oldest of Bloomfield's children, Jake, had been a math wizard. Matt's old roommate, Jake, was a math genius—and, Matt knew, adopted.

It should be absurd. They were talking the sixties, a full decade before the first successful test-tube baby and almost two decades before the Human Genome Project started work on human DNA sequencing. But he also faxed the new report to Jake, in the middle of the night.

"So did you read it?" he demanded the next day, pacing

his office when Jake called. He'd put down his House tally sheets to take this call; that's how important it was.

"Yep," said Jake, solemn and tired. "I read it."

Matt hated to ask; his college friends were more like family to him than his parents. But Jake was the one who'd involved not just him but the damned White House. "So this isn't just about the World Bank heist, is it?"

Silence met his question. Then Jake said, "No. But that's part of it."

Matt thumped the heel of his hand against the doorjamb. He wasn't sure which bothered him more—that Jake had withheld information or that he might really be one of the *World Inquisitor*'s weirdos. "So what else is it about?"

"I can't tell you." Jake sounded apologetic. "Not yet."

"I went out on a limb for you, pal."

"I know that. I appreciate it."

"Carey spent the weekend in North Carolina. Alone."

Again, there was silence. Then Jake drawled, "Is that a problem because you're afraid she was in danger, or because you wish you'd spent the weekend with her?"

"*Was* she in danger?" The POTUS monitor on Matt's desk beeped, and he glanced impatiently at it. The president was on his way back across town from a big luncheon where he'd been building yet more support for this Friday's House vote.

"I doubt it," hedged Jake. "I don't know."

Matt resumed pacing, tethered by the phone cord. "So just who kidnapped your brother, Zach? Bank robbers or spies?"

"I wish I could tell you, but too much is at stake just now. I'll understand if you want to pull out."

"No." Matt rubbed a hand over the back of his neck, shaking his head. "I'm not pulling out. But the second you can, I get full disclosure. Agreed?"

"Thanks, Tynan." Jake sounded weary. "I owe you."

Matt considered how great things had been between him and Carey before Code Proteus. Then he remembered her shaky voice over the phone Sunday night. "Not even your superbrain can begin to conceive of how big you owe me, Ingram."

Jake neither denied nor confirmed his superbrain. "I'll be in D.C. next week—unofficially. I'll call you."

"You'd better." But this was Jake. Angry or not, Matt said, "Look, if you need anything—"

"I know who I can trust," Jake assured him. "Thanks."

As they hung up, the monitor on Matt's desk beeped again. He checked it as always, dozens of times a day. POTUS's limousine was pulling up to the White House.

A chill crept into Matt's gut as he stared at the monitor, wondering why he'd never noticed that before.

POTUS. Proteus. Just two letters difference.

Was it coincidence? Or were there more sinister reasons for such a similarity between a top-secret experiment of the subversive sixties and the Secret Service's acronym for the president of the United States?

Was the president in danger?

Then, to top off his Tuesday, Janeen Sullivan called.

Wednesday, June 18

"So he didn't want to talk about it?" asked Rita at a midweek lunch with Carey. They'd met at the cafeteria of the National Gallery of Art in the Smithsonian complex. "Men!"

Carey loved the Smithsonian. She wasn't so sure about talking about Matt behind his back.

"No. At least, he *said* he didn't."

Rita paused with a forkful of artfully torn lettuce halfway to her mouth. "So you think he *did* want to talk?"

Carey shook her head, wary of oversharing. "Let's just say he's sent some mixed signals, and leave it at that. There's more to life than Matt Tynan, right?"

Even if he'd admitted to worrying about her all weekend. Even if she'd already gotten her check for what she'd spent on her trip to Belle Terre—she doubted Kip would have enforced that kind of a rush or delivered it same-day. Even if Josh O'Donnell, at Carey's interview yesterday, had said, "You gotta let me hire you, or my name's gonna be mud in the West Wing."

Apparently he'd called Matt as a reference, and Matt's recommendation had sounded like a threat. "Hire her or else."

O'Donnell had laughed about it, maybe even exaggerated.

Carey wasn't so sure. She'd taken the job, though she wouldn't start for another two weeks. His current assistant, who looked forward to traveling with her retired husband, had budgeted through the end of the month. It was a great job, doing important work for the nation's children, and if the president's education initiative passed in the House on Friday and the Senate within another week or so, they would need all the good assistants they could get. The job was still in the White House complex, in the Old Executive Office Building. Her security pass would be pink, not blue, but at least it was a pass. Even without Matt Tynan, she was still involved. But she missed him.

Rita was talking. "…a big favor, but it would really help my friend out, and you'd enjoy yourself."

Carey flushed, to have drifted. "I'm sorry, what?"

"I'm asking for a favor. A friend of mine is going to the state dinner tonight, but his date canceled last-minute. He asked me to find him someone with security clearance."

Carey tried not to groan. "A blind date?"

"To the White House. You've never been to a state dinner, have you?" It was a low blow. Rita knew Carey had never lost the awe of a tourist in this beautiful city. That was why they were lunching at the National Gallery.

"I was there for the Christmas party," Carey admitted, but it wasn't an argument. She'd *loved* the White House Christmas party. Matt had danced with her, and every other woman there. Still, it was a cherished memory of hers.

"But you haven't had the full dinner experience. C'mon, Carey, you'd have fun, and you'd really be helping my friend. He hates to go stag to these things. Even the married women hit on him, and congressmen try to fix him up with their sisters or daughters, and it puts him in a bad spot."

Carey laughed at the image. "Matt's had the same—"

Then she stopped laughing and narrowed her eyes. Rita *wouldn't!* Would she?

Apparently she would. Without Carey even having to confront her, Rita shrugged. "Damn, you *are* smart."

"You're fixing me up with *Matt?*"

"Yes, and it's one of my most scathingly brilliant ideas. You'd get to enjoy a state dinner—one to honor teachers, by the way, which is perfect for the newest employee of the Office of Special Education Programs. And Matt couldn't weasel out of talking to you. From the way he's been skulking around the office, he damned well needs to talk to someone, and last time I checked, you're the only person who's privy to whatever top-secret project has him in a funk. Ms. Peanut flew off to Greece last night, and he really did ask me to grab him a date to protect him from the bimbos and the yentas."

"A date, not an ambush. Matt wouldn't have asked you without someone specific in mind, and I doubt it was me."

"If you must know, he asked for my friend Susan, who

works for PBS. But she would bore him silly. You, however, are the best thing that ever happened to him. I'd have fixed you up long ago if you hadn't been working together. Now you aren't.''

She made it sound so reasonable.

"C'mon, Carey,'' Rita pleaded. "I've got a gift certificate for a free spa afternoon and makeover at Rodolphe's, and some designer gowns that may need pinning up but would look great on you. Don't think of it as a date with Matt Tynan. Think of it as a chance to dress up and eat yummy food off old china.''

Carey had never been so tempted. But... "It's not fair to spring this on him.''

Rita shook her head. "He's right. You *are* too good to be true. Watch out, Carey, or I'll start thinking you're one of those mutants Geraldo's been going on about.''

Like Jake Ingram, she thought. Carey choked on a sip of water but luckily caught her breath. "Sometimes I can't tell if you're really his friend or not.''

"I'm an ex-lover, which is a completely different thing.'' Rita leaned across the table, surprisingly earnest. "Trust me here, Carey. I know Tynan better than any woman in the world, except Ambassador Samantha Barnes and maybe you. And I have a decent idea what he needs. That includes getting some top-secret stuff off his chest and *not* seeing you as his secretary for once. I wouldn't qualify even if I didn't already have a date. So give him that chance.''

When Carey hesitated, Rita pounced. "Here,'' said the press secretary, pushing an envelope into her hand. "Take the gift certificate. It's about to expire, anyway. I'm going to tell Matt I've got him a date, and let him think it's Susan. If you want to blow the surprise, go right ahead. If you want a dress, show up at my place around six. We can ride together. If you don't show, no hard feelings. Okay? I've got to get back to the office.''

And before Carey could protest, Rita had dropped a bill on the table and headed out of the sunny cafeteria, back to the West Wing, where Carey no longer belonged.

Carey peeked into the envelope, saw the original price scribbled on the certificate and gulped. Her rent wasn't that high! This was the kind of money sophisticated, experienced women spent on an afternoon of beauty, not a plumber's daughter from Kansas City. But according to the date, it *was* about to expire. An even worse crime than extravagance, in her family, was letting things go to waste.

For a full minute she considered playing along with Rita's scheme. But this was Matt. Even when she didn't like him, she respected him. So, with sinking reluctance, she retrieved her cell phone from her purse, made sure nobody was sitting near enough to be annoyed, and pressed speed dial No. 2.

A familiar voice said, ''Matt Tynan's office. This is Kip.''

''Kip, it's Carey. Is Matt there? I need to tell him about something.'' Such as that Rita wasn't fixing him up with Susan from PBS. It would be too much to hope that he would agree Carey should be his date, but he deserved that chance.

''Oh.'' Kip lowered his voice. ''Matt's not here right now. Could I take a message?''

He would've sounded wholly believable if just then Matt hadn't called something to him about sending out for lunch.

For a long moment Kip didn't say anything. Neither did Carey, clenching her jaw in order not to. If she said something, it would be far too rude for the National Gallery of Art.

Embarrassed, Kip tried, ''I mean, he's in a meeting.''

Carey took a shaky breath, understanding all too well. ''Did he ask you not to put through any calls from me?''

"You know I can't answer that. Look, let me take a message, and I'm sure if it's important—"

"No. Never mind. I'll…" She looked at the gift certificate in her hand. So Matt wanted to play it that way?

So be it. "I'll catch him later," she said.

Damned state dinner.

If Matt could have found a way to get out of it, he would. Not that he had anything against honoring educators. But his temper had gotten so short, he feared making a misstep if he didn't get over his Carey withdrawal soon.

But he had to attend. The sad truth was, even the nation's top teachers didn't have the kind of prestige to draw A-list guests quite the way a visiting dignitary or Hollywood producer did. Hence the importance of President Stewart's initiative. Matt wasn't about to join the handful of weasels who'd suddenly developed fever or sick mothers. And Matt had three mothers he could've chosen from.

He had to go. But he probably wasn't doing Rita's friend, Susan Whatshername from PBS, any favors.

Rita was supposed to swing by in a limo, with her date and with Susan, at seven-thirty. Matt was showered, shaved, combed, dressed in his tuxedo and waiting in his apartment lobby by seven-twenty, trying not to notice his male neighbors checking him out, when his cell phone rang.

He flipped it open. "Talk to me."

"I got delayed," said Rita, on the other end. "So I sent your date ahead in the limo. It should be there anytime, plate number XHQ-66J, so when you see it—"

"Yeah, there it is." He took the revolving door, phone still to his ear, as the long, black car slid to a stop under the building's front awning. "Thanks for deserting me, pal."

"Like you can't handle yourself around a woman."

"It hasn't been a good week." But Matt quit complaining before the driver opened the door for him. His bad mood wasn't Susan Whatshername's fault. "Hello," he greeted, sliding into the back-facing seat and gesturing with his telephone. "Rita just called to explain—"

It wasn't Susan Whatshername.

Matt forgot how to form words. He almost forgot how to breathe, as his confusion was immediately followed by awe. It was Carey.

Wasn't it?

She looked luminous. Her golden brown hair had been drawn back, only a few artfully loose tendrils tickling her jaw and nape, setting off her earnest face more beautifully than ever. She wore a silvery gown with a low-drape neck and triple spaghetti straps over each shoulder, long and elegant in its simplicity. It clung to her slim curves before falling into a long skirt, split high on either side to reveal even longer legs. Carey's feet, delicately crossed, sported high-heeled silver sandals with ankle straps.

Matt could see the ghost of her half-hidden pink toenails through silken hose. Those were definitely Carey's feet.

Carey, who was no longer his employee.

The limo driver shut the door beside him.

Vaguely aware of Rita's voice in the distance, like an ant's, Matt shut his telephone. He didn't care about Rita. He didn't care about the dinner or the job, or even Jake Ingram's super genes. He'd tried to stay away, and it hadn't worked. Carey was here, looking downright edible. And he had no intention of being distracted by other women, Rita included.

Don't make promises you can't keep, he thought, desperate, as the limousine eased into traffic.

Carey swallowed visibly and started to lick her lips but stopped, probably remembering her makeup. It was great makeup, highlighting instead of disguising her fresh beauty. "I tried to call and warn you," she said. She sounded like his Carey.

Matt looked at her feet, at those delicately painted toenails, and let his gaze climb slowly back up her. Were those legs real? "Then I'm glad I wasn't taking your calls."

Her eyes flashed with annoyance. Matt remembered what Rita had said about Carey being able to chew him up and spit him out. Could it be true? Were those strings he'd feared an illusion? "Why weren't you? I could have had something important to say."

"You always have something important to say." His gaze lingered on the long, delicate hands in her lap, then lifted to the gentle folds of that drape neck hanging low over her breasts. The silky material looked almost as soft as her skin. His hands ached to test both. So did his mouth.

"Then why wouldn't you even talk to me? I thought we could at least have a working relationship, but if you don't care…"

Damn. Matt gestured to the seat beside her, widening his eyes in question. Wary, she nodded.

He shifted himself to her side of the limousine and turned to face her. Now he could see her up close, feel her warmth against the limousine's air conditioning, smell her sweetness. She smelled edible, like berries, and her skin looked as lush as the silk she wore. A woven silver choker encircled her slim neck, with matching silver chains hanging maybe an inch off each ear. The need to take her earlobe in his mouth dizzied him in a way he really, really liked.

"I care," he admitted, taking one of her hands in his. She felt more like a lifeline than an anchor. "I've just tried like hell not to, for your sake."

"For *my* sake? You think I can't handle myself?"

"I was your boss," he protested.

"Not since last week," she reminded him.

He could have argued that they'd still been working together on Code Proteus. He could have argued that he didn't want to screw up her life, that her strings scared him. He could have argued any number of logical things, if she didn't smell so damned good. Instead all he said was, "You look like moonlight."

Her ruby lips parted slightly at the compliment. He wished he could think of something even more poetic to say, but at least this was true and simple. Like her.

He began to massage his thumb softly into the hollow of her palm. The raw silk of her silvery dress brushed the back of his hand, as sensuous as he'd imagined, but not as sensuous as her.

She looked down, her lashes shadowing her eyes a moment, then faced him directly. "Weren't you expecting the PBS lady?"

"I didn't want the PBS lady." He leaned closer, breathing her in. "I wanted you. I've done my damnedest not to, but here you are, and the hell with it. I'm done."

When Carey took a shaky breath, the folds of her gown's neckline shifted gently. He began to rub soft, adoring circles onto her inner wrist. "Done?" she asked.

"Done." Matt cocked his head to better watch her eyes. "I tried to do the right thing, but that's never worked real well for me. I tried a retreat and…" He had to laugh quietly at his own clumsiness there. "I made an ass out of myself."

"And now?"

"And now," he confessed, "I'm done fighting. I'm done telling myself I'm not supposed to do this. That's your job. And I hope like hell you really can take care of yourself, Carey Benton, because I'm done doing it for you."

Her eyes widened as he leaned in. But he kissed her, anyway, feeling her mouth soften beneath his, and her eyes drifted happily closed.

Ten

This wasn't the first time Matt had kissed a woman in a limousine. He was now glad for the practice as he slid one hand behind Carey's waist and his fingertips skimmed bare skin. The dress was backless, leaving her naked from the nape of her neck to the small of her back. His body responded to her near nudity, hard and immediate, and yet he was willing to savor this teasing preamble for as long as she needed. Weeks. Days. Hours.

It couldn't hurt to hope, could it?

He slid his other hand to cup the back of her neck, careful not to muss her hairstyle, teased her lips open beneath his, and tasted her mouth. Delicious. Sweet. Real. She still didn't protest. She buried a hand into his hair, her fingers digging against his scalp, so he dipped his tongue more boldly into the hot wetness of her mouth.

She moaned happily. Oh, yes.

Carey.

Caught in her, unsure he ever wanted to pull free of these strings, Matt slid the hand behind her up her naked back, his thumb teasing under the edge of her gown to test a round edge of a breast. He had to shift his weight on the limo seat to adjust for his delicious, throbbing discomfort. Endless nights with many beautiful ladies of D.C. couldn't compare.

The divider between the front and back of the limousine slid down a discreet inch. "Turning onto Pennsylvania Avenue,'' announced the driver. The window reversed direction to close again.

Pennsylvania Avenue. Sounded familiar. Oh, yeah.

Reluctantly, Matt pulled back from Carey, detouring a few times to nuzzle her neck, then her cheek, before he finally managed to achieve a slim distance. She leaned her head back into his hand and gazed up at him, looking sleepy and sated. And that after mere kissing. Okay, after Fourth-of-July level kissing.

He wondered what she would look like after a long, hot night of intense lovemaking. No rushing, he told himself. Not with her. "Pennsylvania Avenue," he repeated solemnly.

Her eyes widened. "Oh! Is my hair—"

"It's beautiful." He flipped down her mirror so she could see for herself. Messing up a woman's hair right before a big society event was a mistake a man made only once. "You are gorgeous. Freshen your lipstick, and nobody will know a thing."

Unless you keep looking at me like that, he thought. If she did, hiding the evidence of their kisses would be the least of his problems.

Carey smiled then, the effect like carbonation in his bloodstream, and she reached out and touched his mouth. "Oh, they might guess something."

He grinned back. "Luckily, these limousines are set up for any contingency." And he flipped down his mirror, too, dug a linen handkerchief from his breast pocket and carefully wiped traces of Carey's lipstick off his mouth. Beside him, she opened her mouth in that funny way women did to reapply their lipstick, and he grinned at how homey the moment suddenly felt, like sharing a bathroom, but smaller.

"Here," she said after capping her lipstick. She finger-brushed his hair back into place, then straightened his tie for him, which felt even homier. "Am I all right?"

Easy question. "Too good to be—"

But she interrupted him, staring out the window. "Oh, Matt!"

He looked to see that they'd pulled through the gates onto the floodlit grounds, part of a line of cars edging toward the north portico of the White House. The building stood ahead of them, lit to alabaster brightness against the looming dusk.

He glanced back at Carey. She'd worked there—granted in the less-ornate West Wing—for a year. And yet her face held a wonder he'd lost countless Christmas mornings ago. He looked back at the residence, trying to see it through her eyes, its elegance, its significance, its dignity.

He liked seeing it that way. It made him feel proud.

Surprisingly similar to how Carey made him feel.

"So when was it built, Carey?" he teased, glad for a few more minutes to rein in his body before they made their own entrance.

"The cornerstone was laid in 1792," she whispered, all but pressing her nose to the glass. God, she was cute.

"And who was the first president to live here?"

"John Adams."

"All right, during which…uh, who…"

Carey glanced over her almost-bare shoulder and took pity on him. "What important person never slept in the Lincoln Bedroom?"

There had been many, of course, though he knew the one she was fishing for. Instead he answered, "You."

He wondered if he could change that. He and the president had a good relationship, but he doubted it was that good.

Carey blushed and looked back out the window, but her eyes were bright. And turning away exposed how intricately her hair had been woven in on itself, and the whole long, beautiful curve of her bare back.

Matt leaned closer to her, to watch the White House over her shoulder, and answered, "Abraham Lincoln," against her shoulder.

She shivered and smiled, and not, he thought, because he was technically correct since the Truman renovations.

"Well, if that turns you on," he murmured, drawing his cheek slowly down to her shoulder blade, "Harry Truman."

It probably was the sweep of his breath, not the name, that made her arch her back and sigh.

He wasn't taking any chances. "William McKinley," he whispered playfully into her spine.

Carey folded her arms along the base of the window and sank into them, graceful as a ballerina, as she enjoyed his caresses. Or his random recitation of their nation's leaders, one or the other.

"Thank you for not being angry, Matt. Thank you for this."

He traced a finger across the folds of silk that draped the small of her back, peeking. "Martin Van Buren."

"There are only four cars ahead of us. We'd better talk about something less—"

"—patriotic?" he suggested, skimming his fingertips back up along the edge of the material to the three little straps that fanned across her right shoulder.

She shook her head, languid. "Less provocative."

"We're talking about dead presidents here, Care."

"I know." She turned to face him, her expression a mix of desire and reluctance, amusement and desperation. "So what chance will I have if you actually start trying?"

She wasn't going to ask him to be the mature, responsible one anymore, was she? He'd tried it. He'd failed miserably. "I have never forced myself on a woman, Carey, and I never will. You can say no at any time—and I mean *any* time—and I'll listen. That's okay. But you're the one who said you could take care of yourself. You're the one who showed up here looking so incredible.''

Like moonlight. But he didn't want to repeat himself.

He swallowed and pushed back on the seat, frustrated and annoyed. ''I'll believe you can handle me only if you believe it.''

Carey listened solemnly. Then her shiny lips turned up into a blinding smile as she whispered, ''Millard Fillmore.''

''Oh, baby,'' growled Matt, and lunged closer for another laughing, lipstick-smearing kiss.

And then she woke up.

But it didn't happen that way. Carey hadn't fallen asleep on the massage table at Rodolphe's and dreamed this. She was really standing in line with Washington's elite, adjusting to the sporadic flash of cameras. She was really edging along the marble entry corridor with its vaulted ceiling, chandeliers, red carpet and portraits. She was really holding Matt Tynan's arm.

If ever a man had been born to wear a tux, it was Matt. Not that she would mind whatever he wore or didn't wear.

Carey couldn't project that far into their evening without feeling dizzier than even his kisses had left her, and more than a little aroused. He'd left no doubt what he wanted from her, whether she could say no or not. But why would she say no?

Except, of course, for him not loving her.

He'd said she looked like moonlight. His arms and his kisses had been heaven, more than she'd ever hoped for...except for one thing. It wasn't permanent. She'd be an idiot to think it was love. This was Matt Tynan! But he was still incredible.

His shoulder brushed hers as he leaned close to point out another First Lady portrait, and maybe just to press close to her. His bright, dark gaze savored her.

Carey flushed and followed his forefinger, dizzy again. She focused on the splendor around her—the haunting representation of Jacqueline Kennedy, which Matt had indicated, the gold and bright crystal of the chandeliers. He'd implied they could enjoy themselves no matter how the evening ended up. Couldn't they?

Or would she ruin her ability to survive without him?

The opulence of this place alone was worth savoring. It was so unlike when Carey had taken the public tour and guests entered through the main entrance hall. Now they passed the grand staircase, also carpeted in red and lined with portraits, these of the presidents themselves.

"Look, Carey," teased Matt, with a low laugh. "Is that a picture of Dwight Eisenhower?"

She wasn't about to kiss him right here. But she narrowed her eyes and butted his shoulder with hers, and from the way he flashed one of his boyish grins down at her, that satisfied him. She liked feeling his body with hers. Maybe too much. It made her think about later, which kept her deliciously off balance.

She struggled to focus on the moment.

Then they reached the East Room, and Carey gasped. She'd seen it on the tour, and at the Christmas party, but not like this—all crystal and candles and class. "It's beautiful!"

Rococo ornamentation topped the high ceiling, arched over each door and tall, draped window and over each giant fireplace. At some point in the past, someone had painted everything, even the copper ceilings; only the heavy doors and golden hardwood floors, now reflecting soft light from candles and chandeliers, had escaped. But even thus subdued, the room was pure, sparkling elegance, full of antiques and flowers and beautiful people.

For a moment Carey felt like an imposter. This wasn't even her own dress! But Matt's hand on the small of her back steadied her, and his ease with people, many of whom he knew, meant Carey only had to smile and remember names. They passed Rita, who looked unbearably smug. They spoke briefly to Josh O'Donnell, her new boss, who seemed truly delighted to see her.

"There's our table," she said, recognizing the number from Matt's invitation. "Are there a lot of empty chairs?"

Matt frowned, noticing. "Maybe people are running late."

"Tynan!" A lean, handsome man about Matt's age waved, tugging a slim brunette with him as he approached.

"Eth!" Matt's smile was genuine as he caught the taller man's hand in a tight grip. Carey suspected that if she weren't on Matt's arm, he and "Eth" would be pounding each other on the back, though the taller man had a fairly snug hold on his date, as well. "Damned if domesticity doesn't look good on you!"

Now she recognized him. "Ethan Williams?"

Williams, a wealthy jet-setter, was another of Matt's good friends from college. He'd been higher on last year's list of the Top Twenty Beltway Bachelors than Matt—probably because of his money—until a sudden marriage took him out of the running. It was his tuxedo that threw her, she decided. She'd seen pictures of him, but he usually looked scruffier and never wore a tie.

Clearly he cleaned up well, although Matt, she mused with an appreciative sidewise glance, didn't have to clean up at all.

Matt looked as comfortable in his tux as he did in jeans. Williams looked as though his neck itched.

"We've met?" Matt's friend reached for her hand.

"Only on the phone," she assured him.

"Eth," said Matt, including the man's wife with his smile, "and Kelly, this is Carey Benton."

"Carey?" Ethan raised an eyebrow. "*The* Carey? A pleasure to finally meet you in person. My wife, Kelly Taylor-Williams."

"Are you enjoying the party?" Kelly was around Carey's age, but shorter and clearly more sophisticated. She wore her dark hair pulled into a sleek bun and a simple, elegant black gown. A single aquamarine hung on a neck chain, nowhere near as flashy as her diamond ring. Clearly both of the mismatched pieces had sentimental value, and Carey couldn't help but approve.

She ducked closer, so Matt wouldn't overhear. "To be honest, I feel a little like Cinderella."

For some reason, that made Kelly smile.

They were seated together at a table so beautiful, Carey almost hated to mess it. Like the others, it boasted a huge floral arrangement of mostly daisies, every petal a perfection, and apples painted with a gilt filigree. A tasseled menu sat open on each crystalline place setting, and the china gleamed so brightly that the plates reflected the print.

Everyone stood as the President and First Lady were announced to enthusiastic applause. Then Matt held Carey's chair for her, adjusting it at just the right moment. She sat like a princess.

"They're hand done," she realized, looking more closely first at their place cards, then at the ornately printed menu.

"Mmm," agreed Matt, watching her as if to savor her enjoyment. "And they prepare the food right here, too."

Carey hit his arm with her beautiful menu, and as he caught her wrist and grinned, she thought she loved him. She'd grown so used to its hopelessness, she had no idea what to do with the echoing possibility of it now. Worrying about sex was easier.

Certainly it was more immediate!

She looked down, then peeked past Matt to his friends.

Ethan Williams had claimed a daisy from the centerpiece and drawn it down Kelly's nose before presenting it to her. Kelly slanted her dark gaze up at him, sharing private messages, and Carey felt a hollowness inside where she wanted to someday feel like that.

That was why she'd never had sex, she thought, taking a quick sip of water from a gleaming crystal goblet with a slice of lemon floating in it. Because love like that existed in the world, and it had seemed somehow blasphemous to accept anything less. And yet tonight...

Matt's left hand found hers, under the cover of the table, and they twined their fingers together. A relationship that had seemed impossible was suddenly, achingly likely. But so, statistically, was the chance of losing it.

Loving Matt from afar, had at least been safe.

But they'd left safe back in the limousine.

Matt loved watching Carey's reaction to their opulent surroundings, the way she traced the edge of the menu, the way she leaned over her plate to see herself reflected in it when she thought he wasn't looking. How did she preserve that wonder, after having worked in politics for a year?

Was it a talent that would fade with age? Or was it uniquely Carey, something she'd keep into her forties, her sixties, her eighties? He didn't generally picture dates in their eighties.

But he liked that she was his date, all the same.

He looked at Ethan and Kelly, intrigued to see his bad-boy buddy so happily tamed. Ethan would get to see what Kelly was like in twenty, thirty, forty years, and he sure didn't seem to mind. Then again, Ethan had been willing to do the deed once before; his fiancée's death had ended that relationship, not cold feet. He'd lost his parents at a young age, too. Maybe that made Ethan hungrier for a family, more comfortable with strings.

Matt, however, had more parents than would comfortably fit into a cab, assuming any of them would ever agree on going in the same direction at the same time. Losing people wasn't so much a problem in his family as just getting fed up with them.

Speaking of which... "Have you heard from Indy, lately?" he asked Ethan while Kelly, between the two men, started a breadbasket circulating the table.

"Not since he sent the wedding gift." Ethan tossed a pair of rolls into the air for Matt to catch, which Matt did, and Kelly rapped her husband lightly in the stomach. "Should I have?"

"Might be interesting. He's moved from small-town America back to Chicago." When Matt handed Carey the second roll, she narrowed her eyes at him in prim disapproval.

Prim, huh? He had the sudden urge to kiss her until they ended up under the table. Maybe she saw something in his grin, because she blushed and quickly turned her attention to her butter dish. Her knife paused before touching the pat of butter. It had, he saw, the seal of the president pressed into it.

Ethan arched his eyebrows. "Chicago? Isn't that where—?"

"Exactly. She-Whose-Name-Must-Not-Be-Spoken lives there."

"S.W.N.M.N.B.S." Ethan laughed. "And wackiness ensues."

Kelly leaned past Matt to explain, for Carey's benefit, "'Indy' is Eric, a banker friend of theirs."

Matt speared a pat of butter right through the eagle and put it on Carey's bread plate, so she wouldn't have to. "We call him Indy because he's from Indiana."

"And because his last name is Jones," added Ethan. "It made sense at the time, us being drunk. We do also call him Eric."

Carey said, "And She-Whose-Name...?"

"Leigh," said Ethan. "She was a few years behind us in college. As close to one of the guys as a woman ever got."

"But with better legs." Thinking of legs reminded Matt of Carey's, and he almost lost his train of thought. He forced himself to regain it. "We started calling her S.W.N.M.N.B.S. around Indy after he blew up."

Carey's eyes widened, and Matt grinned. She'd been researching top-secret CIA projects for too long.

"Not literally," he reassured her with a laugh.

"They got really close," said Ethan. "Might've dated, if he weren't sort of engaged to the girl back home. Not that that marriage worked out."

Matt snorted agreement, before it occurred to him that he was talking to newlyweds. Oops. He tried the engaging smile that most often got him out of trouble. "No offense."

"None taken." Kelly looked clearly amused.

Carey, buttering her bread very carefully, asked, "So what happened? Why didn't Eric and Leigh ever get together?"

"Leigh took off to Europe," said Ethan, "and suddenly Eric wouldn't let us talk about her."

"Blew up." Matt winked at Carey. "In the emotional sense. And he was usually the easygoing, even-tempered one."

"Jake had a cowboy edge," said Ethan. "Indy had a Boy Scout edge."

Kelly rolled her eyes at both of them. "Eric's a very nice man," she told Carey.

"Exactly," said Ethan, as if she'd made their argument.

"Nice," agreed Matt. "He'd rather watch a baseball game than take a walk on the wild side."

"He's the one we called to bail us out when *we* took a walk on the wild side," admitted Ethan.

"To bail *you* out," countered Matt, then reconsidered it. Something about the blue of Carey's eyes while she observed all this made it even harder to lie. "Except that once."

Ethan arched an eyebrow. "Twice."

"They dropped the charges that other time. Doesn't count."

"Another skeleton in your closet?" Damned if Carey didn't have a wicked smile of her own when she put her mind to it. Maybe she *could* handle herself. "Maybe you shouldn't run for office, after all."

Kelly perked up. "You're going to run for office? Local, state or national?"

"None of the above," said Matt firmly, narrowing his eyes at Carey in mock warning. "Anyway, Leigh's a hotshot attorney now. She's been in Chicago awhile."

"Where Eric just moved," finished Ethan. "Interesting!"

Matt said, "I'd love to be a fly on the wall of whatever Starbucks sees those two bumping into each other again."

Ethan leaned past both Kelly and Matt to tell Carey, "I'd contribute to Matt's campaign."

"See?" Carey kicked Matt lightly under the table.

Matt caught her ankle with his. "I'm not a politician."

All three of them raised their eyebrows at that. Even a

few of the other people at their table, beyond the looming wilderness of daisies and gold-laced apples, looked dubious.

"Okay, so I am a politician. But I'm not a representative. Too much responsibility. You're bound to let someone down."

Carey squeezed his hand in silent confidence.

"I'd vote for him just for caring about that," mused Kelly out loud.

"And because he's cute," Carey pointed out, adjusting to the teasing spirit of the conversation with admirable ease.

"Cute?" Matt shook his head. "Not the impression I was hoping for when I bought the tux, Skipper."

For some reason, she smiled at him then, wide, earnest and beautiful, as if she saw someone better than he thought she did—even if she didn't know his stand on all the issues.

His reaction to that caught him in the gut, and he couldn't do anything but stare down at her. He was glad she was here tonight. Glad she got along with Ethan and Kelly. Glad she thought highly of him.

Even if chances were she was mistaken.

He'd called her Skipper. The easy familiarity of the nickname made everything between them even more real. He hadn't called her Skipper since she'd turned in her resignation.

In part not to be rude, Carey turned to two late-arriving guests who were seating themselves beside her. More, she did it to keep her composure in front of Matt. A lot of good a thousand-dollar dress and high-society hairdo would do her if she drooled.

Besides, Kelly and Ethan seemed to appreciate a few minutes to duck their heads closer and murmur privately.

Still secretly holding her hand, Matt quickly joined the conversation, easily charming the out-of-towners, who were also two of the honorees, by the time the soup arrived. He of course knew a great deal about the education initiative, having spent enough time in the Roosevelt Room debating the details.

"Everyone *says* they admire the sacrifices teachers make," he said, finally releasing Carey's hand for the soup spoon, "but too often we equate respect with income, and the income isn't there. Either our society has to change its value system to honor sacrifice more than a paycheck, or we have to start paying you people a hell of a lot more. Probably both."

"Is that you talking, Tynan?" asked a lanky blond man across the table. Carey recognized him as Jeff Jenkins, a *Post* reporter who spent a lot of time in the West Wing's press room, hoping for a story to break. "Or is it President Stewart?"

"Actually, it's Carey here." Matt grinned at her surprise. "But I've heard the president make similar points more often than I can count, Jeff, and so have you. He's also said that we lie by selling education on the promise that it will earn people a better paycheck, as long as what we pay teachers contradicts us. Why not sell education by promising it will educate you?"

"Because," said a bearded gentleman on the other side of the two teachers, beyond the large and perfect centerpiece. Matt had greeted him as Representative Parks, though Carey didn't know from what state. "Education alone doesn't make a difference. The money you can earn with it does."

"No offense, Congressman, but that kind of thinking belittles what these people do." Matt had the unique ability of arguing with a smile, his dark eyes gleaming, little laugh lines forming at the outside corners of his eyes, so that people smiled back even while he cheerfully told them off. "It's about a great deal more than money. It's about having some control over your life, instead of feeling powerless.''

'''Fight fear'?'' Jeff Jenkins was mocking what had become the president's rallying cry since the World Bank heist. ''Name me one real-life person who's fought fear through education.''

Carey couldn't resist jumping in. ''When I was fifteen, my grandmother was diagnosed with early stage Alzheimer's. That terrified her and she got depressed, which was even worse.''

Only then did she notice just how intently everyone was watching her. Even the newlyweds. Even Matt.

Every inch of her right side was acutely aware of his warmth and size and presence. She didn't want to embarrass him, but the only thing more embarrassing than a Nanna story would be a Nanna story without a point to it.

In for a penny, as her Dad would say.

''So Dad and I began to collect information about available treatments, and it made a very real difference for Nanna. She was able to make some changes in her diet and medications that slowed the progression. Her last years were a full, happy time for her, instead of the slow descent into helplessness she'd feared. That was beyond price to us. Education did that.''

Parks shook his head. ''Having the information available made the difference,'' he argued. ''Sounds more like an argument for leaflets or Public Service Announcements than the so-called status of teachers.''

''The information was available while Nanna was depressed, too,'' Carey insisted. ''She quit school early to go to work, so she's never been confident around libraries. All my father and I had that she didn't was the education to know where to look. So in a very real way, every teacher we ever had helped give my nanna five more good years before her fatal heart attack. And yet none of them is paid as much as you, Representative Parks.''

The congressman opened his mouth to protest, but Carey interrupted him. ''And yes, I *do* know how little congress-men earn, and I admire your sacrifice. It's still more than most teachers get, and it garners a great deal more respect.''

Matt leaned close to her and murmured, ''Sic 'em.''

''I think I just did,'' she whispered, uncertain.

The admiration in his eyes confirmed it. So did the way he traced his ankle slowly, teasingly, up her calf.

Better even than the soup! But soon the entrée would be served, then dessert. Then the president would say a few words and dinner would be over. A hot tickle of anticipation slid up her leg from where his knee had caught and held hers.

If she had the chance to sleep with Matt, would she?

Then Ethan asked, ''Have you heard from Jake lately? I imagine he's taking this job personally now.''

But the last thing Carey wanted to think about was Code Proteus.

Eleven

Of course Ethan hadn't meant personal in the sense that now Jake knew he was a genetic experiment.

He'd meant personal in that Jake's adopted brother had been kidnapped shortly after Jake had started to investigate the biggest heist in history.

"Yeah," said Matt, with yet another reason to appreciate Carey's company. She'd doggedly stuck with Code Proteus for him. She knew everything he did about the project, maybe more. They could talk about it.

Not that talking was high on his to-do list tonight.

"Jake called the other week," he told Eth, dishonest only by omission—he didn't say about what. "He sounds pretty tired."

Kelly said she wasn't surprised, and thankfully the conversation turned to the World Bank heist, Zach Ingram's well-being and Jake's floating wedding date.

Catching Carey's gaze, Matt saw her concern—and he wanted her. Wanted to be with her in any way she'd allow. By time dessert was served, he'd decided that even just talking to Carey, holding her hand and brushing her leg were better than sex with someone else.

That was when he knew just how hard he was falling. He would have thought the idea would frighten him. Instead, he felt more stunned.

It didn't surprise him to notice Ethan smirking in their direction. Matt had ribbed his friend enough about his sudden marriage to Kelly last winter—and now look at him. Matt didn't care. He was just glad that the president's comments, once Stewart stood to address his guests, were short: Stewart was glad to see them. He hoped Friday's House vote on his education initiative would help validate the teachers as they validated others. He thanked them for their heroism and said good-night.

"Do you want to wait for the limousine?" Matt murmured into Carey's ear after the applause died down and the guests were standing to leave. "Or do you want to walk?"

"Is it midnight yet?" she asked, dragging her attention away from the centerpiece. He cocked his head, curious why it mattered. She bit her lower lip, then admitted, "Let's head toward the Washington Monument. It's a nice walk."

He laughed, glad for a chance to continue this surprise date as long as she'd let him. "Have you ever been up in the monument?"

Her blue eyes shone at him. "Never at midnight."

"Then let's get going. I can get us in." And with a quick goodbye to Eth and Kelly—and making sure to take their menu and place cards for Carey to keep—they cut through to the West Wing exit. A half mile ahead, the Washington Monument rose, blue-white and majestic in the soft summer night. The dome of the Capitol Building presided over the city from a mile or more to their left.

"That was wonderful," Carey insisted, turning to walk backward as they reached 17th Street. "It was magic. Thank you!"

Matt sped his step to catch her hand. He didn't want her to trip and hurt herself, and he just liked touching her. "Me? I'm betting Susan Whatshername wouldn't want to walk to the Monument."

"I love D.C. at night," she said earnestly.

"That doesn't do a lot for my peace of mind, Skipper."

"Any city has crime," she argued. "But look at it. Take a moment and just *look*."

So he did. His reward was that when she turned to walk forward again, still holding his hand, the move naturally tucked her beneath his arm. She looked surprised, but fit perfectly, as if she belonged there. He was glad to tighten his hold.

Matt had to admit it: the gleaming, floodlit monuments made for a powerful statement. This is where we keep freedom, they seemed to say. This is where we live up to our best ideals.

More often than seemed reasonable to expect, anyway.

"How can you have worked in the trenches for a year and still be this idealistic?" Matt wanted to kiss her hair but hesitated. Was she expecting any of this to be business, or could it all be…limousine? "You know the old saying— the two things you don't ever want to watch being made are sausages and laws."

"You're idealistic, too," she protested. "And you've been working at this a lot longer than I have."

There she went, elevating him again. "*I'm* idealistic?"

"Uh-huh."

"What makes you think I'm even close to idealistic?"

"Because you try so hard. You wouldn't put up with it all if you didn't think you could make a difference."

With her snug under his arm, he half believed he could.

"So how are things going with the House vote?" Carey asked when he didn't say anything. So it *was* business—for the moment.

"It's going to be close, but the numbers are there. I'm worried about the Senate vote that comes later. Last time I talked to Bermann, he actually said that he has the president by the balls."

"Does he?"

Matt widened his eyes at her, incredulous, but Carey just widened her eyes back up at him, uncurling herself from under his arm and walking backward again, her hand still in his.

"No," he assured her, holding on. "It's close, but once we win the House, we should be fine. As long as Bermann doesn't start making statements like that in public, anyway."

"Because then it would turn into a pissing contest."

He laughed. "Exactly." When Carey laughed, too, the sensation tickled through him like champagne bubbles and starlight. God, she really was something. "What?"

"That's why we need more women in charge," she said. "We don't even pee standing up, much less have contests over it."

"Ah, so where do you plan to start?" he challenged. "Local state, or national level? Maybe Eth will contribute."

"I could do it," she decided, brazen. "If I wanted to."

"I wouldn't doubt it for a second." And Matt tugged her back under his arm, where she stayed the rest of the way to the National Mall. He was definitely in trouble here. He'd never felt this content, grounded…optimistic. Not until Carey.

It exhilarated and unnerved him. Why now? Why her?

She was beautiful, sure. Something about her Midwestern wholesomeness gave a depth to her beauty that too many women lacked. Her hair seemed shinier; her eyes seemed a truer blue. Tonight, her expensive hairdo and gown showed her off to perfection. But there was something else, something more. Carey was beautiful because of how she held herself, how she faced the world…and how she looked at him.

Maybe that was why his appreciation of her had crept up

on him so slowly. It had grown with every good-morning, every laugh, every time she trusted him. It had built the longer they went without her becoming needy and demanding, or him screwing up.

But that had been work. He'd always done well at work.

"So did you read my notes from Belle Terre?" she asked from the crook of his arm as they neared the base of the 555-foot obelisk.

He held up a "just a moment" hand and approached the night guard on duty. He wanted to talk about her notes, but it wasn't primary in his mind right now.

"Not yet," he said after getting clearance from the guard to enter the monument without tickets. Carey looked surprised. "I have, but— Let's not talk about that for a minute. Elevator first?"

Let's see how we do without the safety net of the job, he told her silently.

She searched his face, then nodded. "Okay. Race you!" And she took off with a laugh, designer gown and all.

She might have beaten him if she weren't wearing heels. As it was, Matt pulled ahead, reached the monument first and caught her, gasping. Then he walked backward, dragging her into the waiting elevator—and into his arms. Usually, there was a line for the elevator, but not this close to midnight.

He kissed her all the way up to the top.

But he rarely screwed up kissing, either.

Would she sleep with Matt Tynan tonight?

The windows at the top of the Washington Monument were small, yet the view at night was fantastic. But Carey's eyes were closed to D.C.'s twinkling panorama more than they were open.

That was because Matt stood behind her, his arms

wrapped around her, kissing her neck. Kissing her shoulder. Nibbling on her ear, and never once catching her earring.

Delicious sensations she'd barely dreamed of curled through her, up and down her body, from her fingertips to her toes. At times she felt so languid, she couldn't keep her eyes open. He was hard and solid behind her, strong enough to hold both of them up, hungry enough to devour her in ways she couldn't imagine.

He nuzzled past the nape of her neck, changing sides, his breath almost as hot on her tender skin as his mouth. She tipped her head, lengthening her neck to give him more room. This was wonderful, indulgent, insane. She felt like an exhibitionist, despite that he touched nothing inappropriate, bared nothing private—and she loved it.

She was vaguely aware of the elevator behind them. Tourists who'd been there when she and Matt arrived mid-kiss, left. More tourists disembarked, saw them and gave them plenty of room. Only one person, noticing their corner, chided, "Well, really!"

Matt chuckled low into Carey's ear, and she all but whimpered at the sensation. *Yes, oh, yes, really,* her body screamed.

If this was mere kissing, she ached for him to touch her in inappropriate, private places. She'd never understood the attraction of public displays of affection until now. Now here she stood, a living canvas on which Matt Tynan was painting the most incredible, G-rated lovemaking. Well, maybe P.G.

Every time her eyes drifted open, she saw glittering city lights and the gleaming Capitol Building. Every time her eyes fell shut again, she lost herself in him, and his touch, and his mouth, and his need.

She might be a virgin, but she was a modern woman. She knew what that hardness against her bottom was, even before she tried arching against him and made Matt moan in deep, throaty pleasure.

Who was she turning into? And if he could make her feel this way simply by holding and kissing her, what must he be like in bed?

An official stepped out of the elevator and interrupted her thought, calling out, ''Midnight, folks. We're closing down.''

Matt planted a loud smack on Carey's cheek and when he took a step back from her, she almost fell. She felt cold and lost until he looped an arm over her shoulders to guide her back down. At that mere touch, she didn't want to just lean into him. She wanted to hold tight, tuck her head under his chin. She wanted to somehow crawl inside him and never come out.

And she wondered how many other women had felt this way. How many others had he bewitched with his incredible mouth, had he set on fire with his knowing embrace, until they ached and needed and couldn't live without him?

Just how many of those women were now living without him?

She wasn't his assistant anymore. She wore a borrowed gown. As long as she wasn't sure who she was, wasn't it a bad idea to make life-changing decisions? No matter *how* tempting?

She needed better reasons than even feeling this good. She needed better reasons than his attraction to her.

Maybe it was desperation that, once the elevator reached the ground again, had her take a deep breath and say, ''So you *did* read my report from Belle Terre?''

Matt blinked, pulled back. He glanced toward the Capitol Dome, then to her. His smile came and went several times. Of course he'd be confused. If ever a question came out of left field—

But she had to hand it to him. After silently opening and closing his mouth once, Matt cleared his throat and said, "Yeah, I read it the first night. I never would have thought to go by a retirement home. That was something, what you found out, huh?"

He caught her hand and strolled with her in the direction of the Reflecting Pool, beyond which sat the bright, boxy shape of the Lincoln Memorial.

He really hadn't lied about being able to stop—and he was even gracious about it. Had she thought she might love him, tonight at the state dinner? She'd been an idiot.

Of course she loved him. It was literally beyond reason. Her mind was still trying to catch up, still trying to explain it. But her body and spirit were convinced.

She swung their joined hands, unsure what to do with this.

"I faxed Jake the information, too," Matt continued, as if this were a simple business meeting. "And I owe you an apology."

"Me?" Surely not for kissing her again.

"I resisted the idea that Proteus was connected to those tabloid stories when you first suggested it, but I was wrong. If the Freedom of Information reports don't confirm it—what hasn't been blacked out, anyway—Jake Ingram came close. So we may be the only people who know not only that there was a lab, but where it was and the names of the test subjects. And you and I can be pretty sure that one of those children—" he took a deep breath "—is currently investigating the World Bank robbery."

She heard what he didn't say, as much as what he did. "Jake Ingram was adopted?"

"Yeah." They reached the Reflecting Pool. He bent, picked up a stone and whipped it toward the water where it skipped once, twice, three times before going under. The ripples it left caught and scattered flashes of city lights. "He's adopted."

"Oh." She considered that for a minute. "Wow."

Matt's smile, Hollywood-handsome as ever, was wry. "Yeah."

"This is big. As if the *World Inquisitor* is shouting that the sky is falling, nobody knows whether to believe it, and we have the exact time and day." She put her hand on his arm for balance as she lifted one foot and ran her finger under the strap of her shoe. "Except the sky isn't falling at all."

He took her elbow. "You don't think so, huh?"

"No. Everything we've seen indicates that Henry Bloomfield was a good enough man. And Jake Ingram's your friend."

He slanted his gaze toward her, expectant. "That really means something to you?"

"Of course it does." She found a blister on her other heel, too. Running in dress shoes had been stupid. "Do you mind if I take off my shoes and stockings?"

He leaned nearer to tease, "Take off anything you want."

Her whole body seemed to flush in response. She would have to decide, sooner than later, where this night would end. But for the moment she used him for balance as she slipped Rita's heels completely off. She sighed happily as her liberated feet sank onto the dirt path. "Look the other way a minute."

"I'm not sure I can. But I'll hold the shoes."

Well, he was honest. Handing him the heels, Carey turned away and reached up under her gown, finding and unhooking the small buttons of her garter belt to unfasten her stockings. Then she slid them down her legs and stepped free. The night air on her bare skin felt as wonderful as the dirt under her toes.

Maybe she knew who she was, after all.

She turned back, and Matt's eyes were gleaming at her. His need all but radiated from him. But he was waiting for her—as promised. "Let's find a trash can for these," she whispered.

"Hand them over." He stuffed the wads of nylon into his jacket pocket. Even without the kissing to curl her toes, she could get used to having Matt around just to hold things for her.

Kissing was better. Still, she took the safe route. "Why do you think the sky *is* falling? What do you know that I don't?"

Matt hesitated. "I'm worried about the president, Care."

"What?"

"I only thought of it yesterday. Why the name Proteus sounded familiar to me. It wasn't from Greek mythology at all."

"But it is," protested Carey. "He's the son of Poseidon."

"That's not what I meant. I... It sounds like POTUS."

Carey saw the similarity now—and Matt's concerns. "Oh."

"The only difference is an *r* and an *e*. Not together."

"R-e as in 'regarding'?"

He laughed harshly; this was really bothering him. "Or Rural Electrification, or the Rebelian Empire, or even rhenium—which, by the way, is a heavy metal used in catalysts and thermocouples. I looked them all up, and none seems more likely than the other, but they all sound like bad news. So I have to decide if I tell the president and break my promise to Jake, or if I stay quiet and risk the leader I was hired to serve."

"Hey." She stepped up to him, slid her arms around him and kissed him. She feared she might do it wrong. Always before, he was the one who'd initiated their touch. He'd kissed her at the restaurant. He'd made love to her shoulders and back in the limousine. He'd painted kisses across her while she'd looked out at the glittering cityscape of the nation's Capitol.

But from the way Matt caught his breath and looped his arms around her to hold her in place, he wasn't disappointed.

So she tried again, rising onto her bare toes, tilting her mouth up to his, catching his lower lip between hers. He angled his head, opened his mouth to her, and she lifted a hand to the back of his head to better hold him in place. It wasn't a practiced kiss, but it was earnest. She felt no less dizzy for it. She was simply learning to savor being dizzy.

When she dropped hesitantly back onto her heels, Matt came with her, leaned his face into the shelter of her shoulder, tightened his arms around her until the embrace almost hurt.

Almost. Not quite. Her shoes, in his hand, bumped her hip. It felt no more practiced than her attempt at a kiss.

Carey caught her breath, marginally, and said, "The college named it that."

"Mmm?" asked Matt, from where he was still curled into her, still holding her as if he never meant to let go. She wished that were true. She was also beginning to wonder if it should matter.

"Emory University. And maybe Henry Bloomfield. They're the ones who came up with the name Code Proteus, not the CIA. And that was back in the early sixties. Even if there is a connection to POTUS, it's nothing new. Chances that something drastic will happen, if you take a few days to think through the possibilities—"

He laughed, and straightened, his eyes bright. "How did I live without you for so long?"

"Well…" She didn't want to throw stones, but she had

to show him she wasn't ignorant here. She had to let him know her eyes were open. "There are rumors, you know."

"I've heard that." He used his shoeless hand to brush some hair from her face, his eyes savoring her, drinking her in. "You should probably know, some of them are even true."

"Like the pink roses?"

His mouth fell open, and he turned away, but he caught her hand as he did it, paralleling the edge of the Reflecting Pool as he began to walk. If she didn't know better, she would swear he was blushing. After a moment he asked, "You noticed that, huh?"

"Or the female impersonator?" she teased, and he laughed.

"Completely false. I was good at recognizing men in drag long before my current residence, and though I would not besmirch the art form, it does nothing for me personally."

As long as he was being so forthcoming, there were other rumors, too. "The vasectomy?"

"Ah," he said, and took a deep breath. "That."

"Rumor has it—"

"I'd just joined Stewart's campaign, back in California," he said, squinting at the Lincoln Memorial. "And when I made the news, an old lover filed a paternity suit. Tests showed I wasn't the father, but I figured the more public I got, the more likely it was to happen again, so I…took measures. Supposedly it can be reversed. But anyway, that one's true. What else?"

But suddenly she felt she'd gone too far. So many of his goals were so different from hers…but not tonight. "What about that administrative assistant who used to work for you?" When he cocked his head, brows together in confusion, she tugged on his hand, stepping closer to him again. "Carey something, right?"

"Oh, her." He slid an arm around her again, ducking his forehead to hers. "You mean that incredible woman from… Wyoming, isn't it? Too good to be true. Looks like moonlight."

She sank happily into him. "Anything going on there?"

"You'd have to ask the lady," he whispered back.

He really wasn't going to force the issue. And that was what truly decided her. Not only did she love Matt—foolishly or wisely. Not only did she want him with a hot, empty ache. She trusted him. She trusted him to tell her the truth, even when she asked him about sensitive topics. She trusted him to guard her privacy, as best he could. And she trusted him with her body. Completely.

She didn't know if his affection would last. But who could tell the future? Either way, it was time.

"I want to go home with you," she whispered, pressing herself more certainly into the front of him. Breasts to tuxedoed chest. Thighs to thighs—including a hardness against her belly that took her delicious, full-body dizziness to new heights of expectation. Nose alongside nose, and lips a breath away from lips. "I want to go home with you and make love with you."

Twelve

Matt hadn't been this nervous about bringing a woman home since, well, long before he stopped bringing them home.

From the point when he'd first kissed Carey, more than a week ago, he was improvising. His usual rule was hotel rooms. But Carey wasn't usual. So although his high-rise apartment had all the charm of your average empty box, he brought her there.

Her wearing his tuxedo jacket. Him carrying her shoes.

"So the rumors are true," lamented his neighbor, Karl, as Matt and Carey passed, arm in arm, in the hallway. The man sighed woefully. "Not that there's anything wrong with that."

Matt laughed, and unlocked his door for Carey.

"It's not much," he admitted, following her in. She turned in a slow circle, looking around. The furniture was rented. He'd never gotten around to putting up artwork. The most interesting features were the view and the extra telephone, one of those famed direct lines to the Oval Office that senior staffers got.

Carey said, "I wasn't expecting animal prints and a trapeze."

He dropped his cell phone into its charger, by habit, and used a remote to turn on the stereo. Jazz music wove into the room. Then he went to her, looped his arms around her silk-clad curves and bent his forehead to hers. "Props are for wimps."

When Carey stretched her arms up over his shoulders, his tuxedo jacket fell to the carpet. Matt kicked it out of the way so that he could hold her, swaying into a slow dance, enjoying his straight-down view of her cleavage. Hell, he was enjoying everything about her. He angled in for another heart-melting kiss. While they danced, and kissed, he fidgeted to undo her upswept expensive hairdo until the waves hung down her back again.

A strange timelessness seemed to wrap them. Despite his real, imminent need for her, he felt no other urgency. For her, he truly could wait forever. It would be sweet torture.

But the way they were sliding against each other in their slow, sensuous dance, he wouldn't have to. "Carey, are you sure?"

In answer, she kissed his chest where he'd ditched his tie and unfastened the top buttons of his shirt. She kissed his throat, then the soft spot under his jaw, then below his ear, then nibbled on his earlobe. "Are you questioning my ability to decide for myself?"

He couldn't imagine questioning anything about this woman, ever again. So he slowly danced her into the bedroom. At some point, she unbuttoned his shirt, biting one of his buttons and laughing. At some point, he eased those fanlike spaghetti straps off her shoulders so that the silvery softness of her gown dropped to a shimmering puddle at her bare feet.

Carey met his stunned gaze—vulnerable, trusting, wearing nothing but jewelry, tiny green panties and a garter belt. Her breasts were small but full, somehow as innocent as a work of art, smooth as a sculpture. But she was real and here, slim and warm and curved and waiting for him. Matt had never seen anyone or anything so beautiful. When he kissed her this time, sliding his hands onto her nakedness just to reaffirm her reality, she sank into his touch with something like relief.

Surely she knew how incredible she was!

He told her, anyway. Then kissing replaced thinking. Matt laid Carey across his bed, and they kissed. He stretched out, shirtless and barefoot, beside her, worshiping her with his hands and mouth, and they kissed. At some point she tugged at his belt, and he stripped quickly from his trousers. At some point he pulled her tiny panties and the garter belt over her hips and down past her long, long legs and adorable feet, so that she lay naked next to him. Then he worshiped her some more, until they were both damp and flushed, until the taste of her sex filled his mouth and she gasped his name. At some point she slid a hand into the flap on his straining briefs, her palm wreaking sweet torment as she explored his hardness, gently, as if she'd never held a man's erection before. He lost the briefs.

And still they kissed, getting better and better at it.

This went beyond sex. This was lovemaking—him and Carey. It made all the difference. It was perfection.

"Now," Carey began to plead, after a heavenly infinity together. She writhed under the weight of his bare leg, rubbed her hands hungrily over his chest. Her neck arched with impatience, long strands of her hair like taffy across his pillow. When Matt slid his hand to the damp heaven between her legs, she pushed his wrist away. "No, Matt. Please. Now."

So he reached over the side of the bed for his trousers, got a condom, and slid it on with practiced ease. "Now," he promised, settling his weight onto her. She didn't spread her legs wide enough until he nudged them apart, not thinking, just feeling, just kissing. "Anything you want, Carey."

He adjusted himself to slide into her at last, and she felt tight. Wet, yes. Ready for him. But so tight.

He began to hesitate. Maybe began to wonder. But Carey slid her hand onto his bottom, and he thrust instinctively, and it felt so good, so close, so right—

Until he realized she'd been a virgin.

She wished she hadn't cried out—it barely hurt, really— but he was so…big? She had no basis for comparison, but he felt big pushing into her. It surprised her, was all.

Matt's lips faltered on hers, midkiss. His eyes widened in near horror. She really wished she hadn't cried out.

"You…" He'd gone unnaturally still, despite being inside her. She didn't want him still. She wanted him to keep loving her, to keep making her body hum and explode. "Carey?"

He couldn't stop now. He *couldn't!* He was the one who knew what he was doing.

"I'm okay," she reassured him, pressing a palm to his rough cheek, straining up from beneath to kiss him again. Kissing Matt already felt as natural as breathing. More. She kept forgetting to breathe, as if holding her breath could hold these new, voluptuous feelings tight inside her forever. "I'm wonderful. Please, Matt. You said anything I want."

And after searching her eyes for a long moment, he ducked in for another hot kiss and began to move on top of her, around her, inside her—and gave her the world. She opened herself to him, all of herself, so gladly. His breath, his hands, his lips and tongue, the satisfied noises he made deep inside his chest, and the hard heat of him rocking deep into her.

Whether or not he loved her, she loved him. That should be enough, but she still wanted more, and somehow, body to body, he gave it. Then she was shouting, shuddering, clutching him to keep her safe as the world crashed around them. Matt shouted, too, arching his body, then sinking on top of her.

She should have remembered to breathe.

She didn't pass out but much of what happened immediately after blurred into the strange, wonderful hum of Matt's kisses and caresses. He rolled onto his side, pulling out of her, and she wanted to protest, but she couldn't even talk. She felt like she was floating on waves. He did something with the condom, then reached across her to pull the coverlet over them. Then he wrapped his arms around her and rested his chin on her shoulder, and just breathed.

He was breathing hard enough for the both of them.

The CD was still playing lazily from the living room.

"That…" Once she could form words, she turned her head to better see him. "Oh, Matt. That was…"

"Your first time," he finished, an edge to his roughened voice. So it wasn't just her cry that had upset him. She blushed, hoping her inexperience hadn't turned him off. Or worse—was he afraid she would try to wring some kind of commitment out of him, just because she'd been a virgin?

"Begin as you mean to end," she teased, trying to keep things light. But that could mean she meant to never make love to anybody else. Not that she wanted to. But damn it, she was trying to sound worldly! "I mean—"

"You couldn't have mentioned it?" His arm was still tight around her. He kissed her temple, her jaw, and his gaze caressed her with aching gentleness. Even if he was angry, he didn't seem angry at her.

"It wasn't that big a deal," she insisted, and winced. "I mean, *tonight* was, you are, but this being my first…" Maybe she shouldn't talk until her world stopped moving. "Never mind."

He widened his eyes. "Never mind?"

"I'm happy," she insisted. That was an understatement. Lying here, cocooned with a naked Matt Tynan, was like a dream—the ultimate happily-ever-after to her Cinderella night. Even if it wasn't ever-after, just after. "Don't spoil it by being angry."

He studied her a moment, then asked, "You're really happy?"

"Mmm-hmm." She kissed his chin. "Aren't you?"

"I've never been—" But he stopped himself, looked away. "I didn't even know I could feel like this. I—"

I love you. She could almost hear him say it, and propped herself up to better catch his dark gaze. She thought she saw an I-love-you there. Then Matt said, "You're special, Carey."

She'd known from the start that he wasn't the kind to commit. That was why she didn't say to him what was on her lips. *I love you.* She didn't want to scare him.

"Thank you," she said instead.

She wouldn't ask for the future.

Even if she couldn't imagine a future without him.

Thursday, June 19

The shrill beeping of Matt's alarm clock woke him from the best dream of his life. But as he propped himself up on one elbow and slapped the clock to silence, he felt the warmth and curves of a female body against his. He went completely still.

"Mmm?" a soft voice asked sleepily—and he rolled gratefully back to her. It hadn't been a dream. Carey was here.

"Go to sleep, Skipper," he whispered, finding her hair in the dark. Carey nuzzled into his chest, and he felt...

There were no words for the still sense of completion he felt. Or maybe there was one. *Love.* He loved her.

He'd almost told her so last night, but Matt had caught himself. Those were serious words, I love you. They carried serious repercussions. Whenever he heard them from a short-term girlfriend he felt guilty and awkward. Even when his mother, the real one, spoke them, they carried a price. I love you—come visit. I love you—call more. Find out if Stan's really cheating on me—you know I love you.

Better that he spare Carey those silent expectations, at least right off. If somehow he managed not to screw up, if somehow she was willing to be with him for more than a few days, weeks, months, he'd deal with the issue again.

He slid a hand to the small of Carey's naked back instead. He kissed the soft spot behind her ear—at some point, she'd taken off her earrings. She arched against him, still asleep. If they could make it a few months, maybe she would want a relationship—an *us*—as badly as he suddenly did. Then he could say the words without using them to bind her up in strings.

He wondered if this was karmic payback.

The alarm went off again, and he hit the off button. He didn't care about the White House. He didn't care about anything but staying here and making love to Carey.

"Mmm," murmured Carey into his neck. "You don't want to be late, do you?"

Matt bit back a wry laugh, kissed her, then reluctantly disentangled himself from the heaven of her body to get out of bed. He would avoid being clingy if it killed him.

But he kneeled back on the bed to lean over her and kiss her again. "You are a strict mistress, lady. No pun intended."

"I just know—" she yawned "—that you hate to be

late." And she turned her face into the pillow where his head had been.

For a long moment Matt just stood there, naked, and watched her sleep in his bed. This was good. This was right.

Only once he stepped into the shower and turned on the water, and the radio, did he try the words. "I love you, Carey."

They felt good and right, too. Easy, even.

He'd finished brushing his teeth and the radio was announcing "WDCN traffic and weather every fifteen minutes," when a tapping on the glass side of the shower startled him.

He slid open the door and leaned out, water running into his eyes, to see Carey standing there, her hair wonderfully fluffy. She'd wrapped his sheet around her like the sloppiest toga ever. She had his beeper.

"Your pager and your cell are going off," she told him, blushing. She'd never looked so good. "I thought you'd—Matt!"

That last was because he caught her in his arms and pulled her into the shower with him. He took the pager from her hand and tossed it toward the hamper. Then he slid the glass door shut, pressed her against it and kissed her while hot water jetted around them.

This really was heaven. Too-good-to-be-true was true.

"That…" Carey seemed to have trouble deciding whether to talk or kiss, and was trying to do both. When she wrapped welcoming arms over his neck, her soaked toga started to fall, but Matt caught it with one hand. Since he never brought women home, he had no condoms in the bathroom. Better to keep a little barrier to his enthusiasm, here. "I think it was the Chief of…"

Her voice vanished beneath a happy moan and the traffic report. He had better uses for her mouth, anyway.

During a brief moment when his tongue wasn't in it, Matt said, "You resigned, Carey. You don't have to take my messages."

"I think it's important," she insisted, then ducked her head into his shoulder before he could kiss her again. "You brushed your teeth," she accused.

"Sorry?" He lifted long, wet hanks of hair away from her face, laughing sheer joy. He adored her hair. He adored her. "If I knew it would bother you…"

She laughed, too, and he caught her mouth with his again, and they kissed through the rest of traffic and weather. It was getting harder to hold her sheet up for her—and not just because of how very heavy the waterlogged material was getting.

The radio droned on. Bond market—bad. Stock market—worse. Maybe he would call in sick, drag her back to bed, and—

"Is education elitist?" asked the radio announcer. "Bad news for President Stewart's initiative, with rumors that fourteen representatives previously on record as supporting his pet bill, which goes to vote tomorrow—"

Matt stiffened. Carey said, "Go." And with a final, fast kiss, he climbed out of the shower, shutting the door behind him so she could finish her clean-up. He stopped long enough to grab a towel, dig his beeping pager from the hamper and toss her a fresh toothbrush from the medicine cabinet. "Heads up!"

She shrieked—didn't she know what "heads up" meant?—and he watched the fuzzy outline of her great figure bend to retrieve the toothbrush off the shower floor. "Thanks," she called, sarcastic.

"You're welcome," he called back, heading into the bedroom. "And I love you," he added, in a whisper. It was surprisingly easy to say. And it was going to be tough to guard against.

But in the meantime, a new ringing added itself to the demand of his myriad communication devices.

The direct line from the Oval Office.

Carey felt deliciously…physical. Better than after the best workouts. She felt special and a little cosmopolitan, to have woken up in a man's apartment instead of her own.

But mostly she felt in the way.

As she got out of the shower, wrapping a towel around her hair and another around her body, she realized that she had nothing to wear but the raw silk dress from the previous night. Matt, stuck on the phone and pacing, looking neat and pressed in trousers and a starched shirt, noticed her picking up the dress and shook his head. Hindered by the telephone cord, he pointed at his chest of drawers until she found a drawer that held T-shirts and fleece shorts with drawstrings.

With a smile of thanks, she took them back to the bathroom to get dressed—as best she could without underwear. She hadn't worn a bra last night, the dress being backless, and she didn't want to search his bedroom for her used panties.

She'd chosen a University of Chicago T-shirt, because it made her think of him. It was too big on her, of course, as were the shorts, but at least the drawstring kept them on.

It was going to look even worse with those strappy heels.

By time she went back out, she'd combed her wet hair. She wished she had a blow-dryer and makeup. She folded Rita's expensive dress and found her panties. Matt, now in the kitchen, had shaved and put on shoes, a suit coat and a tie.

She felt even more like a vagrant.

"I, uh, don't have any coffee made," he apologized, bending to look into his refrigerator. The man certainly could wear a suit. "But there's beer. And Pop-Tarts."

He looked back up and made a face.

"I'll be fine until I get home," she assured him.

He shut the fridge door and gathered her close against his chest and kissed her again. Even with her hands full, she sank into the minty, warm welcome of it. Her fears that he might regret last night were fast evaporating. So why was she still edgy?

"It isn't supposed to go this way," he complained, sliding his clean-shaven cheek on hers. He smelled of sandalwood. So did she. "You deserve breakfast in bed, and flowers and—"

His cell phone rang, and he growled. "Talk to me." When he saw the shoes in Carey's hand, he frowned and shook his head.

She nodded.

He shook his head and pointed at her feet. He'd noticed last night's blisters. "I'm about to. Maybe half an hour out."

Carey whispered, "You can't ride the Metro barefoot."

He whispered, "You aren't riding the Metro." Then he scowled back at his phone. "Yes, normally I am fifteen minutes away, but there are special circumstan— Screw you, Rob."

Rob was his boss, the Chief of Staff.

Carey found her sparkly purse, adding it to her armful. Upset as he sounded, she didn't want to argue over high heels.

"Bitching about it isn't going to get me out any faster," Matt warned Rob, heading for the door, then waiting. "Yes. As soon as I can. I don't know. Goodbye." And he shut the phone.

Carey went past him into the hallway, barefoot. "You don't need to drive me home."

"I'm not just dropping you off at the train station."

"Then I can take a cab. Matt." She put a hand on his arm as he locked the door, made him look at her. "You were working on the initiative when I started there a year ago. I know how important tomorrow's vote is."

Matt sighed, his shoulders sinking—but she could see she'd convinced him. "Come on," he said, but instead of heading for the elevator, he crossed the hall and knocked on the door.

"What are you—" But she stopped asking when he took her hand and used it to pull her up against him, under his arm.

The door opened after his third knock, and it was the neighbor from the night before, a small man with an earring. "It's not even seven o'clock," he protested before he saw who it was. Then he stood straighter. "Man, Tynan, you did it wrong. In my fantasies, you don't have a woman with you."

Matt said, "You've got small feet, don't you, Karl?"

"Yes, but you shouldn't believe the rumors— Oh, honey." Karl had just seen the shoes dangling from Carey's fingertips. "You poor thing. Hold on a minute."

In short order, she had socks, a pair of Nike runners, a plastic supermarket bag for her extras, and the assurance that Matt was welcome to return them *any* time he liked.

"I owe you," Matt told his neighbor.

"I wish," sighed Karl, closing the door.

"I still hate this," Matt admitted, leading her back to the elevator. "It's not right. Last night was right."

She smiled at the memory, relieved when he smiled back.

"Have dinner with me," he insisted as the elevator arrived. "Galileo, the Willard Room, wherever you want to go."

"You don't have to impress me," she assured him, while he pushed the button for the lobby. "I'm already impressed."

He rewarded her with a boyish grin. "Even without the animal prints and trapeze, huh?"

She nodded and they kissed some more. But once they reached the lobby, she made him go on to the parking garage, only winning that argument by accepting a twenty for cab fare. "I can hail my own taxi," she insisted with more vehemence than she'd meant to. "Go save the nation or something, okay?"

"Okay." But Matt leaned slowly over as the garage elevator doors shut, as if he didn't want to stop looking at her. "Dinner!"

Then she stood there, alone in the lobby of his high-rise apartment complex. She wore overlarge clothes and no underwear, had wet hair and a supermarket bag full of last night's clothes in her hand. She'd never felt like such a hick.

Matt hadn't seemed to mind. So why did she suddenly feel so empty?

Carey sat on an upholstered bench, long enough to put on Karl's socks and shoes and wondered what was wrong with her. She'd just had the most amazing night of her life. She was in love. He wanted to see her tonight. So why wasn't she spinning in happy circles?

Whatever the reason, she couldn't stay here all morning. So she gathered up her belongings and headed out to the Metro.

Even now, she wasn't a taxi kind of girl.

Thirteen

Most days, Matt loved working in the West Wing. This was not one of them. From the minute he strode through the lobby security check—after the lot security check and the entrance security check—he had too much to do and even less time to do it.

More important, Carey wasn't there. Not anymore.

"Morning," greeted Kip, standing as Matt swung into his office. "Rob had me clear today's calendar, which means major rescheduling. I've penciled in some possibilities that need confirmation ASAP. The A.P. printout, the numbers from Texas, a Delmonico update, the tally sheets and a P & C card from Rita Winfield are on your desk. Your mother left two messages for you to please call her. And the senior staff is in the Roosevelt Room to discuss those lost votes. You heard, right?"

Still walking, Matt looked ceiling-ward and barked out a laugh. He looped through his office just long enough to grab the more important papers and to check his Secret Service POTUS monitor. Not surprisingly, it read Roosevelt Room.

"I figured as much," said Kip, as Matt passed him in the other direction. "Do you want me to bring in some coffee?"

"Thanks. And, uh, Kip, I need you to score something for me, but it's personal."

Wonderfully, soul-deep personal.

News in the Roosevelt Room confirmed the rumors. One day before the House vote on the education initiative, the numbers had turned against them. Matt used a daily tally sheet listing each representative beside a column for Yes, Leaning yes, Undecided, Leaning no and No. They needed two hundred and eighteen votes to carry, and yesterday's numbers showed them at two twenty-five. But last night, reporter Jeff Jenkins had noticed empty seats at the teachers' dinner. Suspicious, he'd made some calls from the men's room. This morning's *Post* revealed that fourteen assumed Yes votes had done an about-face. The president's initiative, on which he'd been elected, suddenly looked to lose by seven votes.

Politics was never simple; it had happened in a dozen ways. Representatives had become more financially conservative since the World Bank incident. A congressman from Silicon Valley was protesting an item against planned obsolescence in school computers. A new lobbyist group, People Opposed to the Scholarly Elite, claimed that the initiative discriminated against high-school dropouts. And good old M. H. Cantrell, the tabloid reporter who'd turned on Carey, was doing radio talk shows. His message? If the government meant to "educate" children by tampering with their DNA, as it had in the sixties, the American people wanted none of it.

To postpone the vote at this late date was its own defeat, since they would need months to regroup. But if they called roll, could they win? If not, next week's Senate vote wouldn't matter.

"We've got twenty-four hours before we have to postpone," decided President Stewart after listening to the shouting and blame. He turned specifically to Matt. "This is trouble, Tynan. Shoot it."

"Aye, aye, captain." But as the meeting was breaking up, Matt lingered for a long, still moment before charging off at his usual one hundred and fifty percent. Stewart's administration had teetered on the edge of failure before. They'd be there again. Usually that was part of the challenge. Today it felt more like an annoyance.

In contrast, for the first time, Matt had spent a life-changing night in the arms of a woman he actually loved. A woman whose judgment he trusted, who'd known him over a year and hadn't yet been disillusioned. Maybe Rita was right. Maybe Carey had hidden strengths that could keep even him from messing up or, God forbid, moving on.

But he had work to do and he reined in his thoughts. Striding back toward his office, Matt thought to open the personal and confidential card Rita had left for him—and stopped, right there in the hallway.

"Step two," she'd written. "Don't hurt her."

He suspected she meant to be funny. He didn't laugh. What had happened to Carey being able to chew him up and spit him out?

Worse, the suspicion that he might have to cancel dinner didn't feel like a good beginning for the Don't-Hurt-Carey plan.

Carey, cleaning house in preparation for Matt coming to pick her up, tried to feel casual and worldly about last night. Other women had sex every day, right? But last night hadn't been merely casual, not for her. It had been momentous.

Even if, to judge by tabloids and White House gossip, women—other women—had sex with Matt Tynan every day.

Carey winced at the thought. But she'd kept his calendar. Matt worked up to eighteen-hour days, often through the night. Unless he was grabbing quickies in the coat closet or the bathroom...

She remembered how he'd dragged her into the shower,

fit and tanned and glistening wet and so wonderfully, incredibly naked. Jaw shadowed with a night's beard. Hair dripping rivulets into his dark, laughing eyes. His smile widening as he bent to her.

The concept of quickies made her uncomfortable in more ways than one—not all of them unpleasant.

That didn't keep her heart from sinking with resignation when she saw the courier truck stop on the street in front of her apartment. "Oh, no," she whispered. "Oh, Matt, *no*."

She didn't want to be one of the many, even if she was.

The deliveryman climbed out the back with a large box affixed with Fresh Flowers labels. Carey just stood there beside her window seat, still wearing Matt's T-shirt, her hands in yellow rubber gloves and her hair pulled back into a plain ponytail—and she prayed the flowers weren't for her.

But the solid knock on the door betrayed her. Trying to laugh at herself—what woman wouldn't want roses from Matt Tynan?—she crossed the room, fumbled off her cleaning gloves. But she couldn't laugh. She could only act by rote.

Yes, she was Carey Benton. Yes, she would sign. Thank you.

In a moment she had a huge box in her arms, the sweet scent of fresh flowers surrounding her. She put it down on the coffee table, still sealed, and felt foolishly miserable. Would she like it better if, unlike with his other lovers, he *didn't* send her roses? Except….

She eyed the box. Didn't roses generally come in a long, slim box instead of a big, square one? And wouldn't they smell more like…roses?

Suspicious now, she found her box-cutter and slit open the top of the carton—and beheld a huge spray of perfect daisies and filigree-gilded apples. She dropped the box-cutter to the floor, pressed a hand to her mouth, and everything got blurry.

It was an arrangement from last night's state dinner. Not roses. She was a different, after all!

Once she lifted the arrangement from its box, Carey found the card. She sat on her window seat with its T-shirt pillows and its glimpse of the distant Capitol Dome to read the scrawled handwriting that was as familiar to her as her own.

"To remember the best night of my life," it said, "Until tonight. Matt." The card smelled like apples.

She loved him so much, the immensity of it lodged like an ache in her chest. The rest of her day was a blur of more Proteus research and a call from her new boss at the O.S.E.P. asking her to meet with him and a reporter for lunch the next day. She could not know what would happen with Matt in the long term, she told herself, so why make herself miserable by worrying about it? She loved him, and he was taking her to dinner, sending her flowers—not roses!—and making the kind of love to her that she'd thought only existed in her fantasies.

She would savor this newfound joy however long it lasted.

She hoped it would be longer than one night.

"Hold my calls," Matt told Kip at four-thirty. He felt rumpled, tired and hungry. An open carton of Chinese take-out had sat on his desk for hours, but he'd barely managed to snatch bites. He felt useless. He had a headache. But this was worse.

Kip said, "Except for Representatives Doyle and Weaver, right?" Matt had been trying to get hold of those two since that morning. They weren't at their homes, weren't in their offices, weren't answering pagers or mobile phones, and he needed them.

"Not even Doyle and Weaver." He reconsidered that. He still had a job to do, damn it. "Well, if it's Doyle or Weaver, throw something at the door to let me know and stall them."

Then he shut his door, flopped back in his chair and only reluctantly punched in the number he'd been longing to call all day. When Carey answered, her hello sounded so happy, so hopeful, that he felt sick.

"I'm sorry, Carey." That was the most important thing he had to say, so best to get it out fast, before she hung up on him.

"Matt? What's wrong?" She sounded less happy and hopeful.

In two words, he'd done that to her. New record. "I've got to cancel for tonight. I wish I didn't, God in heaven I wish I didn't. You've got every right to be angry with me."

Hell, *he* was angry with him! A fat lot of good professional honor would do him if Carey wrote him off as unreliable this early in their dating relationship. The first time he'd *wanted* a relationship—wanted it more than he ever would have believed—and he was standing her up the night after he'd deflowered her.

Carey didn't say anything. He scrubbed a frustrated hand through his hair, feeling even worse. He was nowhere near as sure of his ability to salvage things with Carey as he'd been with Janeen. And hell, he'd even screwed up with the peanut heiress! His only hope was to keep talking. "Carey?"

But when she said, "The vote, huh?" her voice had no edge at all. She sounded like his Carey. Disappointed, maybe, but not accusing. She even sounded concerned.

"Yeah," he admitted, cautious. "I've been at this all day,

and it still— You're on a secure line, right? Not a cordless?"

"Yes, Matt. You're safe."

Funny, how poignantly he felt the truth of that. Matt sighed and leaned back in his chair. Tight, tired muscles in his shoulders slowly started to ease. "It still looks lousy. Some of the reps are digging in their heels, and others are flat-out avoiding us. If I stay late, I might be able to catch a few of them at home, especially on the West Coast, and I'm still waiting for others. Carey, we lost Allen."

"From the president's own state? Stewart got him elected!"

"Yeah, but some computer moguls paid more for his campaign, and they suddenly don't like parts of our language stating that new equipment should be able to run old programs."

"But how can lower-income schools keep upgrading if they have to replace their whole library of software every time?"

"Exactly, not to mention the learning curve." He rolled his shoulders, then his head, switching sides with the phone. "God, Skipper, it's so good to hear your voice."

After a moment's silence she asked, "Really?"

He laughed. "Not as good as if I were there right now, and you were naked, maybe covered in peanut butter, but so much better than the rest of my day has been, you wouldn't believe."

"Peanut butter, huh? You sound hungry."

"Only for you," he assured her, his voice thick. He heard the hitch in her breath, as though she felt the same. "Hey, Carey?"

"Hmm?"

"Herbert Hoover," he whispered, and laughed at her dramatic, happy moan. "I've missed you, you know. In the office."

"I've missed it, too. Are you sorry I resigned?"

"After last night? Hell, no." Maybe if he got done by nine. By ten. By midnight. Maybe he could swing by her place....

And what? She deserved a hell of a lot more than a drive-by.

Carey asked, "So did Allen conveniently not notice his constituents were against this until now?"

All that, and brains, too. He agreed that the timing was even more screwy than the lobbyists who claimed that the bill would make dropping out a federal crime. She recognized it as an ambush, almost as easily as he had—though unlike him, didn't think that was his fault—but neither of them was sure who'd orchestrated it. Neither wanted to jump to conclusions.

Neither wanted to get off the phone, either. But if Matt was missing another night with her, just to get more work done, he'd better get some damn *good* work done to justify the sacrifice. "You should go out tonight," he suggested, still feeling guilty about that. "Do something fun for both of us."

"I can handle my own social calendar, thank you," she teased. "Except the parts that need you there."

He winced as he said, "I'd suggest tomorrow night, but—"

"Tomorrow night's the vote," she finished for him, and he hurt with loving her. "The president will need you."

"Saturday, then. Anywhere you want to go. The beach. Mount Vernon. Shakespeare in the park."

"The zoo?" Her delight made him laugh. "I like seals."

If he were Ethan Williams or Jake Ingram, he'd *buy* her the damned zoo. They'd have to make do with visiting. "It's a date. I lo—'' *love* ''—look. Uh, I look forward to it, Carey.''

She agreed, and he managed to hang up without laying premature demands on her. If he couldn't do this right, he shouldn't do it at all. She deserved that. She deserved the world.

Matt couldn't believe how great Carey had been about him breaking their date. He was a little less relieved about that when he called back, three hours later, and got her machine.

It looked as if she'd taken his advice to go out, after all.

So why did that suddenly bother him?

Honey Evans screamed—actually screamed her delight—when Carey made her confession. Several people in the boutique where they were shopping, at the Old Post Office Pavilion, glanced at them in annoyance.

''I don't believe it!'' she exclaimed in a now-hushed whisper. ''You and Tynan having wild monkey sex!''

Carey dropped her face into her hands. ''It wasn't like that. *Isn't* like that. And no,'' she added sternly, looking up as she heard Honey take a breath for more questions. ''There are some details I'm not revealing, so don't even ask.''

''Spoilsport. You *know* it's a subject of debate downstairs. Maybe if you settle the matter, they'd shut up about him.''

Carey turned back to the rack of gowns she'd been perusing, hesitating to even consider something so expensive. ''I didn't sleep with him to get you inside information. I slept—I'm *sleeping* with him because I love him.'' There. She touched a sweep of blue silk, smiling. She'd said it out loud and everything.

Honey shook her head. ''Oh, you don't want to do that.''

"It's too late. I do."

"He doesn't like women who get clingy. That's the number one reason he drops them. Everyone says so. And I don't want to have to listen to your pitiful noises once he moves on. You'd be better off seeing him as a nice accessory. Not the whole outfit."

Carey already scowling about the "everyone says so" comment. "This is the opinion of people who have so little to do, they debate about the size of a man's—" Then she blushed.

Honey blinked at her and said, "Penis. If you can do it, you can say it. See, this is why I worry about you. And, FYI, that last part was *my* opinion, not theirs."

Carey turned deliberately back to the gowns. Matt's office had reimbursed last weekend's expenses, so she had some cash. "You've been to the Willard Room. Would this look good there?"

"Nothing that wouldn't look good on a corpse looks good in the Willard Room. And in case you didn't notice, I just said I was worried about you. Take advantage. It won't last long."

Carey smiled at her, and Honey groaned. That was clearly not the response she'd expected. "I'm going to try this one on," Carey decided. "Will you tell me if it's okay?"

"Not for the Willard Room."

"Maybe for Galileo."

"Okay. Italian food's good." As Carey took the dress to the fitting room, Honey trailed, randomly plucking mismatched items of clothing off the racks they passed. They took adjacent booths.

"I don't want you worrying about me," Carey said, stepping out of her shoes and stripping off her jeans. "I understand why you're worried. I know his reputation as well as anybody. But if there's going to be a chance, even the smallest chance, I have to believe in him. If I'm wrong, I'll be wrong either way. But if I hold back, I could *make* it wrong.''

"Or if you go all needy, you could make it wrong." A purple feather boa settled across the partition between their two booths. "Trust me. I hate needy lovers. They're so whiney.''

"I have no intention of whining." Carey finished stripping to her panties, then paused, staring at her body in the full-length mirror. She'd never obsessed about her body. Sure, there were things she'd change, but she stayed healthy, and her clothes fit. But now, imagining it the way Matt had looked at her last night—how hot his gaze had felt as he spread her out under him, the way his breath had stuttered in his throat—she looked sexier, to her own eyes, just remembering it.

Honey said, "You know what you should do, now that you don't have that virginity thing holding you back? You should start jumping other men. You know, test-driving them. That way you can make sure lover boy is even worth all the angst, and he won't have any reason to say you're suffocating him.''

"I'm not going out with other men, much less jumping them.''

"Kip said at lunch that he got two calls from guys who saw you last night and thought you still worked for Tynan, so they called there to ask you out. You were a real hit.''

"I'm not test-driving anyone. And virginity never held me back. Not being in love held me back." Carey slid the rustling blue gown over her head. The way it caressed her body reminded her of last night. She was going to be mighty uncomfortable if she didn't stop remembering last night quite so…completely.

A yellow smoking jacket appeared across the partition,

beside the boa. Then Honey asked, almost quietly, "Did it hurt?"

"You mean, did *he* hurt me?" Carey still wished she hadn't cried out. "No! It surprised me, how…" Snug? Full? Firm? Honey's more lurid interests would have to go unfulfilled. "Well, I can see how it could be uncomfortable, with the wrong man. Or if I hadn't been so…ready. But it was everything I'd hoped. I kept forgetting to breathe, it was so good."

Honey said, "I only ask out of concern for you. It having been your first time and all. Some women say it hurts, the first time. Not that *I* ever had that problem, I was so ready, but I thought if you wanted some suggestions…"

"He was wonderful," Carey assured her friend. "I was and I am deliriously happy. All is well."

"So why are you out shopping with me, instead of having wild monkey sex with the man of your dreams, huh?"

"I told you. Because of tomorrow night's vote."

"Huh." Carey didn't like the sound of Honey's *huh*. It made her want to defend Matt… except that his reputation kind of spoke for itself, more loudly than she could ever manage.

Instead she just said, "Okay, tell me what you think."

She stepped out of her booth, and Honey, wearing a top of sparkly turquoise netting, peeked out from hers and said, "Well you'd look good in the Willard Room. Or at your own wake. It can pull double duty, as long as you keep your figure. Buy it."

Carey grinned her thanks and looked at herself in the three-way mirror. It *did* look good. And this time, it would be hers. She couldn't wait for Matt to see it on her. And take it off her.

Honey called, "What about that vasectomy rumor?"

Carey laughed and said nothing.

Fourteen

Friday, June 20

"Sir, you may be missing the big picture here...."

"Congressman, I don't have to remind you..."

"Ma'am, you ran on an education platform yourself...."

Matt wasn't the only one on the phone; even the president was making calls to win back votes. They weren't just pressing the Undecided and Leaning no representatives for help, either. They were even contacting long-held No voters.

"The president is expecting a certain amount of loyalty...."

"Yes, but what do *you* think about the language...?"

It felt a lot like the week before an election, back in the good old days, in any number of storefront campaign headquarters. Matt loved this kind of challenge. So why did he pull up information about the National Zoo on his computer while wheedling Congresswoman Judy Riley? And when Judy suggested they meet for lunch, to discuss the matter more personally, why was he so quick to decline?

Carey. That was why. Because he missed Carey. Wanted Carey. Was terrified of screwing up with Carey. He knew he could change minds and get votes. Sticking it out with one woman, though, was a challenge.

Carey set a tough standard, being too good to be true.

Kip leaned through his open door. "Senator Bermann's assistant called. He wants you to come by his office."

Matt stared, and not just because of the come-to-me power play. "He's got to be insane. Does he know what day this is?"

"He said you'll want to talk to him before tonight's vote, so I guess so."

Everything became clear, then. Ambush.

The phone rang. Matt picked it up. "Talk to me."

"Are you still mad about the state dinner?" asked Janeen Sullivan, because his day wasn't complicated enough.

"No. As a matter of fact, Wednesday worked out really well. But I've got to go, Janeen. This is a bad time—"

"It was naughty of me to cancel last-minute. But I'm coming back to D.C. on Sunday, and I hoped I could make it up to you."

Matt waved at Kip to close the door. "Janeen, I thought we were clear last week. We aren't dating anymore."

"'Dating' sounds juvenile. I know I moved a little fast for you, but Greece cleared my head."

"I've gotten involved with someone else, Janeen."

"Someone else?" Even as Janeen questioned him, Matt scowled at his watch. He'd better at least hear Bermann's offer. "That was fast. But hey, I can share. As long as you don't bring her along when you're out with me."

That annoyed him, even if Janeen didn't know she was talking about Carey. "No sharing. Find someone who can appreciate you better than I do."

Janeen sighed. "Well, you know where to find me once you turn free agent again."

Matt hung up, pissed.

As he left the office, shrugging on his suit coat, Kip raised a curious eyebrow. Kip didn't ask, and Matt didn't say. On his way out to his car, one of the new female guards at the security check called an enthusiastic, "'Bye, Matt!"

He recognized her from when she'd worked security at the Capitol. They'd dated more than a year ago.

"Hey, Marlo." Was recalling her name a good thing or not?

Bermann was in the Dirksen Senate Office Building. On his way in, weaving through the human tide of bureaucracy at work, Matt passed a redheaded aide in glasses. She blushed and waved at him over her armful of manila folders. "Hi, Matt."

He'd dated Gwynn, too.

It was like the freaking *Christmas Carol,* right here on Capitol Hill, and Matt was stuck with the ghosts of liaisons past!

He really was a player, wasn't he? How many women *had* he dated, anyway? Stunned, Matt almost walked into a marble column.

How could he be anything but trouble for Carey?

It was almost a relief to step into Bermann's office and distract himself with simple, cutthroat politics.

"Hear tell you boys at the White House have got yourselves something of a crisis," the Missouri senator drawled. "Now, I don't mean to overstate my influence, but I suspect that if I talked to a few of the boys from my state, they might be willing to rethink matters. *If* I were of a mind to interfere, that is."

The game required Matt to ask, "And what might put you in that frame of mind, Senator? Hypothetically speaking."

"I believe," said Bermann, leaning back in his chair, "that you're familiar with a certain base in the town of Harper."

Matt shook his head. Unbelievable. "So if the president

keeps the base open, you'll put in a few good words for the initiative?''

The senator nodded.

''You do realize that if we win this vote on our own, you may have to vote *yes* next week just to save face with the party, don't you?''

''As long as this stays between the two of us, I might,'' agreed Bermann. ''But I'm a gambling man. If you lose tonight, my vote next week won't matter a good doggie damn, now will it?''

Gritting his teeth at his own foolishness in not seeing this coming, Matt agreed to take the offer to the White House. ''But don't hold your breath…sir.''

''I never do, boy. I never do.''

As he left the office, Matt recognized that more than the day's revelations were responsible for the sinking sensation in his stomach. Skipping breakfast was haunting him, as surely as was his sexual past. Only one could be easily fixed. He swung by the Dirksen cafeteria to grab a cup of their famous bean soup, hoping he wouldn't run into the curvy blond checkout lady whom he'd dated, too.

That was where he saw Carey having lunch with *Post* reporter Jeff Jenkins—and his world slammed to a halt.

Carey's new boss was running late for their meeting. But Carey and Jeff recognized each other from the White House, and from Wednesday's state dinner, so they got a table to wait.

''I don't understand how you can write the story before the representatives have even started to vote,'' Carey said, feeling remarkably comfortable with the reporter. That had little to do with Jenkins, and everything to do with her— and with Matt.

Last night's phone conversation, and Matt's willingness

to share his frustration about sensitive information, suggested that there really was more than sex pulling them together. She knew better than to get her hopes up, but...

The idea gave her an extra boost of confidence all the same, even with Jenkins. "Won't whether the vote passes make a little difference to your story?"

"Journalists think on their feet," Jeff explained, leaning across the table on his elbows. "Basically, I write two stories. My editor will hold on to both versions until the final vote. But I figured the O.S.E.P. might have a good quote on its importance, whether in triumph or defeat. And to be honest, Carey, I kind of wanted to see you again."

She blinked, unsure she'd heard him right. "Excuse me?"

"I guess I'm an idiot not to have really noticed you until Wednesday night. But you were something! *Are* something. And since I needed a quote for my story anyway, I figured—"

"Jeff," interrupted Carey. She felt uneasy. And flattered. "At the state dinner, I was with Matt."

"Well, yeah," Jeff started, then stopped himself. "You mean, not just business? It wasn't, like, a goodbye dinner?"

More like a hello dinner, she thought. But even as she sucked in a breath to set Jeff straight, Carey hesitated. Were she and Matt *out?* For people to know they were together, not a week after she'd resigned, would raise eyebrows. Then there was the matter of Matt pushing Josh O'Donnell so hard to hire her. It wouldn't be the first time a White House politician had gotten in trouble for using his position to get his lover a job.

Biting her lower lip, she looked off across the cafeteria. Matt had more at stake. He should make this decision.

And there Matt stood! He was paying for something, ignoring a clearly interested cashier to send dark glances her way.

Carey waved, amazed at how even a good mood improved as he crossed the cafeteria toward her. "Here's Matt now."

Only then did she notice how tired he looked. His shirt might be one of the new ones he kept in the filing cabinet, for overnights. The creases of his suit weren't as crisp.

He still wore it better than any man in this room. Then again, Carey now knew what he looked like under it.

She stretched out a hand on his approach, too impatient to touch him to wait. He caught it, tight, as he reached the table. "Carey," he said, his voice clipped. "Jeff."

She recognized the anger in his smile. The way his eyes gleamed. How the flash of his teeth seemed vaguely threatening as he looked Jeff up and down. He didn't release her hand.

"Tynan." Jeff Jenkins sounded wary.

"Matt." Carey finished their roll call. She'd missed him, a necessary but constant ache she hadn't felt since her homesick days as a college freshman. His lack of enthusiasm disappointed her. But he *was* midcrisis, and it didn't change what she had to say. "I'm glad you're here. Jeff was just asking whether Wednesday night was business or personal between us."

Matt's gaze dropped to her, and he stepped even closer to her chair, his hip brushing her arm as he turned his tight smile back to the reporter. "It was personal, Jeff," he answered—and just that fast, they were an item. He didn't hesitate or equivocate. Carey hadn't realized, until she felt the incredible lightness of relief, how much she'd feared he would. "Carey and I are dating. As a matter of fact—" His smile, when he turned it to Carey, still had a worrisome glitter to it. "Can we talk, Carey? It'll just be for a minute."

She nodded, letting him pull her chair out. Still clutching

her hand, he left a foam cup on the table as he led her toward the cafeteria exit.

Carey felt increasingly confused the farther they went. When they reached the hallway and he kept walking, she tugged her hand loose. "Matt, where are we going?"

"Away from that jerk." He glared toward the cafeteria, as if Jeff's very presence stained the whole establishment.

Carey stared at him, unbalanced. He was almost acting jealous.

But no. That was ridiculous. "Excuse me?" she asked.

Matt stuffed his hands into his pockets, shifting his weight as if to meet an attack. "And what's with you having lunch with him in the first place? If you were angry about dinner, you should have said so. I don't know what I could've done about it, but—" He shook his head, scowled toward the ceiling for a moment. "You could have said something."

Carey's world fell still. It was true!

"You're *jealous*?"

He scowled at her, both of them standing there in the hall as politicians and aides and interns circled past them.

"You're jealous," Carey repeated. "Of me and Jeff Jenkins."

He cocked his head, narrowed his eyes. "Should I be?"

She laughed. Matt Tynan was jealous, because of her!

Matt withdrew his hands from his pockets, spreading one in protest as he shook his head. "It's not funny."

"Oh, yes, Matt. Yes, it is funny." Then, unable to watch him suffer even from his own foolishness, she put a hand on his arm. "Answer your own question, silly. *Should* you be jealous?"

He hesitated. She sensed his wall of anger weakening.

"What have I ever done that would make you think that you can't trust me?" she prompted. "That I would lie to you, or do something behind your back? That I am not truly happy?''

She blushed at the admission, but refused to look away. Every hour without him since Thursday morning had felt endless. She didn't want to stop watching his handsome, troubled face.

He closed his eyes as he sighed, long and tired. But when he looked at her again, ducked closer to her, his eyes had cleared, warmed. He whispered, ''I'm a jerk, aren't I?''

''No,'' she protested, trying to memorize his face to carry her through until tomorrow. ''You're just acting like one.''

''You've got some innocent, Carey-esque reason for meeting with Jeff Jenkins, don't you?'' He looped his arms loosely over her hips, and she liked that as much as the validation.

''Mmm-hmm.'' Their foreheads touched, giving them minute privacy in the midst of the marble hallway. ''And you're here for your latest round with Senator Bermann, aren't you?''

''How'd you guess?''

''I'm too good to be true, remember?''

His loose hold on her waist tightened, pulling her to him, and he slanted a careful kiss across her lips. Carey arched happily against him as he followed that with a hungrier kiss. She slid her fingers into his thick, dark hair, holding his head down to hers. If anything was too good to be true, it was this. Their next kiss deepened, hot and promising and excited.

Then Matt turned his face into her shoulder, his heavy breath tickling her neck. ''Damned vote,'' he gasped.

''Where's a nice coat closet when you need one, huh?'' Fingers still in his hair, she traced the shape of his ears with her thumbs. Her hands framed his face when he squinted up at her, unsure of the joke.

Since he *did* have the vote to deal with, and she had an interview to give, Carey decided not to clarify that particular fantasy just now. She chose a new one. "Come to me afterward."

"After the vote? It could go late."

"After whatever celebration the president has once you win." Now *she* kissed *him,* and that turned out wonderfully, too. "I don't care how late. I just want to know you're coming."

Matt chuckled, low. Still, when he said, "I don't deserve you," there was no amusement in his dark, searching gaze.

"Shouldn't I be the judge of that?" She might have kissed him again had a familiar Bronx voice not interrupted.

"Hey, Tynan! Save the kissing up for the representatives. My assistant's got some actual work to do. Sheesh!"

Carey slowly turned to face her new boss, her cheek brushing Matt's linen shirt. Just as slowly, she readjusted to the steady stream of busy people around them. She supposed she should be embarrassed.

She wasn't. Matt cared so much about her, he feared losing her. And he was coming to her tonight. Probably.

From the way his eyes simmered down at her when she peeked up at him, he certainly would try. But he was also a politician, with responsibilities elsewhere this afternoon. So, with a shrug of defeat, he dropped his hold from around her and stepped back, dragging a hand down her arm. "Don't rub it in, Josh," he warned O'Donnell, before adding to Carey, "I'll see you then."

"I look forward to it," she told him as their fingertips caught, then parted, and he strode away. It was true. Every cell in her body looked forward to it. Every string of her heart.

Some of the people in the hallway sent looks that seemed

almost pitying, as if Matt would hurt her. Well, she could survive that.

She could survive anything for him.

Even him.

The staff and President Stewart watched the roll call on C-SPAN, on a TV in the Roosevelt Room. Assistants and interns came and went, as if checking the score during the seventh game of the World Series, but the senior staffers never left.

Against: 211 to 208. Allen, from the president's own state, voted against them. So did the representatives who'd been honestly against them all along. Several who'd been honestly for them stayed loyal: 216 to 216. It was up to the final two undecideds. Jorge, with whom Matt had played racquetball the previous week, voted yes. Suddenly it was up to Congresswoman Judy Riley, whom he'd refused to meet for lunch.

He'd left his lunch on Jeff's table, but he felt better nourished from those few minutes with Carey—her kisses, her touch, her simplicity—than he would have from the soup. Better yet, she wanted him to come by. Tonight. No matter how late.

The word "yes" flashed across the screen, and the room—now packed—erupted into cheers, whoops, hollers. Everyone surged to their feet, hugging and back-slapping, Matt included. For years they'd worked for this. Years! Now it had happened.

"Excellent," President Stewart kept saying, clasping hands with each of his senior staffers. His eyes were suspiciously bright. "Excellent! Good work, people. Matt, good save."

"That credit goes to Judy," he said. "Her district doesn't list education high on their priorities."

It was Rob, the Chief of Staff, who interrupted their celebration with the voice of reason. "People, listen up! I'm not sure how many of you remember your high school civics classes, but the House of Representatives does not a law make. We've still got the Senate to deal with."

"Next week," said Stewart firmly. "By God, these people deserve drinks and a weekend off. The drinks are on me."

"And," called Rita over the new round of cheers, "Senator Bermann was our main obstacle. He all but told Matt that if the bill passed in the House, he'd have to forfeit and vote yes."

"*If* we can keep a lid on our disagreements for another week," Matt reminded everyone.

"Which you've done wonderfully up to now," Stewart assured him. "Don't go looking for trouble, Matthew. We get enough without creating it. Now, who's for drinks?"

But, despite the intoxication of triumph that permeated this place, these people, Matt wasn't for drinks tonight.

Matt was for Carey.

Parking in D.C. was rarely good; that was the main reason he'd found an apartment building with a built-in garage. After driving to Carey's as quickly as was legal, Matt circled her block three times, looking for a space. Finally he parked not ten feet from her front stoop—and what looked to be a few feet less than the required twenty-five from a corner stop sign.

He would take the ticket.

Her lights were on. He'd barely knocked on the door when it opened. Then she was in his arms, right there on the stoop. She felt like heaven and smelled like springtime. Like apples and the almost imperceptible scent of daisies. And Matt was home.

He was home in her comfortable, lived-in apartment with its modest aquarium and its T-shirt pillows. He was at home in her bed, where she immediately led him. He was at home in her arms, and then in her warm, welcoming body.

In all his restless life, he had never known such peace.

Then, at 5:23 a.m., his mobile phone woke him.

Fifteen

Saturday, June 21

Matt woke immediately to a distinctive riff of beeps. He groaned, then inhaled a delicious lungful of Carey. He had her warm, soft body in his arms, her smell on his skin, her taste in his mouth. He'd never slept so soundly or so happily. He could die a happy man without ever knowing another woman.

So this was what love felt like. Gentle. Sure.

He didn't want her to wake up—not for a job that forced him to both stand her up and put her off. Women liked special attention. Carey was more important than any of them, but all she was getting was sex—the best sex of his life, but still. If she stayed with him, who knew how often his work would interfere?

Not tonight. He reluctantly climbed out of her bed, scooped his trousers up from the floor and slipped, naked, out to Carey's apple-scented living room.

"Rita," read the green-lit display on his phone as he thumbed the answer button.

"No," he said firmly, pitching his voice low.

"Presumptuous, aren't you?" demanded the press secretary. "I haven't even asked for anything."

"No. It's Saturday, and I'm not coming into the office. Unless someone's dead," he qualified. "Is anybody dead?"

"No."

"Good. Then I don't care if mutants have taken over Wall Street, if Bruno DeBruzkya has been named grand high poobah of the EEC, or if World War Three has started. I'll deal with it later. I'm taking Carey to the damned zoo so she can see the damned seals."

"Gee, that's sweet. Listen," said Rita, "we've got a leak."

Matt glanced toward the bedroom door and lowered his voice further. "How soon can I ask her to marry me?"

"*What?* Matt, did you hear me? We've got a *leak*."

"Then thank goodness we haven't been selling arms to Iran or breaking into any offices at the Watergate. I need a woman's perspective on this, Red, and Sam's long-distance. Not to mention recently widowed. So you're it. How soon can I ask Carey to marry me without scaring the hell out of her?"

"What happened to you being commitment-challenged?"

He considered that, reluctantly. Something about being with Carey made him anxious to believe in happy endings, but truth was truth. "I think I'm trying to outrun that," he admitted.

"Don't outrun it, face it. With her. Carey doesn't scare easily. Tell her you're in love with her, tell her why you're worried, work it out together. If you two actually end up married, you'll want the practice."

He could do that. Hell, he could do it at the zoo. He could buy her balloons, lots of balloons, and watch the seals, and simply trust her. Just as she'd trusted him, all along.

The idea felt strange in his gut. But good strange.

"Hey, Romeo," interrupted Rita. "Since the zoo doesn't open for another couple of hours, would you please focus here? Last night won't mean crap if we lose the Senate."

Finally the seriousness of her call registered. And she was right; he had a few hours before the zoo opened.

"Okay, so talk to me. What kind of leak?" He shook out his trousers and stepped into them, switching the phone to his opposite ear when he needed to change hands.

"Jeff Jenkins has an article about the vote in the *Post*."

"Well, sure," said Matt. "I saw—" But some strain of self-preservation, after years of politics, didn't let him finish. *I saw him with Carey yesterday.*

No reason to mention Carey's connection. "I guess a House vote still constitutes news. What's wrong with that?"

"Ahem," said Rita, and she began to read a passage. "'The president's education initiative faces an even greater threat in the Senate. On the afternoon of the House vote, White House advisor Matt Tynan was at the Dirksen Senate Office Building courting one of the bill's more influential detractors, Senator Wendell Bermann, Missouri.'"

True, they'd tried to keep Bermann's name out of this, so as to not corner him. But... "That's it?" asked Matt. "That's not too damning. Anyone could have seen me. I didn't sneak in."

Rita continued to read, "'Though Bermann has underplayed the extent of his opposition in the press, he has gone so far as to boast to Tynan that he has the president 'by the balls.'"

Matt sat on Carey's sofa, bare-chested, trousers still unzipped. Oh, hell. "How'd Jenkins get that quote?"

"So it's a legitimate quote? He said that to you?"

"Yeah, in one of our calls, but I can count the number of people I've told about it on one hand." Rob. Stewart. *Carey.*

Matt glanced back toward the bedroom and frowned. That was ridiculous. Sure, Carey had been with Jenkins...

And she'd confirmed that Matt was visiting Bermann...

And, in fact, she'd never denied his suspicions about Jeff. *Answer your own question,* she'd told him. Should *you be jealous?*

She'd never actually said he shouldn't.

He shook his head, stood, paced to her bay window. This was crazy. He trusted Carey more than anyone—although that was damned dangerous for a man in his position. He had more face-time with the president than anyone short of the Chief of Staff or the First Family. It made him vulnerable.

When Carey learned that he wouldn't date his assistant, she'd quit. Surely that didn't mean—

"So have you started talking in your sleep, or what?" asked Rita.

Matt ran a hand through his hair. Reality was fragmenting on him, just like when he'd learned that his friend Jake was the product of secret government experiments in genetics.

He *had* to trust Carey. If he couldn't trust her, he couldn't trust anything. If he couldn't trust her, then love was stupidity, and the idealism of monuments and zoos and balloons and Midwestern wholesomeness were all lies. Just as he'd always suspected.

No. Just as he'd *known,* since childhood.

Maybe she *was* too good to be true.

"Matt?" prompted Rita.

"No," he said. This was crazy. What little evidence he had was pure circumstantial. He'd known Carey for a year, and she'd never lied to him. Even if she hadn't mentioned her virginity until it was too late. And that time she'd said she hadn't called him from the library, when she had.

Damn.

Rita said, "No, you haven't been talking in your sleep? No, you still aren't coming in? Give me something here, because when I do my press briefing today, you can bet I'll be asked about this. And now that Bermann's threats are public, he sure as hell won't be voting yes next Friday.''

"It'll be a pissing contest.'' Matt used Carey's words from the other night. Any compromise on either side would now look like failure. All deals were off.

"Exactly. So what are you going to do?''

Matt tried to consider it—and couldn't. ''I'll call you back,'' he said and disconnected the call.

Then he just sat there, in Carey's homey living room, his elbows on his knees, staring at the slowly graying world outside her window. She had a partial view—a glimpse, really—of the Capitol Building from here. She'd always been interested in politics as much as office management, hadn't she?

He felt guilty for even suspecting her. He felt gullible for feeling guilty. He was tired of working into the night, every night, tired of plummeting from near triumph to likely failure at a moment's notice or a single newscast.

And he was deeply tired of being alone when the sun rose.

He didn't want his suspicions to be true. But he hadn't wanted it to be true when his mom said she was leaving. When he learned his dad had been having an affair with his secretary. When his mom had said Matt couldn't go with her, that it was more important for a boy to live with his father. He hadn't wanted it to be true when his dad cheated on his first stepmother, or when his discovering sex had almost ruined things with his friend Samantha, or when he suspected his second stepmother was flirting with him. He hadn't wanted it to be true when his friend Eric, adopted into one of the most normal families Matt ever got to visit, lost first his father, then his mother. He hadn't wanted it to be true that Jake Ingram was a genetic mutation surrounded by spies.

But it had all been true. Every lousy bit of it.

He'd always known what was true. Maybe that was why he'd always suspected, on some level, that Carey couldn't be.

His phone beeped its little riff again. Rita.

"What?" he demanded, answering.

"And good morning to you, Mr. Grinch. I've got something I thought you'd find funny, but if you don't want to hear it…"

"No." Matt braced his forehead in his hand, sorry for his tone. His stupidity. His uncertainty. Everything. "What is it?"

"Not to be outdone by the *Washington Post,* our favorite rag, the *World Inquisitor,* also has breaking news involving you. Are you ready for this?"

Matt didn't say anything. He sensed he wasn't ready, but that he had to hear this anyway.

Rita read, "'Government Confirms Code Proteus Project.' That Cantrell guy claims to have found a 'top-level government worker' to confirm the existence of a secret lab, and he's actually named it. This is of course the project that 'White House troubleshooter Matt Tynan has been investigating.' Now he's calling his secret mutants 'Proteans.' Isn't that a hoot?"

Matt turned off his phone, and felt hollow.

He guessed he couldn't trust anything, at that.

Carey woke and stretched blissfully, and reached for Matt.

He wasn't there.

She frowned and sat up. She had to sweep hair out of her face to see, but he wasn't in the bedroom. When she looked over the edge of the bed, his clothes weren't there, either.

For a moment she wondered if she'd dreamed him last

night. Dreamed him coming to her door after midnight. Dreamed him trailing her to her bedroom. Dreamed him kissing her, undressing her, loving her, burying himself in her until she'd screamed her pleasure, then waking her to do it again, together in the darkness. No fantasies could surpass such contentment.

Her body felt tender and sensitive in all the right places. Her bed smelled of sandalwood. So did she. He'd been here.

Maybe Mr. Pop Tarts and Beer had commandeered her kitchen to try to make breakfast? Maybe he'd gone out for bagels and pecan cream cheese?

She fisted her hair back into a scrunchie and put on her short, terry-cloth robe. Then she padded into the living room—and found Matt. Fully dressed in his now-rumpled suit and tie.

He hadn't gone for bagels. He wasn't waiting for the zoo.

The pain in his dark eyes, when he raised them, called to her, even as the force of his accusation held her back. "Was it just for the information?" he asked, his voice hoarse.

Carey shook her head, confused. "What?"

"The job," he said. "The sex. You never did let me take you off the Code Proteus project, did you? Every time I tried."

That was when she felt the first warning. This wasn't the same Matt who'd made love to her last night. "I don't understand."

"*You* don't understand?" He swallowed, hard, and stood to pace. "I trusted you. Not just…" He gestured toward the bedroom, dismissive, as if that had meant nothing. As if she could have been anybody. "Not just that, but with national security. With the presidency. With Jake Ingram's reputation, maybe his life, and *you* don't understand?"

Chilled, she tugged her robe more closely around her, wishing it hung longer. "No," she said, despite her heart thudding so hard she thought she'd choke on it. "I don't understand. You think... You don't trust me?"

"You only went to the press after you resigned," he said, as if figuring this out as he went along. "Maybe that's my fault. I made you think we wouldn't see each other again. Cut off your source. What did you have to lose? Once you sold the story, it was too late to take it back, so you had to distract me."

"Sold what story?" Now she did follow the pull to his side and, despite his anger, searched his face for some hint. "About what? I haven't gone to the press about anything. Matt—"

"Could you at least say how much you've told?" He shoved his hands into his trouser pockets, ducked his head, then scowled at her through his eyelashes. "Give me the chance for damage control?"

Who *was* this man who didn't trust her, who wouldn't listen? Carey felt sick, deep in her gut, deep in her womb. She'd taken him into her heart, her home, her bed, her body. She'd trusted that she knew who he was.

If she didn't know who he was, how could she really love him? That frightened her worst of all.

"I can't tell you anything if I don't know what's going on," she insisted, watching him pace some more. "Clearly you're upset. I get that. But, Matt, I've walked into this thing midway, and I could use the Cliffs Notes. Tell me what happened and maybe, if I'm actually involved, I can explain it."

"So I can just believe you again?" He grinned, his best go-to-hell grin. "I've got more important things today, thanks."

And suddenly Carey understood. Not what he was angry about, whatever he thought she'd leaked to the press, but why he was so ready to believe it. Why he'd believed the worst of her and Jeff, yesterday, too. The truth broke her heart—for him.

He was leaving her so she couldn't do it first. Protecting himself. And he didn't even seem to realize it, any more than he'd seen it in his years of serial relationships.

"Let me get on some clothes, and we'll go to breakfast," she suggested. "Someplace neutral. Then you can tell me everything, and we'll look at it together, okay?"

"No," he said simply, pulling his car keys out of his pocket, shifting them to the other hand. "I've got to get to the office. I should've left already, but it seemed wrong to—to just sneak out. And I didn't want to wake you…for this."

He frowned at a spot on her bare floor, wiped the back of his hand angrily across his mouth, then squinted up at her.

She took a deep breath, trying to get air around the lump building in her chest. His pain and hers. "Then call me later."

He headed for the door. "I don't think so."

She didn't follow. "Why not?"

He spun on her. "Because I can't trust you, Carey. I can't trust your discretion, and I can't trust your motives. I don't know. Maybe you just let something slip. Or maybe you've been feeding information to reporters the whole time and this—you and me—was just another way—" He closed his mouth on what he'd been about to say, but it was too late.

He actually thought she'd seduced him for information.

Now her heart broke for herself. She'd thought she knew him. Thought she loved him. But what counted for good sense in Kansas City clearly wasn't a match for Top Twenty Beltway Bachelors. She'd been an idiot to think she could play in his league.

Her eyes burned. But courtesy, as her nanna used to say, was commanded. "Then go. Get out of my home. If you ever stop running from yourself long enough to figure this out, give me a call. Start with an apology. Then we'll talk.''

Matt stared at her for a long, accusing moment, then left. He slammed the door behind him.

Carey moved to the bay window, stunned. She watched him tear a ticket out from under his windshield wiper, climb into his car, slam that door, too. Then he peeled away, the roar of his engine echoing through the quiet morning streets.

She was clutching her stomach, as if to keep from throwing up. She was trembling. After several long moments she found her remote control and fumbled it on, turning to CNN, searching desperately for news beyond the passage of the House vote. Nothing gave her a hint. She checked on C-SPAN, then the local channels. Then, desperate for answers, she went to her laptop and pulled up the online issue of the *Washington Post.*

House Says Yay, read the headline. Senate Bigger Battle. It was by Jeff Jenkins.

Several parts of the article could have come from her— or any number of people. Surely Matt knew she hadn't leaked anything about Bermann! The less she understood, the angrier she became.

Only when the noon news reported a fluff piece on Proteans did Carey realize the double-whammy that had hit Matt this morning. M. H. Cantrell, the conspiracy-minded reporter for the *World Inquisitor,* had somehow found specifics about Code Proteus. He gave Bloomfield's name. He gave years, including the dates of birth for the five young Proteans. And he was claiming to have as his source a "top-level government worker."

The son of a bitch! Furious, Carey tried calling Cantrell, unsure how she'd learn his source but determined to do just that.

She couldn't get through.

She considered calling Matt, to protest her innocence yet again, but hesitated. Why would she be any more believable now than when she hadn't even known what was wrong?

Besides, he *did* owe her an apology. If she went after him, sympathized with his misdirected anger, she wouldn't exactly be fixing the problem. Even if he came back to her, she'd have shown him it was all right to distrust her, and she couldn't do that.

It wasn't all right. It could never be all right.

Not even for him.

So she waited for him to call her. Desperate to stay busy, she forced herself to go back to researching Code Proteus. She'd let the project fall by the wayside these past few days.

What with falling in love, taking a lover…losing him.

Now she had all too much time with which to conduct her latest search in newspapers from coastal towns in Georgia, from the early eighties. She hoped to learn that Violet Vaughn and her little Proteans hadn't died in the rumored boat accident. She hoped to find a story full of implausibility and intrigue.

By evening—with no word from Matt—Carey finally located a report on the accident. Credible witnesses had seen the woman and four children get on the boat. They'd seen the boat explode.

That was when Carey finally wept, for lost hopes.

Whether Violet and Henry had loved each other or not, they'd died horrible deaths. Whether Matt was capable of loving her or not, he wasn't living up to that potential—and she knew better than to accept less. And if the senator's stupid quote was enough to bring down something as important as the president's education initiative, then maybe Washington, D.C., wasn't the place Carey had hoped it could sometimes be.

Maybe there were no happy endings.

So after washing her face with cold water and blowing her nose, Carey made some efficient, heart-rending phone calls.

The last was to Honey Evans.

Violet watched from the shadows under a striped awning at the agreed-upon sidewalk café, as her son Jake arrived. He was taller than Henry had been, his hair darker. She'd never seen anyone so handsome.

He had two men with him. At least one of them, she thought, was a government official. Both wore jackets, despite the warming summer morning, that could hide shoulder holsters.

After her experience with rogue CIA agents, Violet had no great trust of intelligence operatives. Despite how her whole body ached to go to Jake's side, to drag him away from these men, to safety, she forced herself to remain hidden. He was no longer a boy, certainly no longer hers. He knew what he was doing.

Sure enough, Jake waited until the men were settled at a bistro table across the patio from where she waited. Then he raised his deep blue eyes, as if casually scanning the crowd, and immediately found her. His taut face softened.

Letting herself trust him, Violet emerged from the shadows and took a seat. Jake came to her, then, taking the hand she reached toward him and squeezing it as he sat. It was not the hug she longed for. Then again, they were obviously being watched.

"Friends of yours?" she asked, sliding her gaze that way.

"One's my bodyguard, Robert," said Jake. "After what happened to Zach, it seemed the smart thing to do. The other's Lennox, my FBI contact. It's…complicated."

"Do you trust them?"

"As much as I trust anybody just now. I'm sorry I don't have much time, Violet. I'm not even officially here."

"No, of course." She raised her hand to her throat and, for the first time in months, removed her necklace. She unclasped it, and poured its three treasures into her palm. "These rings belonged to your father—that is, to Henry Bloomfield and me," she explained. "They weren't official, of course, but...I stopped wearing mine when I married Dale Hobson."

Jake waited for her to get to the point.

"I didn't remarry for a long time," she added, hoping he understood. "And it was for his daughter, Susannah, as well as him. He was a fine man, and I did love him, as best I could."

"Hobson?" clarified the man her oldest son had become.

"Yes. How I loved your father had nothing to do with 'doing my best.' He became my life. And he gave me five perfect children. I don't mean biologically perfect," she hurried to add at Jake's wariness. "Your perfection came from the miracle of love. The five of you healed his wounded heart. You gave me back my soul. We had never known such happiness as those years with you five. I want you to believe that."

Jake looked away—maybe far away. But all he asked, gently, was, "And what's the key for?"

Violet glanced again at the two men across the patio. Her instincts sensed danger—danger to her and, worse, to Jake. And yet she did trust Jake. He'd taken on more than should be asked of any one man. Gretchen and her husband were busy turning a small island into a state-of-the-art safe house. With any luck, they'd find that their lost Faith and Mark were equally competent.

Perhaps among them, they really could rescue poor Gideon from the clutches of the Coalition.

Violet began to explain the key. "You know that immediately after Henry's death Agnes and Oliver—the Coalition scientists—took the five of you. That's when they brainwashed you to forget us."

"After having implanted the hypnotic suggestions that Maisy Dalton has been trying to deprogram," said Jake wryly. "I know."

She nodded. "I barely escaped. When I tried to rescue you, none of you recognized me." She'd wanted to die herself then. Already reeling from the blow of Henry's murder, the indignity of being kept away from his funeral, and the powerful drugs, she'd almost given up. But not on her children. Never on her children. "I had to steal you away by force, and we escaped together."

"Except for Gideon," finished Jake. "Achilles, I mean."

The mastermind behind the World Bank heist that he'd been charged to solve. Of all her heartbreaks, that wound still cut the deepest. "No. They kept me from saving Gideon."

"So what has that got to do with the key? I'm glad to see you, but the timing isn't great."

"Your father didn't just hide the van and new identities," she explained. "He kept two sets of files. Only we knew where the real files were. The ones we left for the Coalition to discover were doctored imitations. This key is to a safe-deposit box in Arizona."

Jake's eyes widened. "With the real Code Proteus files?"

She nodded and pressed it into his strong, capable hand. "It's time for you to have it, before anything—" Again she glanced toward his lurking companions. Why did she feel so threatened? "Nobody has a better right to it than you."

Jake squeezed her hand before pulling his away, the key safely tucked inside. "Thank you, Violet."

"The bank—" But her voice stumbled when both of the

men, across the patio stood and started toward them. No! Both reached under their jackets. God, no!

Then Jake followed his friends' line of sight—and dove across the table at her. "Violet, get down!"

Their table went over with a crash. Violet fell to the ground, Jake's body shielding hers from a new threat. Not his friends. Someone else! A woman screamed. Gunshots broke the summer morning.

Beside them, a display window crumbled in on itself, raining pebbles of glass onto them. Chairs and bistro tables toppled as more people took cover. Violet struggled to get out from under Jake, even as the crack of more shots hurt her ears. A man, the one Jake had identified as Lennox, crumpled not three feet away, between them and the shooter.

Blood soaked the back of his jacket. Exit wounds.

"Stay here!" yelled the bodyguard, and he took off after the shooter. Finally, Violet saw the man who'd come so close to killing them—and she recognized him. He'd been outside her hotel room. Outside the arcade, at the mall. He'd been following her for weeks...and she'd led him right to Jake.

Jake lunged toward Lennox, even as one of the café patrons knelt beside him. "Call nine-one-one!" the woman shouted. "I'm a nurse, but this man needs a trauma center!"

Lennox's mouth worked, shaped the word no. His eyes, glazing, still managed to find Jake's. Jake leaned closer, his face drawn as he heard more. Then the nurse pushed him back.

"He needs room!" she insisted. And Jake backed slowly away, giving her all the room she wanted. Lennox's desperation softened; he seemed to nod. That was what he wanted.

"Come on," growled Jake, taking Violet's hand. As witnesses clutched each other, some crying, and bystanders pushed forward to see what was going on, Jake managed to blend himself and Violet into the crowd, carefully going the other direction. In moments they'd all but vanished from the center of excitement, toward the Cleveland Park Metro exit.

"'You're too well known,'" spat Jake, looking over his shoulder. "That's what he said. Lennox is dying from bullets meant for me, and he's worried about publicity. Christ, I hate this. I hate all of it!"

"I know," said Violet. "I'm sorry."

Jake looked surprised. Then he put a hand on her shoulder. "No, Violet. That wasn't your fault. Look, you'd better get going. We're more of a target when we're together."

His words were truer than he knew. "But your bodyguard—"

"He'll know how to find me," Jake assured her. "I just hope he gets that son of a bitch. Now go. Please. I'll see you soon."

Violet hesitated, then obeyed. As she stepped onto the escalator, descending into the underground station, she looked over her shoulder for one last glimpse of her Jake, tall and strong in the bright sunlight. Then he vanished, hopefully to safety. Perhaps he was right. Perhaps his bodyguard could take out a Coalition agent sent to kill him.

But if he didn't, the killer knew where she was staying. The Coalition spy would return for her.

She almost hoped he did.

Then he would have her to deal with.

Sixteen

Late Monday morning, after the worst weekend of his life, Matt's office door opened to Kip insisting, ''You can't do that!''

Then a thick, manuscript-size envelope flew past his head. A heavy one, to judge by the force with which it hit the lamp. Matt doubted that was due to the strength of the small, curly haired blonde standing in his doorway, though the way her eyes blazed at him in undisguised malice, he could be wrong.

''Sorry,'' said Kip, shouldering into the office and tugging futilely at the woman's arm. ''Honey, you really shouldn't—''

''Shouldn't?'' She jabbed at Matt's assistant with a mean elbow. Kip wisely let go. ''*Shouldn't?* As long as we're talking about things that should not happen, let's mention men who seduce innocent virgins and then not only dump them but make stupid accusations while doing it! How about we talk about *that?*''

Oh. Now Matt recognized her. Carey's friend. He'd seen her in the White House's common areas, but he'd steered clear of her because she looked like trouble. ''It's okay, Kip.''

''Okay?'' repeated Honey Evans, as Kip discreetly backed out and closed the door. ''You're a bastard, Tynan, and *nothing* you've done to Carey is okay.''

"I appreciate that you're upset." He'd dealt with hysterical women from a young age, including his mom. He had a knack for it. "But if you knew the whole story, you—"

He dodged when she pitched another large envelope his way.

"There's the rest of your stupid files," announced Honey, over the crash. "Carey made me swear to pass them on without peeking, when I drove her to the airport. Me, I would have burned them. On your car. But that's the kind of responsible, honorable idiot she is."

Honorable. The word sliced through Matt, sharpened by his increased doubts of the last few days. Even worse was another word. "Airport?"

Carey had left? For good? From the start he'd feared he would ruin her life, and now, even if she *had* betrayed him…

Against that, it was easy to ignore something as trivial as a very junior member of the staff yelling at him in his office.

"She went home to Kansas City. Congratulations for chasing her out of her favorite place in the world and back to the boondocks. You should have stuck with your kind, Tynan. But clearly you can't tell one woman from another, because if you knew Carey Benton, you'd know that she doesn't…doesn't…"

She wasn't hysterical. While she searched for the right word, Matt appreciated how flat-out furious she was as she righteously defended her friend. Still out of line. But earnestly so.

"She doesn't bleat!" exclaimed Honey finally.

Matt blinked at her. "Bleat?"

"Did she give me details when I asked? She did not. Would she reveal her confidential work? She would not. She is one of the few truly decent women in this city."

When Honey Evans narrowed her eyes, Matt wondered

if he should really worry. Then again, if her ranting assessment of Carey's character was right, he deserved to worry.

It sounded right. It *felt* right. Hell, it felt like something *he* should be saying, not Evans. But what if he believed it, and was wrong? Who else could have leaked such damaging information, a mere week after Carey resigned?

He picked up one of the large envelopes Evans had hurled at him, and saw his name written on it, in Carey's handwriting, and the initials C.P. The realization that she'd returned her own copies of the Code Proteus files cut deeply.

She really was finished with him, wasn't she?

His intercom beeped. "Matt," said Kip. "There's a call from Jake Ingram on line two. It sounds serious."

Honey's eyes widened. "Did he say Jake *Ingram?*"

"No, he didn't." Pointing a silent warning at her, Matt picked up the phone. "Talk to me."

"Matt?" It was Jake, all right. To someone who didn't know him, he would have sounded as steady as ever.

Matt knew better. "What's wrong?"

"I'm on Connecticut Avenue. There's been a shooting. An FBI agent took a bullet meant for me, and my bodyguard's gone after the killer. They've brought in an ambulance for the agent. I'll need to make a statement. But given the circumstances, I doubt it's wise for me to walk back into the crowd and introduce myself."

"What's the closest intersection? What quadrant?" Matt scribbled it down as Jake told him. "I'm on my way."

Then he hung up, looked at Honey Evans and lied through his teeth. "That was my stepmother. I have to go."

"What?" she challenged while he grabbed the address and his suit coat. "Your stepmother is named Jake Ingram?"

"No, she's named Jackie Graham. Get your ears checked."

"I know why you won't tell me whatever's going on," she said, following him out. "You think women can't keep their mouths shut, right? Just like you thought with Carey, you rat bastard."

Matt paused by Kip's desk. "That was my new stepmother, Jackie. I'm going to go pick her up at her hotel. Got it?"

"Got it." Carey had chosen her replacement well.

"Oh, yeah?" demanded Honey of Kip. "What's her *last* name?"

"Well, of course it's Tynan." Good save.

"And her maiden name," added Matt pointedly, "is Graham."

"Well, sure," agreed Kip, catching on. "Jackie Graham Tynan."

"I hate you," Honey told Matt. "I'm glad Carey left. You had a shot at a real class act, and you blew it. There isn't much I can do to you worse than that, but don't think I won't try."

"So you've said." Matt waited for her to leave the office first. "Carey's the innocent victim, I'm the jerk. Point taken."

"You really don't get it." And Honey stalked off to wherever it was she worked, calling out one last, truly inappropriate name through the halls of the West Wing.

Matt hesitated. Then he looked at Kip, who was watching intently. "I've got a special project for you. Find out where those leaks came from. Tell nobody but me."

If it had been Carey, he'd sit on it. But not if it wasn't.

Unable to face even the possibility that he could have destroyed his happiness like that, much less the injury he may have done Carey, Matt headed out to help his friend Jake.

* * *

"Mom!" wailed Carey's youngest sister, Annie, in that pitch only teenagers could master. "Carey's watching C-SPAN again!"

Carey sat cross-legged on her family's worn sofa, barefoot and pony-tailed, wearing shorts and a large, stolen University of Chicago T-shirt. "I'm still waiting on a phone call," she said, her gaze on the screen. "What do you want to watch?"

"Anything but that!" insisted Annie.

Their other sister, Liz, home from college for the summer, paused in the living room to twist her mouth at the octogenarian speaker who currently held the Senate floor. "You can take the girl out of D.C.," she teased, "but you can't take D.C. out of the girl."

Then Mom appeared in the doorway between the living room and her garage office, wearing an apron over her jeans and a wrist brace to help prevent carpal tunnel syndrome. "Carey, is there even anything scheduled from the White House today?"

"No," admitted Carey with a sigh, chucking the remote control to her bratty youngest sister. "Heads up!"

Annie caught it and began to surf channels, pausing on game shows and soap operas.

"Cheer up, Carey," said Liz. "Maybe there'll be some huge executive scandal, with all sorts of press conferences, and you'll be able to see Matt Tynan standing there in the background looking all *GQ* and serious."

"Gee, thanks." Carey rolled to her feet. "I'm sure the White House appreciates your positive thoughts, too."

"Hey, between family and country, I know where I weigh in."

Mom said, "I, for one, would prefer Carey spend her visit

doing something more productive—like upgrading my e-mail program like she promised?''

''Your wish,'' said Carey, heading into the office, ''is my command.'' Her dad's idea of refurbishing the garage was to add insulation, put in a window air-conditioning unit and a space heater, and buy desks and computer equipment. The floor was still cement, mottled with old oil stains, cool under Carey's feet.

''It's good to be queen,'' agreed Mom, following her.

''So you're definitely going back?'' asked Liz, trailing. ''If I actually get that internship I'm applying for—''

''If I got in, you can get in,'' Carey promised, perching on the typing chair and inserting the new CD her mother handed her. ''And yes, you'll have a place to stay and food to eat, even if it's just peanut butter. I'm definitely going back.''

''Good. I was afraid…well…'' Liz winced, unsure how far to go. The whole family knew the basic story, that Carey had taken a new job, dated Matt, then broke up. She wasn't good enough at hiding her feelings to try keeping that much from them. But only Liz, with whom Carey shared a room, knew she and Matt had been lovers. Only Liz knew Carey's full heartache.

No matter what face Matt wore—playboy, boss, hero, jerk— Carey still loved him. But apparently that wasn't enough.

''I committed to Josh O'Donnell at the O.S.E.P.,'' Carey reminded Liz. ''Even if I wanted to quit, it wouldn't be right.''

Mom said, ''And I raised my daughters better than to throw aside their lives for their boyfriends.''

Carey smiled ruefully at the word ''boyfriend'' being applied to suave Matt Tynan. She finished the installation process on the computer, showing her mother the step where Mom always got stuck. Then, to make sure it worked, she checked her own e-mail.

When she saw the return address on one of her new messages, she leaned closer: MHCantrell@WorldInq.com.

She couldn't click it open fast enough. He was returning her call via the Internet, leaving an exchange at which she could contact him. She wrote down the number and logged immediately off. Her parents still had a dial-up modem.

"Is this line—" she started to ask, then caught herself. Their home line wasn't scrambled, but it was relatively secure. "I'm going to make a long-distance call, but I'll pay for it."

"Is it Matt?" asked Liz, leaning closer as Carey dialed, and Carey shooed her back for privacy. If the e-mail *had* been from Matt, she wasn't sure what she would do. Every fiber of her wanted to reach out for him, by e-mail or phone or, best yet, with her own two arms. Every bit of her wanted to reassure him that not every woman would leave him the way his mother had, and to hold on until he felt safe enough to stop suspecting her. The idealism that adored zoos and historical monuments couldn't help but believe that if she could just hold him long enough, love him hard enough, he would come around, apologize, love her back.

Good sense, however, knew that no matter how honorable she was, how efficient she was, how much she cared, some things were beyond her scope of control. Matt Tynan was one of them.

But slimeball reporters were not.

The other line rang, then picked up. "Cantrell."

"Hello, Mr. Cantrell. This is Carey Benton. We talked the other day?" And, more innocently, several weeks ago. But he seemed to have forgotten how he'd tracked her name back to Matt for use in his article.

"I remember. Have you thought about everything?"

She said, "But you promised a phone number."

"You promised me some information, as well," he hedged. And she had. Sort of. Desperate times and all that.

"The deal," Carey insisted, "was for you to go first."

She hadn't spent a year inside the Beltway for nothing.

Matt pulled up to the corner that Jake had indicated. He didn't like Jake being without his bodyguard. Too much was going on that he didn't understand—but Matt understood danger.

Then Jake appeared beside the car, ducking to look in the window, and Matt popped the locks. In barely a moment, they were easing down Connecticut Avenue—past police cars, strobing blue lights and yellow tape marking the crime scene.

"So have you heard anything?" Jake sank back in the seat as if exhausted. A lean Texan with thick black hair and bright blue eyes, he looked haggard. "From the hospital?"

Matt had risked using both his mobile and his connections to make the needed calls. "I'm sorry, Jake. He was DOA at Bethesda."

Jake closed his eyes. "Damn."

"He was a good guy, this Lennox?"

"Stand-up, all the way. But even if he'd been a jerk…"

"Yeah." Lennox had died for Jake. Even Jake Ingram's brand of competence couldn't easily gloss past that kind of guilt.

Matt said, "He was an agent doing his job."

"I don't know if my bodyguard could have caught the killer."

"It might negate his job security, huh?" Matt tried to joke.

Jake laughed, harsh. "C'mon, Tynan. You don't think I'm up against just one guy, do you? I'd need a bodyguard even if I'd caught and killed the bastard. I've put protection on my parents, my brother, Tara. This Coalition that's after me is bigger than Code Proteus. It's bigger than the World Bank heist. You can't imagine."

So Matt hadn't been paranoid when he'd worried about Carey making phone calls, driving alone to North Carolina, digging up information on Proteus. Little good it did him to be right, when he was right about having put her in danger.

Maybe she was better off without him in Kansas City. Safer, for sure. She might even be happier.

He wasn't. He was already forgetting what happiness felt like—except that it was intricately tied to Carey Benton.

Matt took Dupont Circle with practiced ease, driving toward his high-rise. "You'd be surprised what I can imagine, Jake. The imagining may be worse than the reality. I deserve to know more."

"Are you sure you want that responsibility?" Jake slanted a calculating gaze in Matt's direction. "It's pretty big."

Responsibility. Great. But Matt was already up to his neck in it. Maybe it was time he started acting responsibly, instead of just being responsible. Maybe if he'd done that with Carey...

"Try me," he said.

So, Jake, sounding relieved, told him everything.

Another day, thought Carey, parking in front of a small, boxy house from the post-World War Two building craze. Another interview with a senior citizen.

She carefully locked her brother Ricky's car, which she'd borrowed for this trip across the bridge from Kansas City, Kansas, to Kansas City, Missouri. Then she waved at a white-haired couple who were sitting on their front porch swing next door, enjoying the midmorning coolness and holding hands.

They smiled and waved back.

Carey wondered if they had ever gone sight-seeing at night, then spent the time kissing instead. When had their hold on each other's hands softened to such assured ease? How long had they shared a bed, shared a life, shared a world?

Her throat ached. She missed Matt. And she didn't know what to do with that awful emptiness that loomed in her future, except to chide herself for her idealism and to keep busy. So she headed up the walkway to number 275 and knocked.

The elderly man who answered was comfortably plump, with a cowboy-style handlebar mustache and wire-rimmed Santa Claus glasses. "Yes? Are you the Miss Benton who telephoned?"

"Yes, sir, Mr. Sloane." She shook his hand. He had a good grip. "I appreciate your willingness to talk to me. Especially since I can't pay you the way the *Inquisitor* did."

"Oh, that. Pshaw. How about we sit out here on the porch," he offered, indicating two white-painted iron chairs. "Wouldn't want the neighbors to talk about me entertaining a pretty young lady like you in private, now would I? What would I tell Myrna?"

"I'm sorry." Carey sat. "I thought you were widowed."

"That I am, darling, but that doesn't mean I don't talk to my sweetie every Sunday in the churchyard." Sloane sat across from her. "It's not so different from when I was serving in the Navy, gone for months at a time, writing letters. Love like that, it lasts. I know Myrna's waiting for me when I finally go home."

Carey smiled, unsure she could speak past the lump in her throat. That was the kind of love she'd always wanted. Why had her heart chosen Matt Tynan, if he couldn't give her that?

''But you wanted to hear about the information I sold to that weasel Cantrell,'' continued Sloane. ''He said he'd keep my name quiet—'deep background,' he calls it—but I knew better. Didn't have no choice. Needed a hearing aide, and Medicare wouldn't cover it. Anyhow I wasn't surprised he told you.''

Carey was. In fact, she'd made quite an enemy of M. H. Cantrell. Then again, since he was the same tabloid reporter who'd used her to name Matt in an earlier story, they'd been enemies already. She'd offered to tell him everything that she'd passed on to the president, from her private research into Code Proteus, if he first told her where he'd gotten *his* latest information. When Cantrell learned that she'd passed absolutely nothing on to President Stewart, and since quitting the White House couldn't say whether or not anybody else had since debriefed their Commander in Chief, he'd been furious.

But by then, she'd had Mr. Sloane's phone number.

''As I told you when I called, sir, I'm working alone, but I might share whatever you tell me with certain staff members in the executive branch of the United States government.''

''I appreciate you being up front about that,'' he said, eyes sharp behind his glasses. ''Would these be folks you trust?''

Carey remembered how hurt Matt had looked before he'd walked out on her. Though she couldn't excuse his suspicions, she did understand them. And though she couldn't trust him with her heart, she still trusted him with her country.

''Yes, sir. People I trust a great deal.''

''I'm glad to hear that. You know, I didn't give that weasel Cantrell any more information than he could've gotten through Freedom of Information, if he'd just known where to look.''

"I noticed." That was one of several reasons Matt had suspected her; what she'd gotten through the Freedom of Information Act closely paralleled much of Cantrell's recent scoop. "What I was hoping you could share with me is how *you* knew where to look."

Sloane grinned. "Darling, I didn't have to look at all. I knew. Back in the sixties, I worked in D.C. myself, as an aide in the Senate. Worked for a first-time congressman on the Senatorial Intelligence Committee overseeing CIA budgets, Proteus included."

Carey felt the stillness of expectation settle over her. "A Missouri senator knew about the genetic experiments being done on children, while they were still going on?"

"Man's been in office ever since," agreed Sloane—and Carey said the name at the same time he did.

"Senator Wendell Bermann."

Violet Vaughn adjusted the seat of the used Ford that she'd just bought for cash at a suspicious car lot in Maryland. She'd left her own pickup back in Colorado weeks ago. Ironic that, in all the chaos that her life had become, she could still enjoy the idea of a cross-country road trip.

Especially if it drew the bastard who had killed Jake's FBI friend away from the trail of her children.

Adjusting the mirrors she noticed the dark car, which had followed her here from the hotel, parked up the street.

Violet nodded to herself with resigned satisfaction.

Follow me, you son of a bitch. Follow me.

Seventeen

Jake's story was unbelievable.

And yet Matt believed it. For more than an hour, safe in his high-rise apartment, Matt learned about Jake Ingram's erased childhood as a genetically enhanced experiment. Jake spoke of spies, kidnapping, murder. He discussed lost siblings, all presumably walking time bombs of posthypnotic suggestions, only one whom he'd found, and one whom Jake had been hired to bring to justice.

"And on top of all that," finished Jake, staring down at his beer can, "Tara's madder than a wet hen about postponing the wedding. Have any suggestions, Casanova?"

Jake's cell rang before Matt could respond. Just as well. Mere weeks ago Matt would have arrogantly accepted his role as a supposed expert on women. He would probably have teased Jake that the problem had been getting engaged in the first place.

Now that he'd screwed things up with Carey, he understood Jake's worries all too well. Maybe Matt did know women. He just didn't know about commitment.

Or love.

"Yeah," said Jake, on his cell. "Uh-huh. It figures. No, at least you tried. I'll see you there." Then he hung up. "That was Robert, my bodyguard. Lennox's killer got away."

"Damn." Jake's world just got darker by the minute. "You need me to drop you off somewhere?"

"Yeah. Thanks." As they stood, Jake put his hand on Matt's shoulder. "I mean it, Tynan. Thanks. You really came through for me in a crazy situation. I know it's a lot for you to swallow."

"I work in politics," Matt reminded him. "You'd be surprised—" But his throat closed on the rest of the joke, sickened by his own hypocrisy.

He could believe that his friend of eighteen years had just discovered his true identity as a top-secret mutant. But he couldn't believe that Carey Benton, the most wholesome person he'd ever known, the woman he loved, hadn't betrayed him?

Honey Evans had been right. He was a bastard.

In light of that, what better place for him than the Hill?

By Thursday, sleep had become a rare luxury. Amid the usual foreign and domestic crises, the staff struggled to prepare for Friday's vote. But there were fewer senators to court; Matt could only go down his call list so many times. The education initiative still looked short of even a tie. Already, the West Wing had taken on the air of a funeral home.

A funeral home with constantly ringing phones.

Rita sauntered into Matt's office and sang, "Mail call!"

Matt looked up from his tally sheet, glared at her and looked back down, still scribbling notes.

"Oh, I think you're going to want to hear this." Rita perched on the corner of his desk. "I've got a little piece of intelligence that's gonna knock your socks off. Have some coffee." She put a paper cup and a fax printout in front of him.

He rubbed his eyes, ignoring the coffee to concentrate on the fax. But his eyesight quickly cleared.

Senator Wendell Bermann had served on the Senatorial Intelligence Committee from '65 through '72.

He'd known about Code Proteus from the start.

"Holy…" Matt looked up to Rita. "Where'd you get this?"

"An anonymous source," she said.

Bull. "Then how can we trust it?"

"Anonymous to *you*, sweet cheeks, not to *me*. I, for one, trust this source implicitly." She smiled a saccharine smile. "You know that if the CIA let Bermann hold the purse strings, especially back then—"

"They held his strings," he agreed. Even better. "They'd have had something on him, to make sure he'd play nice."

"So, shall we go fishing for Bermann's dirty little secrets? It would be an insult to homosexuals to imply he was gay. I'm putting money on the idea that he attended Communist meetings. But he can still have a secret love child, or an opiate addiction. Don't you have a friend in the CIA?"

Ethan Williams. Probably. Matt had never flat-out asked. Ethan had never told. "You're suggesting we blackmail Bermann?"

"I most certainly am not. Just that we twist his arm a teensy bit."

Matt thought of Carey. Of how proud she was of this damned city, this White House. He wasn't sure if he would have gone along with twisting Bermann's arm, even a "teensy bit," a year ago. Having known Carey, loved Carey, he wasn't about to now. "No. But I think I can handle this all the same."

He got Kip on the intercom. "Call Senator Bermann and ask him to meet me in my office, will you?" He grinned. "Tell him he'll want to talk to me before tomorrow."

Then he looked up at Rita. "Thanks. Now I just need some face-time with the president, and we're in business."

"Shave first," advised Rita. "And have Kip schedule a haircut for you, you're starting to look like a used-car salesman. You know you've gone to hell without Carey, don't you?"

"Yeah." He dragged splayed fingers through his hair, then looked up to meet his friend's wry gaze. "I screwed up, Red. Big time. I..." But he hadn't been able to confess it to Jake; he sure wasn't telling Rita the details. "I've got to do something. You're a woman, you know Carey. What do I do?"

"Here's a thought," said Rita, sauntering back toward the door. "Whatever it is she asked you to do? Start there. Carey's not exactly a game player."

But it couldn't be that easy.

It had been too easy, thought Violet on Friday as her used car bumped down the dirt road toward her Colorado ranch. She knew these plains, those mountains like clouds in the early evening West, the one-lane bridge that spanned the arroyo. She wanted to believe that her ranch was safe. But she could not.

As she'd hoped, the Coalition assassin's car had tailed her out of D.C., out of the Eastern seaboard, well away from Jake. Knowing that she was in increasing danger alone on the road, she'd tried to lose him in Kentucky. It seemed she had.

Each time she stopped for the night at some rustic roadside motor lodge, she half expected it to be her last. Each new dawn, as she carried her luggage out to the car for another long drive, felt too good to be true. Literally.

She was a biologist, not a spy. She was a rancher, by marriage. She was a mother, a survivor. And it seemed too easy.

Still, she had to get back to the ranch, the one she and

Dale Hobson had worked together for so long. Violet hoped to leave for Brunhia, to spend time with Gretchen, but she could not ask her neighbor and friend, Travis Dean, to keep tabs on the place indefinitely. Official arrangements had to be made until her rebellious stepdaughter, Susannah, could be found.

If Susannah could be found.

The homestead looked neither deserted nor neglected; Travis had been a good friend, as always. Her pickup sat where it always had, on the rutted driveway by the porch. She would bet money Travis had thought to turn over the engine every few days to ensure its running. Not wanting to attract the unwanted attention of neighbors, Violet drove her D.C. car out to one of the machine sheds and hid it there, well behind some other machinery, under a tarp. Just in case.

Her life here had never overlapped with her secret past—not until that morning in April when she'd seen Jake's picture on the news. None of her Colorado neighbors, nor Susannah, deserved to be drawn into her dark intrigues. Better that this car, the most obvious link between D.C.'s Violet Vaughn and Colorado's Violet Hobson, never see the road again.

Winded from the extra exertion, especially after so long a trip, Violet hiked back to the house she'd shared with Dale.

She hadn't lied to Jake earlier that week. Dale Hobson had been a fine man, and she'd loved him and Susannah dearly—with whatever had remained of her heart after Henry's death and her loss of the children, of poor Gideon. This was perhaps the only true home Violet had ever known, with no scientific experiments or intrigues lurking in the shadows. It wasn't where she'd once thought she would be as she approached seventy. But it had kept her safe. It had given her peace.

The least she could do was to leave this ranch its peace.

So Violet did not stop to rest, just in case. She turned on her home computer, on which she kept ranch records, and wrote a letter for Susannah, in case her stepdaughter—who'd run away after Dale's death—ever came home again. Next, she would retrieve some papers she'd hidden, accounts that might be of use to Jake and the others.

But as she stood, and glanced out the window, Violet spotted the dust of an approaching vehicle.

It could be anybody. Her neighbor, Travis Dean. A teenager driving too fast to make a late dinner. Susannah, coming home.

But somehow, Violet knew better.

She wished she had more time. But if wishes were horses, then beggars would ride, right? She'd known something like this would happen from the time the government had taken over Henry's funding. She'd known it since Henry's murder. Since the World Bank heist. It was almost a relief to face it at last.

Every beginning hit an ending, sooner or later.

Friday, June 27

A green yes flashed in the corner of the TV screen.

"Yes!" echoed Liz Benton, her fist pumping the air. She stood and danced around the living room. "It's a tie! Yes!"

Carey, cross-legged on the sofa, didn't feel quite so elated. Maybe because it was all over now. This was the happy ending the president's staff had worked toward since before he'd taken office. She'd helped, both in her work for Matt and by forwarding Rita the information about Bermann. That information might have influenced the Missouri senator's own early affirmative vote.

It was good news for Matt. For President Stewart. For the country.

"I don't get it," griped Annie, who'd paused more to score some popcorn than for the political excitement. "Only a hundred people are going to vote? A tie isn't a win, is it?"

Liz rolled her eyes in disgust.

"Two senators per state, Annie," said Carey. "Fifty states, remember? The vice president gets to break ties."

"And you think he'll vote yes?"

"Yes," said Carey and Liz together.

"Then why isn't Carey dancing?" she asked, still looking confused. Then someone knocked on the door, and Annie hopped up. "Whatever. That's Tasha. We're getting tacos for supper. It's not like I care."

"Well, *I* care," insisted Liz as their youngest sister fled the room. "Why *aren't* you dancing, Hill Rat?"

Carey let her head fall back against the floral-print sofa cushions and wondered how to answer that. Maybe the problem was that, at the moment of victory, she was a thousand miles from everyone she'd worked with toward this.

A thousand miles from Matt.

The whole staff was probably celebrating with the president of the United States, and here she sat, peripheral to almost everything she cared about. She hadn't made a dent in Matt's life, though he'd become the heart of hers. That was her doing. It wasn't how she'd wanted to end, though.

"Carey," called Annie. Liz stopped dancing, surprised.

Carey looked up—and made a soft, vulnerable noise.

It was Matt.

Oh, God. It really was Matt, standing right here in her parents' sunken living room, almost painfully handsome in his suit and tie. A bouquet of daisies hung forgotten from one hand.

He shifted his weight. A fleeting smile touched then faded from his face before he ducked his head and slanted his dark gaze back up to her in a silent plea.

Carey slowly stood, disbelieving. *It was Matt.* Here. In Kansas.

In the middle of the most important vote of his career.

"I'm sorry," he said, his voice broken. "Care, I'm so—"

But she ran to him, wrapped her arms around him and kissed the rest of his apology happily away.

Barefoot. Wearing faded shorts. With her hair in a ponytail.

Hurrying now, Violet made a few more notations on her home computer, printed, then powered down. She slipped out of the house to the storm cellar stairwell and pulled out a loose stone by the door.

It was too late to get anything to Jake. Instead, she had to place her hopes on a different child—one who, until now, hadn't even been involved in all of this. For the second time this week, Violet took off the necklace she'd worn since Henry's death. On it hung the two ruby rings she'd always thought of as their wedding rings. For a last, long moment, Violet gazed at the two golden bands.

Then she lowered them into a white envelope, into which she'd already placed a coded letter.

Her mouth felt so dry, she could hardly lick the envelope closed. Her hand shook as she slid it into the dusty crack in the wall, then replaced the loose stone.

Now she had yet more reason to pray that Susannah came home.

Violet watched from the deep shadow of the outdoor

stairwell as a dark car pulled up in front of her house and a man got out. She felt an aching mix of fear, excitement and familiarity.

It was the man who'd been watching her all these weeks, back in D.C. It was the man who, in trying to murder her son Jake, had killed the FBI agent, Lennox.

She'd been found.

God, Carey looked good. Not just beautiful but healthy, happy. Matt didn't want to ever let go, much less stop kissing blessed welcome—and, he hoped, forgiveness—off her lips.

But the teenager who'd answered the door was staring with blatant interest. The young woman by the sofa had folded her arms in silent challenge. And a young man in jeans and a T-shirt had paused halfway down the stairs. They resembled each other, these Benton siblings. Tall and slim. Blue eyes. Shiny brown hair. They had family values and American ideals...and he was the political outsider in their wholesome world.

The one who'd seduced then discarded their sister.

"Matt Tynan," said Carey, "this is my baby sister, Annie, and my other sister, Liz. And that's Ricky, my brother."

She didn't sound discarded. He'd feared he would find her worn out with weeping, or maybe taut with anger. The way his mother handled romantic setbacks. Not Carey.

From the color in her cheeks, the glow of her gaze as she searched his eyes, she'd clearly survived him just fine. Maybe that should have hurt his feelings, bruised his ego.

He could barely breathe through the relief of it. Through the hope.

"You dropped these," offered Annie, coyly holding up the daisies he'd brought. "They aren't for me, are they?"

Liz said, "Like men will ever bring *you* flowers."

Ricky said, "Hey, we saw you on TV last year, didn't we?"

Carey said, "Put them in water for me, will you?" And, an arm still around Matt's waist, she edged him toward the front door. "Tell Mom and Dad we'll be back later."

Matt asked, "What kind of flowers do you like, Annie?"

Annie's face lit at the very idea of it. "Roses!"

Carey shut the door between them. Then it was just him and her, on the front stoop of her family's nondescript suburban house, Matt's heart sinking. Was Carey so angry with him that she'd told her sisters about Matt's standard, post-sex offering? Was Annie mocking him?

But Carey, her head back to better study his face, seemed to read his mind. "A friend of hers got a dozen red roses for her birthday. It was a very big deal around here."

"It *should* be a big deal." Then, before he lost his nerve, Matt said, "Let me take you out to eat, Carey. Wherever you want to go. I owe you that much, and we…we can talk."

He'd never screwed up this badly. He wasn't sure he could fix it. At least on a dinner date he'd be in his element.

Carey looked down at herself, tugging her lower lip between her teeth in consideration. Matt looked down at her, too. She wore a tank top and shorts. Her long, bare legs seemed to go on forever. He had to swallow hard to keep his hands where they were, one on her soft, bare arm, one fisted hungrily.

She looked cute, with her hair back in a high ponytail.

"I didn't pack my best dresses," she admitted, which seemed odd for someone who'd moved home. "Wouldn't you rather just walk? I know the neighborhood's not exactly scenic."

"It's a great neighborhood." Sure, all the houses looked

pretty much the same, with only subtle variations in their matching lawns, sidewalks, mailboxes and driveways. But it reminded him of being a kid. Back when everything had been safe. "But I'll need to lose the jacket and tie."

"In June?" Carey really didn't sound heartbroken, did she? "Go figure. This is Kansas, you know."

Matt could have joked about expecting to find her in Nevada. Or Idaho, or Deadwood, or Ogallala. Instead he said, "I know."

"I'm happy to see you." She stepped back as he unlocked the rental car. "Really. But, Matt, you could have just called."

"I was afraid I wouldn't get two chances," he admitted, shrugging off his suit jacket and tossing it onto the passenger seat. His tie followed. "I hoped I'd do better in person."

Carey cocked her head, intrigued. "Do what better?"

Now or never, Tynan. "You said for me to apologize. That morning. God knows you deserve that much. And I really am so sorry, Carey, sorry for not believing you, sorry for not behaving better about it, sorry for chasing you away."

She looked surprised, but he had to finish.

"I don't have any good excuses. Maybe I panicked. I loved you so much, I guess I couldn't believe it could be real."

"You loved me?" she interrupted, her blue eyes widening.

So much for not putting *that* kind of pressure on her. If she reacted with the discomfort those words had always before elicited from him, it was probably no less than he deserved. "I didn't mean to say that. I'm sorr—"

She pressed gentle, capable fingers against his lips. She smiled brightly up at him. "You loved me?"

Since she didn't look the least bit panicked or sick, and since it was the truth, he shook his head.

Her hand fell away. Some of her brightness wavered.

"No, Care," he clarified quickly. "I *love* you. Still. And I'm so truly sorry for every—"

She interrupted him by sliding her hands up behind his neck, her thumbs guiding his jaw. She pulled his face closer to hers as she rose onto her tiptoes in clear, glowing invitation.

As Matt kissed her, wrapped his arms around her, the weight of a million fears slid from his shoulders. They had a chance. Carey wouldn't be kissing him if they didn't.

One kiss became two, became four, became countless.

And then, being Carey, she ducked her face into his shoulder, caught her breath and leaned slightly back in his arms. "First," she said, very solemnly, "I love you, too."

He'd never heard such beautiful, welcome words. His throat hurt. His eyes burned. His chest filled with more love, more hope, than he'd thought existed in the world. He bent toward her, determined to kiss her again, to kiss her forever, but she stepped warily back.

"I love you," she repeated. "And second, we have to talk."

"That doesn't sound good."

"Trust me," she assured him, again sliding her arm around his waist.

If he trusted anybody in this world, it was her. So he looped his arm over her shoulders to pull her close against him despite the afternoon heat. She fit perfectly.

He pocketed his keys, and they began to walk together through her world of sprinklers, picket fences and people washing their cars. "Then talk to me, Care," he agreed, kissing the top of her head. "Just don't ever stop talking to me."

* * *

Violet waited, slipping her hand into her pocket for her truck keys. The stranger stepped onto the porch. She could no longer see him, but she could hear footsteps on the floorboards. Sometimes he paused. Likely, he was looking in windows.

His footsteps headed toward the opposite side of the house from where she hid, clearly circling the place. It was the best chance she would get.

Violet bolted out of hiding. She scrambled into her truck, panting. She was too old for this, she thought. When she fumbled the key into the ignition and turned it, the truck rumbled to life.

Bless you, Travis.

She glimpsed the Coalition agent racing toward her just before she sped off. In her rearview mirror she saw him run for his car. Good.

She had no intention of letting him search Dale and Susannah's home, if she could help it. No intention of letting him find her papers or, for that matter, getting hold of her. Jake was too close to locating the other children, and Gretchen was pregnant. The Coalition had proved dangerously skilled at taking over a person's mind. If they got Violet, they might use her to find her children. That must never happen, no matter what.

As Violet led the agent back down the dirt road, faster than was safe, a strange sense of completion washed over her. At least she'd gotten to see Jake, to speak to Gretchen, one last time. That was more than she'd ever hoped. She regretted not seeing Susannah again. She regretted not knowing the fates of the other three of her and Henry's children. But if anybody could find and protect them, it was Jake Ingram.

At least her running was almost over.

Her final hope now was simple. She hoped the agent had not yet reported the specific location of her ranch to the Coalition. If he hadn't, she meant to keep it that way.

She pressed the gas pedal, speeding up, counting on her pursuer to do the same. He did, easily keeping up with her old pickup. Seventy miles per hour. Eighty. Ninety. She could barely catch glimpses of the trailing car through the dust her truck was kicking up. All the better.

When she reached the bridge across the deep arroyo, Violet braked, skidding her truck to a stop across both lanes. She had no time to get out, nowhere to go if she did, so she simply unfastened her seat belt as she watched out her window.

Her trail of dust cleared…just in time to see horror on the face of the other driver as he realized that he could not keep from hitting her.

Violet's world exploded into crashing metal, broken concrete, a long fall. And silence.

Warmth. Softness. Peace.

And, she realized as the world brightened around her and her cares floated away—Henry. Other loving presences surrounded and welcomed her. Her parents. Her sister. Dale. But bright as a sunset, glowing and beautiful, Henry's was the soul to which her essence turned. He held out his hand toward her, in pure love.

Safe at last, done at last, Violet took it.

Henry.

Matt.

Arm in arm, Carey walked with the man she loved—the man who loved her—in the orange wash of the Kansas sunset. She'd been sorely tempted to run back inside, throw on something more sophisticated and let him take her out. Kansas City might not be Washington, but it wasn't the boonies, either. She'd decided not to because she'd finally realized she wanted more than the fairy tale.

This past week had been too painful for her to risk going through it again, not unless it was real. She liked who she became with Matt—more D.C. than K.C., more physically and emotionally complete. She loved who he became for her, too. But if it wasn't real, wasn't possible, then they had to know now.

No matter how painful.

She had to know he loved her, not just Cinderella. And she had to make sure that, after all his protean changes, Matt Tynan was the man she thought she loved, as well.

"You shouldn't have left during the vote," she chided gently. "Not even for me. We taxpayers front your salary."

"My job was over when the senators started handing in their cards," Matt insisted, kissing her hair again. He didn't seem able to stop touching her, stop kissing her. She was having a very, very hard time staying practical against that. "Stewart's a big boy. He didn't need me holding his hand."

"Still." And as far as being practical went, how much of his love came from simple gratitude? Senator Bermann *had* voted yes. "Can I ask you something? Did you use the information about the Senatorial Intelligence Committee to get Bermann's vote?"

Matt asked, "Senatorial Intelligence Committee?"

Then he looked away. Carey's heart ached. He was hiding his answer from her—but why? Had he done something shameful, maybe blackmailed the old congressman? Was he ashamed to tell her how far he would stoop? Surely not Matt! Or maybe…

She studied his profile as he pretended to admire some lawn gnomes, trying his damnedest not to telegraph what he really knew. She recognized that look. She loved that look.

He wasn't ashamed. He was just doing his job, not sharing top-secret information that he didn't know she knew!

He wasn't here because of her competence, or his gratitude. He was here for her.

She snuggled more closely against his side, heat or no heat. "The Senatorial Intelligence Committee that Bermann sat on in the late sixties, overseeing the budget for Medusa and Code Proteus," she said gently. "Which I faxed to Rita."

Matt stopped walking. "That came from *you?*"

Carey nodded, delighted by the open emotions now playing across his face.

"Oh, my God." Matt wrapped both arms around her, scooped her up and spun her in a circle, scattering kisses across her face. "That was you! Even in Kansas, you're too good to be true!"

"Nobody's that good." But even as her feet touched ground again, Carey leaned into Matt's chest, gazing happily up at him, glad he thought it anyway. *He* sure came close. She was finding it harder to stay practical. "But, Matt, how did you use it?"

He kissed her again, long and grateful, then pulled back just far enough to start walking again, his arm tight around her, their hips bumping. "Not the way you might expect. I saw Jake earlier this week, and he okayed me telling the president about Code Proteus. When I did, Stewart gave me the go-ahead to keep looking into the project. Officially. So I asked Bermann, as something of an expert, if he'd help with the project."

He shrugged. "I left it up to him to decide that our work might go more smoothly if he didn't shoot down the most important bill of Stewart's administration, first thing."

She considered him. "Amazing how good people can be when you let them."

"I'm not saying he wasn't worried about us digging up whatever the CIA had on him," Matt confessed, slanting a wary glance toward her. "Just that I didn't mention it."

"See," said Carey, bumping him with her shoulder. She never wanted to stop touching him. "Sometimes I get suspicious, too."

"But I didn't tell you the best part," he insisted, eyes bright. "Bermann has tapes and he gave them to the president."

"Tapes? Like Watergate?"

Matt's grin widened. "Like old, encrypted computer files, from before the age of diskettes. Bermann has a hand-crank pencil sharpener on his desk, he's so technology challenged, but he sure knew about holding on to evidence. Since he didn't trust Medusa, he squirreled away some copies of their files from Code Proteus."

Carey's mouth opened, but she couldn't speak. This was huge! This was exactly the kind of thing Jake Ingram needed.

"And to think, we owe it to you. Even after everything I did to get you off the project, all my stupid accusations."

She hated him beating himself up. "I only fell into that because I wanted to know where Cantrell got his information."

"To show me that you weren't the Proteus leak," he finished with a roll of his head, his voice bitter, his eyes bright. "Which I should never have suspected in the first place."

"Matt," she protested, not releasing his hand.

"And I shouldn't have thought for a minute you'd sell information to Jenkins," he continued. "It turns out the senator doesn't differentiate between mobile phones and land lines. My guess is, whoever gave Jenkins that quote got it from a cell phone capture."

"That's good to know." But she wanted to change the subject.

"I wish I'd trusted you enough to fly out here before *I* knew it. God, Carey. How can I ever make that up to you?"

He honestly didn't seem to believe he could.

"You had reasons," she reminded him, and kissed him when he groaned further protest. Nothing must be left to sabotage them. "And your dad lied to your mom, right?"

Matt blinked down at her. "What?"

"Didn't you once say that your dad lied to your mom?"

"Moms." He made a face. "Plural."

Catching his hand, she began to walk again, to make it easier for him to talk—if he trusted her enough. If he trusted *himself* enough. The sun was sinking below the horizon, leaving streaks of red and blue in the sky, and more and more neighbors were setting out their lawn sprinklers.

They reminded her of the Court of Neptune fountain.

Of Proteus.

"So maybe on some level you figured that's what couples do," she offered. "And since you weren't the one lying…"

"Oh, God." Matt tipped his head back in dismay. "Please don't say I'm doomed to repeat *both* my parents' patterns, Skipper. I'm already worried about my inability to commit."

Intrigued, Carey asked, "What inability to commit?"

He squeezed her shoulders. "You may not have noticed, but I don't excel in long-term relationships."

"Uh-huh." She snuggled more closely into the hollow under his shoulder, so very glad to be surrounded by his warmth and scent and presence again. This was where she belonged, all right. Especially if Matt was thinking about long-term relationships.

She asked casually, "So when did you meet Rita Winfield?"

"About ten years ago. The Smith for California campaign." Matt looked worried. "But we didn't make it three weeks dating."

"How about your college friends? Ethan Williams and Jake Ingram and Indy?"

"Seventeen years, give or take." He frowned. "Why?"

"And you're old friends with Ambassador Barnes of Delmonico, right? I remember, you spent some time with her when she visited last winter, after her husband died."

"I've known Samantha since high school." Matt was catching on. "But it's not the same, Care. Friendships are different."

"How?"

"Because you don't completely screw up someone's life when you mess up a friendship the way you do with a marriage."

Marriage? Carey tried to swallow back a tremor of hope and forged on. "Have you ever dumped a friend? Left a job undone? You've been with the president for years. When Jake Ingram needed you, you jumped right in to help. You're one of the most committed men I know."

"And you're one of the most idealistic women I know," he countered. He looked briefly surprised to see his rental car ahead of them. He apparently hadn't been paying close attention to the turns Carey had been taking, which led them back where they'd started. "That's not a bad thing, Care. I love that about you. But I'm reluctant to risk your happiness on ideals."

She boosted herself onto the trunk of the car. "Then it's a good thing it's my happiness. Mine. I get a vote, too."

He scowled, leaning beside her on the car, unconvinced. Then Carey asked, "Don't you trust me?"

And she won. She could tell by the need burning in Matt's eyes before he closed them, by the set of his mouth, by the lowering of his shoulders. She caught his arm, pulled him closer. Matt stepped between her knees, wrapping his arms tight around her, leaning his head on her shoulder. "I'm not sure I could live with it if I hurt you again," he breathed. "And then there's—"

As if to punctuate his dilemma, his pager went off. He glanced once at it, accusingly, as he turned it off. It must not have been an emergency. "And then," he said bitterly, dipping his forehead to rest against hers, "there's my political work."

"I am intimately familiar with your work, remember? It'll just get crazier when you finally decide to run for office, and I'm okay with that, too." Carey smiled, half teasing, half daring. "At least we'll be able to work together again."

"Maybe you'll run for office," Matt suggested, his eyes crinkling as he grinned. "And I can run your campaign."

"But I like doing support work, remember?" She kissed him, then repeated a favorite phrase from her days as his assistant. "Tell me what you want, and I'll tell you if we can do it."

"I want to spend my life giving you whatever you want."

Carey's eyes stung. Love like this really did exist. "Done," she whispered. "What else? Please, Matt. Let me see all of you."

His eyes burned into hers, full of need and hope and fear. "I want you," he whispered. "I want an us, strings and all. I want a home with you. I want…a family." His voice broke. "God, Carey, if I've screwed that up…."

"Shh," said Carey, kissing his jaw. "You were being responsible, Matt. Do you have any idea how safe I feel with you, knowing how responsible you are? You said the vasectomy might be reversible, didn't you?"

"No guarantees."

"As opposed to the rest of life?" she teased.

He didn't smile. His gaze searched hers, as if barely daring to hope. "I've been looking in all the wrong beds, Carey. And now here you are, and if I'm too late—"

"You're not too late," Carey assured him. "The future will be fine, as long as we're together. That's all I'm asking, Matt. That you face it with me. Like Proteus."

Matt kissed her then, needful and giving and thankful and, yes, practiced. Perfect. And in his kiss, and its loving promises, he did give her the future. He gave her everything.

"Thank you for holding on," he whispered.

"Always," said Carey, doing just that. Holding on tight. "Always."

*   *   *   *   *

*There are more secrets to reveal—
don't miss out!
Coming in September 2003 to
Silhouette Books*

*Pregnant and alone, Susannah Hobson
came home to bury her stepmother.
What she uncovered, instead, was
beyond her wildest dreams....*

THE BLUEWATER AFFAIR
by
Cindy Gerard

FAMILY SECRETS: *Five extraordinary
siblings. One dangerous past.
Unlimited potential.*

*And now,
for a sneak peek,
just turn the page...*

One

Trav distanced himself from the other mourners at the cemetery and watched Susannah Hobson. Violet Vaughn's stepdaughter stood at the graveside, hollow-eyed, dressed in black. She had yet to shed a tear.

Not that he'd expected her to. He'd never met her, but everything he knew about her said she was spoiled, selfish and immature. Tears—even for a woman who had loved her beyond reason—would have been too much of an effort.

"Susannah had just turned eighteen when she left four years ago," Vi had confided in Trav one day last fall when they were riding fence together. "Dale's death hit her hard. I just…well, I always thought she'd work her anger out of her system then come back home. I never thought this much time would pass without hearing from her."

He could have told Vi then what he suspected. It was selfishness, not grief that had kept Susannah from returning home. Most likely it was selfishness that had her trotting her little butt back here now, just in time to bury a woman who had deserved more from her. Because Vi also deserved more from him, he reconciled himself to doing what she wanted. The letter he'd received from her attorney just this morning still had his mind reeling. He doubted if Susannah had had the time to even open her mail today, let alone read it.

He studied the girl's lowered head where she stood by the open wound of the freshly dug grave. The first time he'd seen Susannah's picture he'd thought she was Vi's natural daughter. He was still taken with their likeness to each other—a little stunned by her beauty.

Their eyes were the same brilliant blue. While Vi had worn her hair in a short no-nonsense cut and Susannah's was long and fell well below her shoulders, the color was the same rich, lustrous brown. Vi had been a slim five-seven. Susannah appeared to be about the same height and equally slim. She seemed lost in her loose-fitting black dress that hung on her narrow shoulders like a sack.

It was only after he'd commented to Vi about their resemblance to each other that she'd set him straight.

"Her birth mother died when Susannah was eleven. A rare form of cancer. She's not mine by blood and we had our problems, but I couldn't love her more if she was my own," Vi had said with a sadness in her voice and a faraway look in her eyes that, for some reason, had always haunted him.

What, besides Susannah, had she lost? he'd wondered at the time. Vi had had secrets; he'd never doubted it. Whenever a reference to her past before she'd married Dale Hobson a little more than ten years ago came up, she'd changed the subject. He'd respected that. Just as she'd respected his silence concerning his own past.

Trav shifted his attention back to the dry-eyed young woman. He forced himself to let up a bit. Grief took many forms. He knew that. Just as he knew the pallor in her cheeks came from fatigue. Same thing for the slow blink and dull glaze of her eyes. She was running on autopilot. Her movements were stiff and automated, as though her body was going through the motions but her mind had shut down.

"Amen." The gathered crowd echoed Pastor Dugan in a hushed murmur.

He let out a deep breath. It was done. He said a silent goodbye to his friend, then, determined to pay his respects to Susannah, walked toward the thinning knot of mourners.

He'd almost reached her when Pastor Dugan and Rachel Scott crowded in and flanked her on either side. Trav hesitated then froze when Susannah's head came up and her gaze connected with his for the briefest of moments.

Sorrow. Aching and deep.

He was stunned by the strength of it even as he tried not to react, tried to rein in the tug of sympathy for this beautiful young woman.

Before he could marshal his feelings, she looked away and allowed the pastor to steer her toward the waiting cars. He watched them go, then walked slowly to his pickup and, against his better judgment, followed the stream of cars to the Rocking H where the Colorado version of a wake would continue.

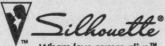

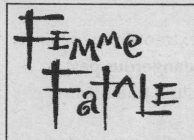

Five extraordinary siblings.
One dangerous past.
Unlimited potential.

If you missed the first riveting stories from Family Secrets, here's a chance to order your copies today!

Silhouette®
Where love comes alive™

FAMILY SECRETS

Five extraordinary siblings.
One dangerous past.
Unlimited potential.

Collect four (4) original proofs of purchase from the back pages of four (4) Family Secrets titles and receive a specialty themed free gift valued at over $20.00 U.S.!

Just complete the order form and send it, along with four (4) proofs of purchase from four (4) different Family Secrets titles to: Family Secrets, P.O. Box 9047, Buffalo, NY 14269-9047, or P.O. Box 613, Fort Erie, Ontario L2A 5X3.

Name (PLEASE PRINT)

Address   Apt. #

City   State/Prov.   Zip/Postal Code

Please specify which themed gift package(s) you would like to receive:

❑ PASSION
❑ HOME AND FAMILY
❑ TENDER AND LIGHTHEARTED

❑ Have you enclosed your proofs of purchase?

One Proof
Of Purchase
FSPOP3

Remember—for each package selected, you must send four (4) original proofs of purchase. To receive all three (3) gifts, just send in twelve (12) proofs of purchase, one from each of the 12 Family Secrets titles.

Please allow 4-6 weeks for delivery. Shipping and handling included. Offer good only while quantities last. Offer available in Canada and the U.S. only. Request should be received no later than July 31, 2004. Each proof of purchase should be cut out of the back page ad featuring this offer.

Visit us at www.eHarlequin.com   FSPOP3